Baba Ali and the Clockwork Djinn

A Steampunk Faerie Tale

Danielle Ackley-McPhail
& Day Al-Mohamed

PAPER PHOENIX PRESS
Pennsville, NJ

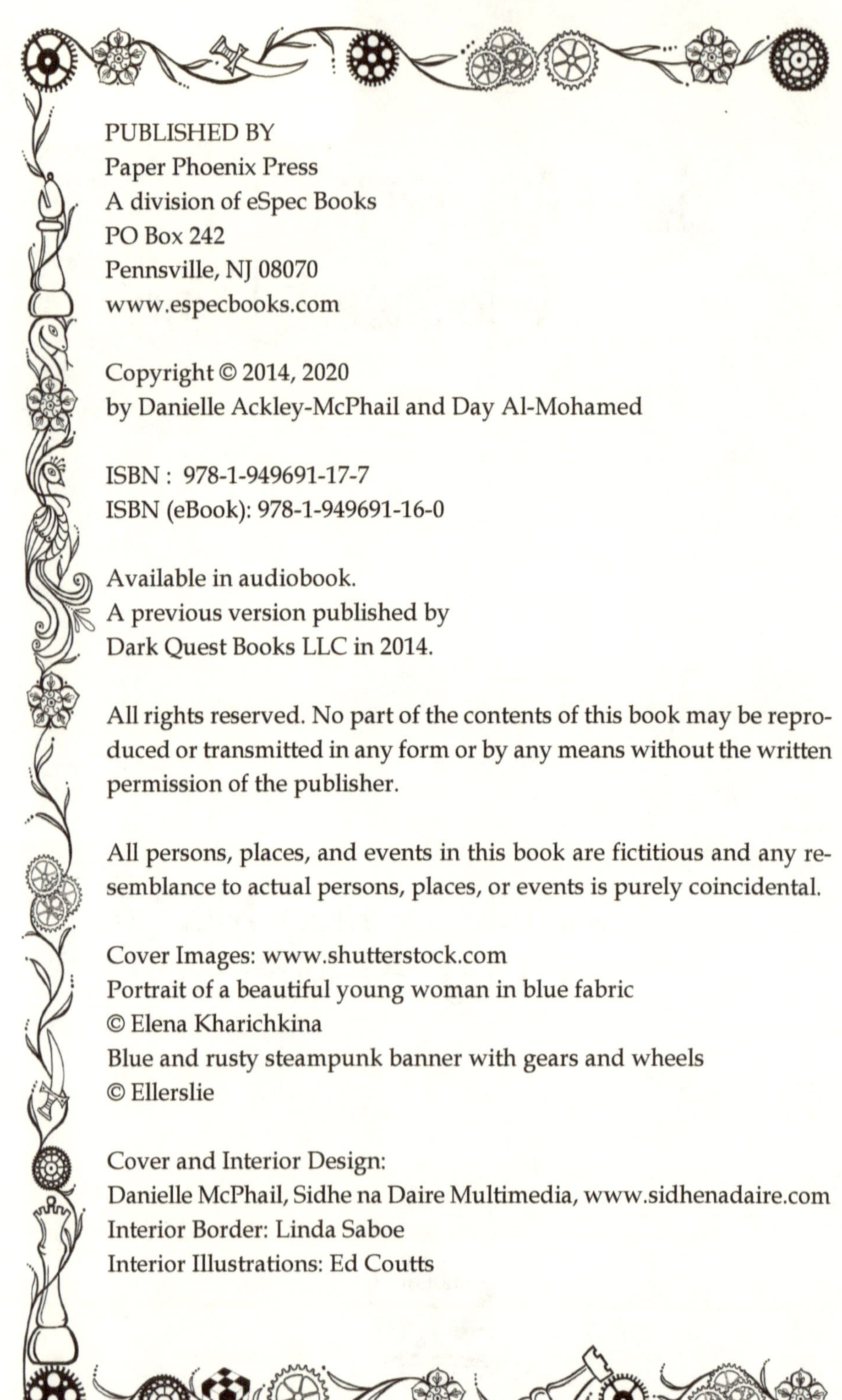

PUBLISHED BY
Paper Phoenix Press
A division of eSpec Books
PO Box 242
Pennsville, NJ 08070
www.especbooks.com

Copyright © 2014, 2020
by Danielle Ackley-McPhail and Day Al-Mohamed

ISBN : 978-1-949691-17-7
ISBN (eBook): 978-1-949691-16-0

Available in audiobook.
A previous version published by
Dark Quest Books LLC in 2014.

Cover Images: www.shutterstock.com
Portrait of a beautiful young woman in blue fabric
© Elena Kharichkina
Blue and rusty steampunk banner with gears and wheels
© Ellerslie

Cover and Interior Design:
Danielle McPhail, Sidhe na Daire Multimedia, www.sidhenadaire.com
Interior Border: Linda Saboe
Interior Illustrations: Ed Coutts

Other Titles by Danielle Ackley-McPhail

THE ETERNAL CYCLE TRILOGY
Yesterday's Dreams
Tomorrow's Memories
Today's Promise

THE CONTINUING JOURNEY SERIES
Eternal Wanderings

BAD-ASS FAERIE TALE SERIES
The Halfling's Court
The Redcaps' Queen
The High King's Fool
(*Forthcoming*)

STAND-ALONE COLLECTIONS
A Legacy of Stars
Consigned to the Sea
Transcendence

THE LITERARY HANDYMAN SERIES
The Literary Handyman
Build-A-Book Workshop
(*Forthcoming*)

Other Titles by Day Al-Mohamed

The Labyrinth's Archivist (Falstaff Books)

Steampunk Titles by eSpec Books

The Clockwork Witch by Michelle D. Sonnier
After Punk: Steampowered Tales of the Afterlife
Gaslight & Grimm: Steampunk Faerie Tales
Spirit Seeker by Jeff Young
The Fall of Autumn by Jeffrey Lyman
The Troll King by Jeffrey Lyman

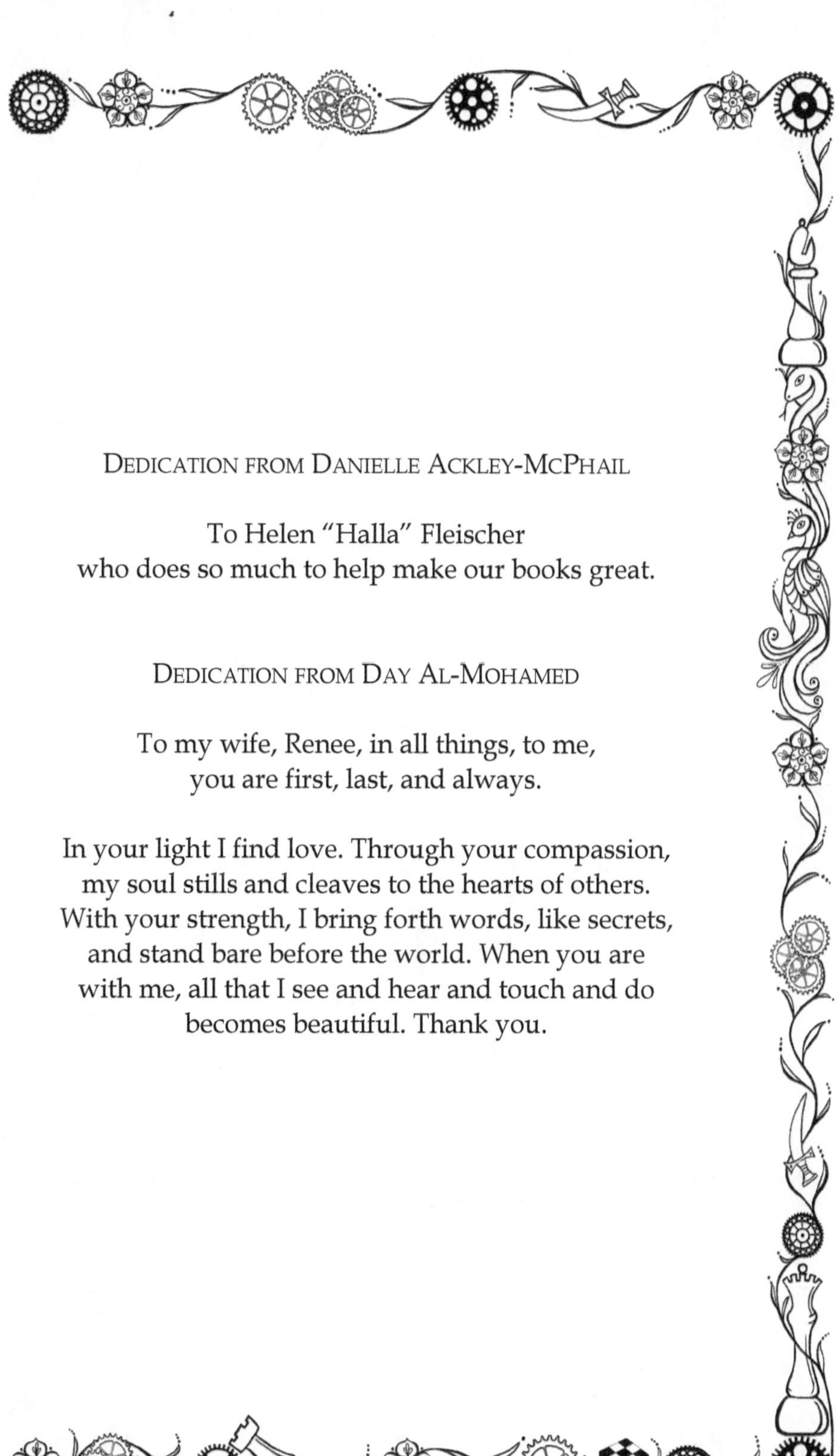

Dedication from Danielle Ackley-McPhail

To Helen "Halla" Fleischer
who does so much to help make our books great.

Dedication from Day Al-Mohamed

To my wife, Renee, in all things, to me,
you are first, last, and always.

In your light I find love. Through your compassion,
my soul stills and cleaves to the hearts of others.
With your strength, I bring forth words, like secrets,
and stand bare before the world. When you are
with me, all that I see and hear and touch and do
becomes beautiful. Thank you.

Come, Best Beloved,

and sit you by my feet. I shall tell
you a tale such as sister Scheherazade
could have scarce imagined. A tale
of wonders, of deeds both great
and grievous, of courage that defies
description, and above all,
Child of Adam,
I shall tell you a tale of love.

The night is for the telling of tales
of which the morning may bear Truth.
In the oldest of days and ages and
times, there was, and there was not,
a great evil that reached across
the desert and beyond...

Chapter One

ALI BIN-MASSOUD MADE HIS WAY DOWN DORSET STREET AT a brisk pace, hunching his shoulders against the damp chill that clung thick upon his person. Though he was but eighteen years of age, on days like this his bones ached as if he carried three times that number of years. His woolen white *thobe* and the darker *besht* robe he wore over it protected him from the worst of the weather, as did the *chafiye* wrapped about his head, but they also marked him as an outsider. Many days, his choice to wear traditional garb made things more difficult for him than the weather itself. In the three years since he had come to England, Ali could have chosen to adopt this foreign land's manner of dress but he was not willing to forgo any remaining shred of the culture he still cleaved to in this wet and foggy place. His body longed for the dry heat of the desert. His soul ached for home and his family…especially his father.

Ali missed his wisdom and patience. And on days like today, even a small word or look of encouragement would have lifted his spirits as a ray of sunshine cutting through the unfriendly English skies.

Ali shivered as the late-spring drizzle pelted his skin. He held the package of instruments he had fetched from the

blacksmith for his teacher tight against his chest. Around him loomed the buildings that edged the street, their brick facades staring at him. Ali felt crowded and smothered. It was so different from the open desert that surrounded his home in Wadi Al-Nejd. Lengthening his stride and keeping his head down, he hurried toward his temporary home, eager for the shelter it offered. His professor would no doubt have a warm fire and hot tea waiting.

Ali tensed as the swift two-step clop of hard-soled shoes approached behind him, but was distracted by the cry of a falcon overhead.

"My word! *Two* in one day. It is a veritable infestation," the stranger muttered. "Out of my way, golliwog."

The man shoved past him. Ali's feet slipped off the edge of the wooden walk. He fell toward the cobbles and into the street. Pain shot up his leg as his knee struck the hard stone. Angry yells and the clamor of hooves and wheels shattered the quiet calm of Dorset Street. Mud splattered his *besht* and covered his one hand where he had tried to catch himself. With his other hand, Ali clutched his package more tightly and whispered a prayer to the Almighty. He scrambled to the safety of the walkway, his body trembling as the carriage raced by without even slowing, the driver yelling maledictions as he passed. Ali's cheeks burned at the stares of those few people on the street.

With quiet dignity he shoved down his anger and continued on his way. Pride forced him to take slow, normal steps, though bolts of pain from his knee coursed through him with each stride. Ali could do nothing else; any response or complaint would be twisted and misconstrued. He had seen this too often. He had even experienced it once or twice, especially when he had first arrived. Throwing angry words and even fists accomplished nothing. Three years had passed and now Ali refused to let his honor, nor that of his teacher and his family be sullied, though the injustice burned him like the noonday sands.

He understood that his father had sent him to this cold place out of a desire for a better life for his second son than he would find in his brother Kassim's shadow. But the well-meaning exile…*apprenticeship*, Ali corrected himself, weighed heavily on his soul.

His feet longed for the shift of desert sands beneath them. His skin ached for the hot rays of a brilliant sun. His heart cried out for people who would accept him as he was and not give him baleful looks for skin that was more brown than pale. But more than anything else, he longed for his family. Neither he nor his father had realized how ill-received he would be by the English artificers and engineers, unable even to enroll at University despite a sharp mind, innate talent with mechanical things, and his father's plentiful wealth. If not for the famed artificer Charles Babbage accepting him personally as an apprentice — an offer made out of gratitude for a past kindness…and perhaps a more recent exchange of coin — Ali would have found his time in England unbearable. The Almighty be praised, his situation was not so. Ali murmured the quick benediction. A gratitude to protect against evil.

The hours spent studying with Babbage filled Ali's mind with wonder and his heart with joy. Like all artificers, the man's mind was a puzzle of machines and engineering and designs that, when the two of them were safely ensconced in the workshop, made Ali desire only to sit at his teacher's workbench and create with him. Such knowledge more than made his venture to this land of the English worthwhile.

Today they were to experiment with a new variation on a "difference engine." Ali's heartbeat sped up and a faint smile appeared at his lips. The machine was complex, its problems daunting and Ali loved every minute. His steps sped up at the thought.

Finally, he reached the wrought-iron fence surrounding One Dorset Street. As Ali passed through the gate, his shoulders relaxed. His head rose, and his chest loosened enough for him to draw a more comfortable breath. Before he could knock, Babbage himself opened the door, his forehead creased and his brow heavy as he scowled. His gaze took in the limp and the torn and dirtied state of Ali's clothing.

Babbage's lips pressed tight. "Again?" He glared down the street; first one way, and then the other.

"I am fine, *Ustad*." — Honored teacher. "The Almighty's blessing upon your household," Ali said in English. His words were clear and unaccented. He and his brother Kassim had learned the language, as well as many others, at a young age, through their merchant father's tutoring. Ali handed his teacher the package he carried, along with a letter he'd collected from the postmaster. Babbage's scowl deepened as he read the sender's name: The Honorable Lady Chadsworth. He *humphed* as he slipped the envelope into his coat, then turned to stride down the hall.

"Well, come on in then," Babbage said over his shoulder.

Ali followed, slowly, careful of his aching leg. No doubt he would awaken with significant bruises in the morning. Despite this, his fingers clenched as if already a spanner weighed upon his palm, all memories of his encounter temporarily forgotten.

Babbage waved toward the stairs. "Why don't you take a minute to wash up?"

Ali glanced down at himself, his cheeks flaming in shame at his disarray. He bowed quickly before hurrying to the scullery that held the house's single pump for fresh water. Collecting a pitcher, Ali carefully filled it and made his way upstairs to the attic chamber granted him as a part of his apprenticeship, along with meals.

Once in his room, Ali removed his clothing and made his ablutions. He winced as he gently dabbed at his throbbing knee with a damp washcloth. It was swollen, the skin scraped and oozing blood. Each step up the stairs had been painful, but the injury was not serious. Ali changed to a clean *thobe*. Eagerness to return downstairs to begin his lesson spurred his pace.

Babbage waited impatiently beside the door at the back of the house, his tall, lanky form tense. Without a word, they stepped out under the covered walkway that led to the workshop, a two-storey affair that seemed a palace in itself compared to how most people in Ali's home city of Wadi Al-Nejd lived. As they entered the workshop, Ali moved to the coldbox in the corner, where they kept items for quick meals. He took out a small pitcher and poured milk into the bowl he'd reserved for the household's brownies. He had learned of the English's magical faeries in a book he'd found in the library. It had comforted him to discover that this soot-grey city, in some small way, echoed the magic of his far-off homeland. Being conversant with tales of the fickle, and at times, malevolent ways of magical creatures, even foreign ones, Ali made certain to ensure these were kept happy.

As he placed the saucer just outside the workshop door Ali sensed Babbage's disapproval. He grinned up at his teacher, knowing the complaint. After three years of this ritual, it no longer needed to be voiced — science versus poppycock and ignorant, savage superstition. Yet his teacher never stayed Ali's hand, his tolerance was good-natured though his manner remained gruff. Ali had to admit he had yet to see a being that resembled the images from the book, but set out his saucer all the same. Faith required belief, not proof.

His task complete, Ali rolled up his sleeves in preparation for work. His gaze went to the roof, constructed from sheets of clear glass. The rain tapped against them in a steady patter. Soft light bathed the chamber, but the hour grew late. They would need lanterns to see their work.

Ali sighed, not overly fond of the paraffin lanterns. He missed the fragrant oil lamp oil of his homeland. English paraffin stank and smoked. Straightening his shoulders and shrugging off his distaste, he circled the room, using lucifer matches to light the many lanterns until the workspace fairly glowed. Once he completed the task, he joined his teacher at the workbench where Babbage had already opened the package of custom-made tools Ali had been sent to collect. They were truly things of beauty, not just tools for efficiency. Wood handles, with cold steel working parts—a mainspring tightener, a brand-new indicator, a set of collets, indexible turrets, and an oddly shaped ratchet. Ali recognized Babbage's own designs among the more standard implements. While many were familiar, several were not. No doubt, he would learn the purpose of the others as they proceeded.

They worked for hours, constructing first paper, then wooden templates from Babbage's notes and assembling them, working out the calculations precisely. That was where Ali excelled, in the implementation of Babbage's designs. Taking something from the theoretical and making it tangible. Ali felt a small bubble of pride as they tested elements of the machine. He longed to take up the new tools and construct the whole of this difference engine, but that was forbidden him for now, though an entire clean-room remained sealed at the back of the workshop, eternally waiting for the master's "grand invention". Even dust was not allowed entry.

In his secret thoughts, Ali feared his teacher would never venture forward, would never take the steps to realize his dream, his spirit broken by an earlier failure many years before, the specifics of which were never discussed.

Ali sought to become a master artificer. And there was yet much for him to learn of theory, mathematics, and engineering through the smaller efforts completed under his teacher's tutelage. This is what Ali's father wanted for him. The skill of the artificer, the knowledge of the scholar, the vision of the inventor; and tools with which he could build a future outside of the family business. A business that would be his brother's inheritance. As the younger son, it was necessary that Ali seek his own destiny. On his own, Ali would have become little more than a machinist or tinkerer. Blessed with this opportunity to work with *Ustad* Babbage, Ali had the chance to achieve the dream his father held for him, which, in his heart of hearts, Ali also wished for himself.

Content, he settled into his work, pausing only for his evening prayers. Other than Babbage's instructions, neither of them spoke. Just as well, Ali found it hard to breathe, let alone talk; the fumes from the lamps and their work made the air heavy. The third time Ali strangled a cough, Babbage ordered him to open the "damnable" window. The air outside was scarcely any better, but at least the evening breeze and the damp from the recent rain freshened the stifling room.

After several hours, they stopped for a bit of bread and tea, Ali preparing the blend his father regularly sent him from his far desert country. Happily, Ali's teacher was quite taken with the full-bodied flavor of Indian First Leaf and so the evening break was a time of comfort and peace in their day. To make it doubly pleasurable, during that time, Ali usually asked questions about mathematics and philosophy. Babbage spoke broadly about the theoretical underpinnings that every artificer needed to know. Time flew quickly and soon they returned to the workbench, ready to toil well into the night.

Before they could take up their tools, something clattered on the windowsill. As one, Ali and Babbage turned to behold a fantastic sight. Perched upon the sill was a falcon. Not one of the small English kestrels. This creature rivaled the majestic raptors of Ali's desert home.

Head tilting for a better view, Ali stepped forward. The movement took him out of the path of the light, allowing the warm glow of the lamps to fall full upon the form in the open window. Gem-bright eyes flashed at him from a sculpted avian face. Drawing a sharp breath, Ali stopped still.

"How extraordinary," Babbage murmured softly. Silently, Ali agreed.

Other than its form, this bird had no foundation in nature. Both "feathers" and "flesh" were purely mechanical, finely wrought from the most delicate of clockwork and hammered metal. Ali noticed a series of gears beneath the wings. They moved both seamlessly and silently. Feathers of fitted bronze, copper, and tin in their natural colors, undimmed, fluttered flat against its back with faint clicks. Ali longed to examine the inner workings.

Both he and Babbage stepped closer. But as a shape moves, so does its shadow; their own reached out toward the marvel before them. The construct gave a sudden cry at their motion and hunched upon its clawed feet, wings sweeping out and upward until they stretched wide into the room.

"Allah, protect us!" Well aware of the damage that could be delivered by the claws and beaks of hunting falcons, Ali stepped in front of his teacher, waving his arms and shouting in Arabic. Behind him, Babbage swore and picked up what sounded like a heavy lever from a pullback motor. But the bird did not strike.

The falcon flapped its wings, showing off the tiny myriad gears. It screeched a high piercing call, repeating it once, twice, three times.

Ali paused, peering past his arms. That wasn't the sound an impending attack. The falcon gazed back at him. It blinked, repeated the cries once more and then launched skyward, disappearing into the night, further establishing its unnatural state. The sill bore deep gouges in the wood and an ornate bronze puzzle box remained where the falcon had lit.

The air grew still as neither of them moved. A frown puckered Ali's brow as he turned his gaze to his teacher. Babbage merely stood there, rigid, his features pale. He gripped the lever so tightly that his hand shook.

"You've seen it before?" Ali wasn't sure if his sentence was a statement or a question.

His teacher swallowed hard, as if forcing something bitter past his throat.

"Fetch it, lad." Despite his lack of tone, the words carried an air of foreboding.

Ali's jaw tensed at the diminutive form of address used by the older man. In light of the earlier encounter on the street, Ali had to remind himself there was no malice in *Ustad* Babbage. The man had the habit of calling any man younger than he, 'lad.' However, his clear refusal to answer Ali's question indicated something else was troubling him.

Ali moved forward, careful step by careful step, though the raptor had already flown away. For a moment, he thought he saw something move in the darkness beyond the window, but could not be certain. Recalling the bird's razor-like claws, Ali's hands clenched into fists. He shook them loose, then reached for the box with one hand as he closed the window with the other. Turning toward the nearest lamp, he brought up his right hand to trace the engraving: his name, scribed in his own language, with a flourish that seemed familiar. Surrounding his name, intricate scrollwork ran from the edges of the top of the box, and down each side. His vision blurred as he stared down at the marks, as if the design rejected his gaze. Ali shook off such foolish thoughts. Surely the oily lamp fumes had addled his brain.

"*Ustad* Babbage…?" Ali didn't understand the significance of the box but perhaps his teacher would. "You've seen it before?" Ali repeated the question, this time more insistently.

Ali held the puzzle box out toward Babbage. The mechanical bird had come to *his* home, left the box on *his* sill. All Ali had done was retrieve it. The lighting dimmed, or perhaps just his vision, and the room shivered.

Babbage's eyes dropped to the box and then lifted back to Ali before sliding away, avoiding Ali's questioning gaze. His lips drew down at the corners. "I would say we are done for the evening, lad. Go on to bed."

Ali tapped the puzzle box.

"Take it with you. It is clear whom it is meant for."

"But…this…" Ali fumbled over the English words. His mind raced and he couldn't translate his jumbled thoughts or emotions quickly.

Babbage met Ali's gaze and held it. "That is *your* name engraved on the box. We can both see that, and no creature, neither mechanical, nor natural, could have found this place, could have found *you* by accident. Do you understand, Ali bin-Massoud?" This was the first time Babbage had used his full name.

Before Ali could inquire further, Babbage turned away, discouraging any further conversation as he set about tidying the workbench and extinguishing the lamps. "I will finish cleaning up here, alone. Goodnight, Ali."

"Of course. Thank you, *Ustad* Babbage." Ali said softly pocketing the cube. Something had come between them and he didn't understand what, nor why.

Ali left the workshop, noting in passing that his offering of milk had been consumed. Any other night he would have searched the foliage for the brownies. Tonight, remembering the flutter of movement he saw outside the window, Ali hurried back to the house. Feeling his way in the dark, he lit a tallow candle at the banked coals in the kitchen hearth and made his way to his room. Setting his candle on the shelf just inside the door, Ali sat upon his bed and stared at the strange box. It smelled faintly of sandalwood and cedar. Awakened by the familiar scent, a fierce longing for his father reared up in Ali's heart. His father had a fondness for such puzzles, though no skill in solving them.

Growing up, Ali had received many puzzle boxes and other mechanical devices as gifts after each trade journey. Most of them he'd disassembled in an effort to discover the secret of their workings. He'd rebuilt each one, though never quite the same as they'd been given to him. The memories of the first time his father brought him a puzzle box rose up, bittersweet.

"My son, I have something for you."

Ali barely registered the words, so tightly were his arms wrapped around his father's waist. This trade journey had taken months and months. Father had never been away for so long before and Ali had missed him terribly.

"Ali?"

He looked up to meet his father's gaze, which fairly danced with excitement.

Ali wiped his face with his sleeve, letting his father's enthusiasm wash over him. "Thank you, Father. May I see?"

With a flourish, his father pulled out a small box made of wood.

"It is called a Himitsu-Bako, a secret box."

Ali's eyes widened at the geometric patterns crafted through the use of a variety of different woods. His fingers gently roved over the box. He could barely feel where the pieces met.

"How beautiful! I promise, I shall tell no one!"

His father laughed, a deep rumbling sound. Ali laughed with him, though he knew not why. "The box isn't a secret," his father said. "It holds a secret."

Then he crouched down, one arm draping Ali's shoulder, the other pointing at one of the shapes making up the design; a small triangle smoother than the rest. Ali peered closer. He ran a finger over the spot and drew a sharp breath as a faint click sounded and the triangle sank inward. Ali brought both hands up to grip the box, his fingers tracing each pattern, pressing the shapes until another clicked, this one rising up. A smile blossomed across his face as he looked up at his father, who grinned back.

Awed, Ali whispered, "What is the secret?"

"You shall have to open the box to find out."

"How?"

"You must discover the answer. You can slide and move the different pieces and push various parts of the surface of the box. But there is a trick. You must

discover the correct order to allow the box to open. Without the correct sequence, it will remain a…" His father's voice trailed off as he looked at Ali expectantly.

"Secret!"

His father ruffled his hair. "You're a good son, and Allah has graced you with intelligence and skill. I shall show you another secret the box holds." He took the box from Ali's hands and turned it over, revealing a scrolled design. He ran a finger over it and the box gave off blue and gold sparks.

Ali mouthed an "O" of wonder.

"These boxes are special. They were some of the first items to ever combine magic and mechanics. Few are blessed with the ability to understand such things, let alone make them." Ali saw a shadow of melancholy move across his father's eyes as he flicked his fingers, following another pattern. This time, the design on the box glowed a deep purple before fading back to its original wood hue. His father gravely handed the box to Ali, who stood even more in awe at his gift. "Do you think you can figure it out?"

Ali nodded his head vigorously, his chest swelling at the pride in his father's gaze.

Ali toyed with the box, sliding wood section back and forth, "Did you bring one for Kassim?" His gaze focused on the magic sparks that rose from the movement.

It was a long minute before his father answered. So long that Ali paused in his play.

His father smiled and ruffled Ali's hair again. Only this time the smile didn't quite reach his eyes, "Ali, my darling boy. You know your brother doesn't care for puzzles."

It had taken him six months to figure out the thirty-three steps to open that first box. He delighted in each magical response nearly as much as he had in solving the puzzle. Inside had nestled a silver coin. The money allowed him to buy his friends candied dates in the market, which was nice, but Ali saw the box itself as the greater treasure. The engineering was beautiful. Complex. It woke a thirst for knowledge in his soul.

Ali had loved *Himitsu-Bako* ever since. They became a special joy that balanced the heartache of his father's many absences. On his return from each trade journey his father added yet another box to Ali's collection, each one more challenging than the last.

Ali had been careful to hide them from Kassim. His brother had smashed that very first Himitsu-Bako. It had been in the middle of a fight. Ali couldn't even recall what the fight had been about , but Ali learned his lesson well. While his brother's actions saddened him, in a way it made the boxes even more special, to be enjoyed only in secret. The only thing that meant more to him than solving the puzzles was sharing what he discovered with his father.

Ali sighed, a long exhalation of air, filling the silence of his room.

He could not say when, or if, he would have a chance to share this *Himitsu-Bako* with his father. It was unlikely Ali would return home anytime soon. He turned the box over and over in his hands, focusing on the puzzle in an effort to push the homesickness aside. He examined every side but his eyes blurred and itched, causing the scrollwork to shift and bend in an odd manner. Was magic at work? It seemed the plates that formed the box were tight-fitted and flush to one another. There had to be some way to shift one of them, to allow the others to move, but he'd yet to discover the secret. He searched for some subtle marker to tell him the starting point, but even touch revealed nothing. Other than his name, he spied indents on two sides and an engraving upon the bottom, delicate and easy to overlook, segmented like a mosaic by the intersecting lines of scrollwork, but he could not be sure. He feared his vision sought to trick him.

He ran a finger over the lines seeking the fine indentations he was not altogether certain were there. His skin tingled, then burned. Ali jerked his hand away when the box began to glow as if afire. Sparks trailed like falling embers from his skin only to vanish in the air. He blinked, then squeezed his eyes shut tight, certain he imagined what they told him. The pattern…the sparks…Allah have mercy, *everything* he'd seen this night from the moment the clockwork falcon appeared in the window, seemed to him the product of a fever dream, or far-flung sorcery from his homeland, because surely such things were not possible here. The English had long forgotten the ways of magic, as evidenced by Babbage's own disdain for providing sustenance to the house brownies.

Ali dropped the box on his bed. He opened his eyes, letting only his gaze touch the object, his mouth moving soundlessly in a prayer for protection. *What magic is this?* The scrollwork had vanished leaving smooth sides, the interlocking plates marked only by his name and an engraving on the base. Ali knelt beside the bed, bringing his eyes level with the box as he peered closer. His injured knee ached at the motion but Ali barely noticed as he examined the etching: a lion before a radiant sun, one paw raised as the plume of its tail lashed the air. He frowned. It was a symbol of Persia. Ali recognized it from the carving on his grandfather's staff, which Ali's father had given to him when he left for England. Ali was sure of it, but this image was different. Balanced on the lion's paw — which should have clutched a sword — the engraver had scribed a different mark, one that looked similar to a spanner. He briefly considered pulling the staff from its place under the bed but found that he was far more intrigued by the mysterious symbol.

He gave in to the impulse to touch, running his index finger over the etching. The metal blazed and the air itself grew hot. Ali yelped and jerked his finger away. His bedclothes began to smolder. Turning swiftly Ali grabbed the pitcher of water from earlier in the evening and poured the remains onto his scorching bedclothes. The Himitsu-Baku hissed and smoked in response. This box would *punish* the user for any errors made in physically attempting to solve the puzzle and open it.

A sound escaped the Himitsu-Baku, a word spoken in a long angry mechanical hiss, and then it went dark. Scrollwork crept back over the box, obscuring the marks once more.

Dropping to the floor, head bowed toward the Holy City of Mecca, Ali's prayers were no longer silent, tumbling from his lips in frantic pleas for deliverance. The sound that had come from the puzzle box was a name, his own. Ali prayed without ceasing, long into the night.

Chapter Two

A CREAM-COLORED STALLION STREAKED ACROSS THE DESERT. White rimmed its eyes and sweat and more darkened its hide, all but where pale foam flecked. The horse ran at a reckless leg-breaking speed, its mane and tail lashing the night air, not stopping until it reached the closed city gates of Wadi Al-Nejd. Prancing and rearing until its front hooves beat upon the barrier, it loosed a ringing scream before dropping its feet to the ground, its head whipping to and fro as its lungs worked like a frantic bellows. In the distance, on a dune overlooking the city, two riders cloaked in dark *chafiyes* and *beshts*, drew up on small, sand-colored desert horses and watched the stallion prance, ignoring the horse's bugled challenge as the stallion whirled in frenzy once more.

"Pray the others have better success capturing the magician's bird," one said to the other in the softest of murmurs. "Or Rassul will have all of our heads."

His companion grunted but said nothing, his eyes locked on the frantic stallion.

At the groan of the gate opening, the watchers withdrew into the twilight. In silence, the riders returned the way they had come, the night breeze whisking away their trail.

Beyond the gate the city guards waited, scimitars raised, while on the walls above archers stood ready, bowstrings drawn taut. For a moment nothing moved, neither man, nor horse. The magnificent stallion was well-known and as easily recognized its master. The guards exchanged puzzled glances. Then, as if startled by a sound the men couldn't hear, the merchant's stallion charged past, riderless, its saddle and pale flanks glistening wet and black with blood in the torchlight.

As the horse galloped wildly toward the merchant's home, the guards raised a prayer to the Almighty for the man's soul.

Kassim bin-Massoud woke to the sound of someone slapping at his chamber door. Rolling over, he pushed at his wife, Malakeh, to go answer. Kassim closed his eyes and buried himself in his blankets. The desert night was cold, but the blankets were warm, as was his wife. Kassim frowned, still half-asleep and irritated at the interruption. He hoped that Malakeh would return soon. He could barely hear her murmurs at the doorway to their chamber. With Father away and Ali in England, Kassim enjoyed his current role as master of the house and the trade, all but for times like this, when duty drew him from the comfort of his sleep. He would be glad when his father returned from his journey, and the servants could once more wake *him* for the slightest disturbance.

Sleep had nearly reclaimed Kassim when Malakeh hurried back to his bed. He stretched and rolled, awake enough to perhaps indulge in coupling, only his lady wife did not slide between the silken sheets and press herself against the length of him. No. The shrew tugged and nagged, her words so hurried he could not tell one from the other, noting only that they trembled querulously from her lips. With a disgusted grunt, Kassim turned away. But his wife set up a keen that jerked him from his rest, all thought of sleep banished.

"Enough, woman! If you cannot be pleasant and warm, go off to your own bed chamber and send me a servant girl."

"Husband, you must wake," her words were urgent, but coming more slowly now. She clutched a length of cloth. "Come away from your bed and see for yourself the tragedy that has fallen upon our household. Allah, protect us!"

Kassim frowned as he reached for his robe and then lit the oil lamp beside his bed. "You make no sense, woman."

She extended her arms. Draped across them was a horse blanket, rank with sweat and something else. From the cloth rose another smell, both sweet and pungent. Kassim scowled and waved Malakeh closer. His wife knelt before him and raised her arms until he wrinkled his nose and drew back from the coppery odor of blood. As the light brushed the cloth Kassim stilled. His breath caught in his chest. It was his father's saddle blanket, used for no other steed but his most cherished, Biaban Govad — the Desert Wind.

"No." Kassim rose to his feet and snatched the blanket to him, noting how a faint trace of blood yet welled from the fibers as he crushed the cloth in his grip.

Without another word he pushed past his wife and hurried to the courtyard where his horsemaster surely waited. Kassim barely took note as Malakeh followed. As he neared, the horse went wild, Kassim's bold stride and the heavy, biting scent of blood causing the stallion to fight its lead.

Biaban Govad pranced, half mad with fear, his reins clutched by the horsemaster, who desperately sought to calm the valuable animal. By the light of courtyard lanterns that had been tinkered by his brother as a gift to their father, Kassim took in the weary state of the creature, the thin gash across its flank, and the deeper one slicing its withers. The blood staining the creature's back told a tale than needed no words. Kassim's grief fought a battle with good fortune. It would seem that his standing in the household would forever rise this night, as Kassim bin-Massoud became master in truth.

He called out to the horsemaster, "What have you discovered?"

Startled, the stallion reared, almost pulling the man off the ground as he helplessly made soothing sounds. Kassim shook his head in impatience but there was little he could do until the horsemaster had calmed the beast.

Kassim let the saddle blanket fall to the dusty ground. "See to the horse. In the morning, send word to the magistrate that my father has met his fate on the desert and is no more," he ordered, his tone solemn even while his chest swelled with satisfaction as the man…*his* horsemaster hurried to do his bidding.

Kassim then turned and shooed his wife from the doorway. He entered the household, already planning the changes he would make to brand it his own. Ali's infernal lanterns would be the first things to go. There was much to be done before that, though. He must contact the imam for prayers. Tradition required burial as soon as possible. He had no doubt his father was dead, if not from the wound that bore such blood, then at the desert's mercy, for surely he'd been grievously wounded. They must, of course, search for the body, but even without it, Kassim would ensure that his beloved father had the greatest *Janazah*—funeral—anyone in Wadi Al-Nejd had ever seen.

The blood-soaked blanket would inspire the proper compassion in those watching. But he would not depend on this alone. He would hire many women to wail and mourn and show how great was his loss. All of the town would see how deeply Kassim grieved for his father. And in this they would also know the power into which he had finally come.

He stopped in the center of the hall and rethought this plan. Power…new wealth…it did not do to broadcast such to the masses. Better, perhaps, to mourn quietly, in solitude, rather than invite the parasites drawn by such things. Only those who must would know of his father's fate, else Kassim would spend all his time deflecting those who would grasp at his inheritance.

Not bothering to wash the blood from his hands and robe where the saddle blanket had stained them, Kassim went instead to his father's chambers to plan…and to begin the long process of assessing his personal wealth. He was not so much interested in the goods of their trade or the coin it brought. Of that he was already well informed, having worked many years at his father's side. No, what he sought was the hidden treasure he'd seen long ago, when just a boy of five.

A gentle breeze swayed the palm fronds overhead. Kassim was grateful for the rustling that masked any sound he might make crouched among the ferns. He watched as Father and Mother reclined on a blanket in the garden, their backs against the sparkling rock said to have been placed there by Grandfather Farzeen. Father called it the heart of the garden. His parents came out here to talk when they had matters they wanted no other to hear, at night, when the ring-necked parakeets roosted in the trees, knowing if any drew near it would disturb the birds. Kassim, however, had been there already, hiding from his nursemaid. He was cross with her for sending him to bed early and without his sweets, just because the extra treat he had hidden for himself drew bugs into their rooms. How was he to know? He frowned. Tomorrow he would get twice

as many sweets and make sure she had none. He could do this. He was his father's heir.

For a while he lay there, letting the sound of his parents' murmurs soothe him. But then their voices rose in pitch. Excited cries disturbed the garden. Kassim was so curious he forgot to keep still. The brush rustled and the parrots fussed overhead. His parents' voices fell silent a moment.

"Who is there?" his father called out softly. Kassim's eyes widened and he pressed a hand over his mouth to muffle his gasp. For a moment he feared Father would rise up to check the garden. He crouched in a tight, little ball. If they found him he would be punished with worse than going to bed without sweets. After a long moment, the birds settled and the low tones of his parents' voices teased him once more.

Soon, Kassim fidgeted again as curiosity itched deep in his belly. Dare he move forward? As the light wind ran fingers through the trees tinkling chimes hung from them, he carefully crept nearer, curious as to what excited his parents. When he reached the edge of the ferns he curled up beneath their curtain of fronds, his head pillowed on his arm and his ear turned toward where his parents lay.

"Are you certain, beloved? Is it true that Allah has blessed us so richly?"

"As certain as I may be, husband," she answered him.

Hearing joy in their voices, Kassim raised a small finger to draw down a length of fern, trying to see for himself what could call for such a response. There was nothing on the blanket between them, but his mother wore an odd smile on her face and her eyes were bright as stars. Kassim watched as his father raised a hand that trembled and placed it on his mother's belly. The look on their faces made Kassim uneasy.

"A child…another child!" his father said, his voice awed. "Allah, be praised!"

Kassim shivered at his father's words. Surely he misheard. They had no need of another child in their household. Was he not enough that his father must have such joy at the news of another?

Father's eyes brightened as he spoke, his voice increasing with the fervor of his words. "Surely this child will have the gift, will have the skill and love for mechanical devices that Kassim and I lack."

Another child?… Kassim hated the words, hated the idea, knowing in the fullness of time his world would change. That he would no longer be the sun and the moon and the stars for his father and mother. He knew it. He could see it already. In their eyes, he was not worthy, even as heir. And mechanical devices? He would never see another without smashing it!

Kassim scowled at his parents, his lower lip jutting out.

He watched as his father drew an embroidered pouch from around his neck and shook out two gems…glittering and black in the light of the braziers. At the sight of them Kassim forgot to be cross. His eyes widened. They were as big as ripe dates. Bigger than any jewels he had ever seen at his father's trade. Fascinated by their brilliance, he watched as his father laid first the stones and then his lips on his mother's belly. "You will restore our honor, little one."

Mother smiled at his father's words, "This child…this child will fulfill the legacy." She stroked her stomach where his father's kiss still lingered.

Kassim's scowl returned and his stomach twisted. His lips trembled and his eyes stung at the tenderness they showed. Tenderness they had never before bestowed upon anyone but Kassim; but now there was to be this other, and already it usurped his parents' affection. Here was the proof. He buried his face in his arm and felt tears dampen his sleeve. But…but he was heir. He was to take his father's place.

He wanted nothing more than to crawl up into his mother's lap and cry and beg her to deny this other child, to tell him that it was not wanted or needed, but to reveal his presence would bring such punishment down upon his head. He lay there in the dark, sniffling and curled in on himself, thinking of gems as large as dates until sleep crept over him.

Kassim gazed about his father's chamber. The low bed was still made, as if waiting for his father's return. A low desk sat against one wall, the dark wood lustrous in the lamplight.

Pulling out drawers and scrolls, Kassim rifled carelessly through the sheaves of records not heedful of the bloodstains his hands left on lists of wares and accountings. He pulled apart books and cushions seeking hidden spaces. Pulling the bedclothes from the frame and the rich tapestries from the wall, Kassim ripped them to shreds. Nothing. He tipped over a bag of coins and upended a box of rare jade from the Far East, but Kassim sought a treasure much more personal than mere riches.

As a young boy, he had thought the stones pretty, never imagining their worth, wanting them only because they were bequeathed to the *other* child of Massoud. The promised child; the special child.

The man he'd become knew them for the rarest of jewels, black diamonds of such clarity the angels would weep at the sight. Any man to possess them would be wealthier than the most powerful sheikh. But even now, for Kassim, those diamonds stood as the icons of all his brother had stolen from him. This was the treasure Kassim sought. They did not come to him the night he'd learned of his father's death, or any night thereafter, but he would not stop searching, as Allah was his witness.

In silence the riders galloped across the desert, their tack silenced and their horses' hooves covered in cloth. Moonlight limned them like specters gliding over the sands. Dread clung to their robes. Swinging down before their mounts had fully stopped, they hurried into their lair, a cavern whose stone roof rose above the desert, a deeper shadow in the darkness.

Handing the reins to others of their band, the men strode to their leader, Rassul Maroun, who sat at a marble table ignoring them as he studied a scrap of parchment. The returning men knelt before him, heads bowed and the backs of their right hands pressed to their foreheads in tight fists. Torchlight flickered over thick silver bands engraved with identical markings visible across their inner wrists: a coiled viper poised to strike emblazoned over crossed *khanjars*. They knelt there on aching knees for long silent moments as their leader finally let his gaze rise from the parchment.

"Tell me of your success," Rassul ordered, his voice rumbling low, like the threat of a pending storm. He stood slowly, aware of the impression he made as his lean, well-muscled body unfolded from the chair to tower above all present. He walked toward the prostrate men, his steps whisper soft. Stopping in front of one, Rassul traced the symbol on the man's wrist before shoving the hand aside to grip the man's chin tight, forcing his gaze upward until their eyes locked.

The man trembled, blinking furiously as he swallowed hard. There was a stillness in Rassul's gaze, something that made grown men fear to disobey him. "The horse fled too swiftly, master," the unfortunate man answered. "We followed but could not draw near enough before it reached the gates of Wadi Al-Nejd. The guards took the beast in and closed the gates." He gulped again, sharp, as if swallowing a plump date. "We could follow no further."

Rassul tightened his grip, almost pulling the man up by his jaw. "Your orders were to follow that beast and learn from where it came, that we might ensure no other holds the secret of our lair."

"Yes, master."

Rassul dragged the man to the table and tapped the surface. "Allah has blessed you with two eyes, that you might see the world. Do you see this?"

"Yes, master."

"Are you certain? Because with the sanctity of our cache at risk, it is important to be absolutely certain."

The man hesitated.

"Would you swear by Allah?" As he spoke, Rassul moved his hand to the back of the man's neck in a lighter grip. Beneath his fingers the thief trembled. "What is it you see?" Rassul asked.

"A m-ma…ma…" The man could not finish.

Rassul *tsked*. "I think you are not certain at all," he said after a moment of the man's stammering. Locking his grip hard on the man's neck, his hand took on a glow of power as he slammed him forward into the table's surface. Bone crunched against unyielding marble and the body went slack. Rassul let go and the corpse slid to the floor, trailing crimson streaks from the edge of the parchment to the rim of the table.

"It is a map," Rassul said as he spat on the body. "May *Allah* forgive you your foolishness…and your failure."

He snapped his eyes upward and locked gazes with every one of his men, including the dead man's partner, who still knelt, as yellow piss slowly pooled around him.

"All of you. You sought immortality. You bound yourself to me. Learn from this, in case any of you are uncertain."

Casually, Rassul stepped over the body and once more perused the map. "Wipe out all knowledge of this map. Destroy any copies. Do this before all other things."

He grabbed the map and held it to the nearest torch until the parchment blackened, then curled, giving off a pungent stench as the flame consumed it. In a gesture of disgust he crumpled it, still burning in his hand, until there was nothing left but the ash that stained his palm.

Without another word he left the chamber, his thoughts on much graver concerns. The intruder had carried an ornate box, one Rassul recognized. It had belonged to the guardian of Nader Shah's fabled treasure trove. Rassul had killed the guardian, more than one hundred years ago, and secured the treasure—hidden in this very cavern—but had been unaware of the significance of the box. He had thought it just another trinket, a child's toy.

It had only been after he'd ended that blighted soul that he discovered the treasure was ensorcelled in place. Rassul could not move even the smallest seed pearl from where it rested, whether by magical means or mundane. He was certain the box—which had vanished—held the key.

A wise man…a free man would have turned away then and returned to his own life. Rassul could not. He was trapped for all time by a master long-dead. Himself enchanted, Rassul could not leave these desert lands until the Peacock Throne and all the riches pooled before it were delivered to the Shahanshah of the Qajar Empire. He seethed at the thought of toiling for many generations, in exile, for a dynasty he cursed with each and every breath. This was his treasure. He had earned it with blood and sacrifice. He rubbed the onyx ring he had taken from the guardian. Rassul should have long ago died in this place, as the loved ones he'd been forced to leave behind surely had.

And now the box had resurfaced and with it a chance to finally claim his freedom. Yet, before he could take the box from the intruder's cold dead hands, a mechanical beast had plummeted from the sky to snatch the prize away. Rassul's lips curled in disgust. He was a man of magic and the inventions of the "tinkerers" had always disturbed him. Filthy unnatural things.

But his feelings on artificing and mechanics didn't matter. Rassul would have the box. This time he would win his freedom. He sent his best men in pursuit. They would pay with their lives should they return without the box. Immortality did not belong to those who failed in the tasks he set for them.

The letter arrived a little over three months after the box, delivered by the Royal Post carrier, one brisk autumn day. Ali did not hear the knocking at the door. His teacher was off on business and Ali's time was his own. The day maid brought him a travel-stained letter as he sat in the back garden. He'd intended to sketch a few designs in a journal *Ustad* Babbage had gifted him, but instead lost himself in contemplation of the Almighty's glory in the changing hue of the leaves on these English trees. Never before had he seen the color of flame captured so; until the branches seemed on fire, though nothing burned.

This was life passing through time. His marvel at such things swiftly waned, however, as he accepted the missive.

Ali recognized his brother's hand. That in itself spoke to Ali of unpleasantness within. Never had Kassim squandered even a moment to show Ali kindness. Sometimes, in the darkest recesses of night, Ali grieved for his brother. Kassim was a man of wealth and power and influence, and yet, rather than rejoice in Allah's bounty, he cast his gaze always outward, to that which he did not possess. Such pursuits had left little room in his heart for tenderness or joy.

Somewhere in the garden, a songbird trilled contentedly. Ali let himself fall into the sound, so at odds with his spirit. Even before the letter's arrival, since the very night the falcon descended upon them, the household had existed as if beneath a pall of mourning. He and his teacher worked in silence and when Babbage did speak, it was softly, without the familiar gruffness Ali recognized as a shield to the man's heart. Ali was frustrated with his mentor's unwillingness to explain himself and all attempts to return to their previous relationship were rebuffed. Ali did not understand the aura of sorrow that encompassed Babbage, save that he was its focus.

If his teacher's behavior was not sufficient to unsettle Ali, he also feared he was being watched and some nights suspected someone lurked in the garden. Once he'd found spots of blood on the walkway to the workshop. For months now, he existed on edge, so much so that he woke several times in the night and could not return to his rest without checking that the household was secure. He could only imagine what further trials the letter might bring.

Willing peace into his spirit, he rose from the bench, journal forgotten, and retired to his chamber. He closed the door behind him and settled on the bed. Despite the stifling warmth of the sun-heated room, a chill crawled through Ali's belly. He broke the wax seal and pulled out the pale pages, reading his brother's words, written in the language of their people.

Honorable Brother,

As is Allah's Will and the Prophet's, I write to tell you of the death of our father, the Almighty's blessing upon his soul.

You will return immediately and fulfill your responsibility to our household.

Kassim

A cry sliced through the silence, followed by the tearing of parchment. Glass shattered somewhere as the solid oak door slammed against the plaster wall. The world spun and buffeted Ali as he tumbled, reality only loosely holding him in its grasp. He curled in on himself tightly, as a continued keening lanced his ears. His soul wept and raged but could not be heard above the crying.

For a very long time Ali knew nothing but his own heartache.

Chapter Three

CHARLES BABBAGE FOUND ALI AT THE BASE OF THE STAIRS, in the front foyer; gently rocking, but making no sound, his arms folded over his head and his face buried against his knees. Babbage instantly felt a surge of concern. The lad looked upset, but not injured. Had someone accosted him, as had happened too often before? Or had he news from home? There had been mention more than once recently of strangers in the neighborhood…strangers in British attire, but with skin the color of strong tea. Might someone from the lad's homeland been sent to fetch him? Babbage frowned.

Looking around for anything that might give clue to the matter, Babbage noted the maid peering around the door to the parlor, still as a mouse afraid to slip past the cat, her face white and her eyes wide. At her feet lay a cleaning rag and the shattered remains of a crystal decanter. When she saw him, she drew the courage to dash out, nearly making it past him to the front door before Babbage caught her by the arm.

"Tell me, girl, what happened here?"

"I don' ken, sir," she stammered, her accent thick. "The wog…" Babbage's jaw clenched at her unthinking use of the slur. He shook her before she could continue. "The young sir," she corrected herself, " 'e gots a post. I gave it 'im and

went to clean the parlor. Next I know 'e's screamin' like the divil 'isself, then comes half fallin' down the stairs an' stops where you seen 'im."

At her words, Babbage noticed the pieces of parchment scattered around Ali like leaves fallen from a tree. He sighed, his chest tightening as he released his grip on the girl, his attention on Ali. "Go. And do not return. Do you understand me, girl? You are dismissed." His tone was once again flat, unemotional.

Sobbing, she fled without even closing the door. Babbage edged it shut with a quiet *click* then turned toward his apprentice. He knew to a fairly certain degree what news the letter had held. Since the night the mechanical bird appeared in the workshop window he had been waiting for something like this.

Babbage had recognized the box and knew it represented Ali's inheritance. That it had been delivered meant Ali's father, Massoud, had met his end. Old grief darted from the crevices of Babbage's heart to strangle that self-same organ. His wife…so many of his children… his own father…and now his unlikely friend. Babbage had held his tongue and waited for Ali to receive formal notice. He did not want to believe, and likewise had not felt it his place to speak when he had no confirmation. Looking down at the young man Babbage experienced a moment of regret. Perhaps it would have been kinder to let the lad hear the news from a friend's lips.

The regulator clock on the upstairs landing chimed the dinner hour…the time of the lad's required prayer. Not tonight. Babbage watched as first a tremor ran through the huddled form and then a full shudder. He realized the reaction was not grief alone, but in part from cold, as evidenced by the gooseflesh raised on Ali's skin.

Babbage sniffed. The only smell in the air was must and a faint hint of lye. The girl had not even lit the fires against the evening chill. Frowning, he entered the parlor. First he cleaned up the glass, and then he kindled a blaze, before returning to Ali's side. Babbage knelt beside him and reached out. A broken sob answered the light touch of his hand on the lad's shoulder.

"Come, lad," he ordered brusquely, as was his usual manner, knowing to depart from it would not benefit the lad.

Slowly, as if under the influence of opiates, Ali raised his head, then unwound himself from his knotted huddle. The collar of his robe was soaked through and evidence of earlier tears crusted his lashes. His eyes, for now, were glazed but dry, the flesh surrounding them red and swollen. Worry scribed Babbage's expression as he drew his apprentice to his feet and guided him into the parlor, seating him in a chair beside the hearth.

His instinct was to ply Ali with brandy to deaden the ache, but even if such were not in violation of the lad's beliefs, Babbage knew the futility of such treatment for grief. Instead he dropped a blanket around Ali's shoulders and then went to set the kettle for tea. He was torn. Would it be best to use the familiar blend Ali received from home, or would such a reminder anchor him deeper in his melancholy? Babbage hesitated only briefly before taking up the exotic tin and measuring out the leaves.

Surely, at this time, the familiar would be a comfort.

When he returned to the parlor with the tea tray Ali had not moved and the blanket lay slumped around him. Intimate with the reaction, Babbage resolved himself for firmness, knowing little else would penetrate the fog enshrouding his apprentice. First he tested the heat of the tea, waiting long enough for it to cool sufficiently that it would not burn, then he physically wrapped Ali's fingers around the teacup and raised it to grief-numbed lips.

"Drink now," he ordered. When the cup was twice drained and some semblance of warmth had returned to Ali's flesh, Babbage led the lad to a nearby divan and laid him down, covering him with the blanket. "Rest. We will speak in the morning."

The lad's eyes closed as ordered, but tension held his form stiff.

Babbage drew the drapes and fed the fire until the room was nearly over-warm, then he sat in the chair by the hearth and watched over his charge, his heart sitting vigil for his fallen friend as his body did for the son.

Ali woke to salt's sting upon his lips and bitterness upon his tongue. Sweat beaded his skin and somewhere beyond his darkness rumbled a deep, steady snore. Ali lay there listening, part of him noting he remained clothed in his *thobe* beneath a wool blanket, on a surface that was not his bed. Reality returned against Ali's will and his heart ached beneath the burden. The sigh that slipped from him caught in his throat as the words from his brother's letter burned before his closed eyes. He pressed his lips together against any further sound, ashamed at his half-formed memories of earlier. To grieve the dead was permissible, loud cries and wailing were not. He who believes in Allah and the Last

Day need not mourn the dead overlong. Slowly, quietly, he rose from the couch and left the parlor. In the kitchen he rinsed away the tears that had overcome him and freshened himself. After that he fixed a simple meal for his teacher, as was their routine. Today he set only one place. The thought of food, or even tea, inspired his stomach to instant rebellion.

As he set a serving of poached egg over toast at the table, the parlor door opened and footsteps approached the kitchen.

Ali did not turn, instead busying himself preparing tea, losing moments of time as memories of his father swarmed up, as if borne upon the fragrant steam. Memories of mornings on the desert and drinking tea before the fire. As the steps drew closer, Ali raised one hand, warding off assistance. Right now the routine of preparing the meal helped him to focus and allowed him to not be overwhelmed by his emotions. The sound of the chair scraping back from the table eased the tension in his shoulders. For a long, silent moment, Ali focused on the rise and fall of his own chest, drawing deep of blessed air while he listened to the muted sounds of *Ustad* Babbage breaking his fast. When he felt himself steady Ali released his grip and slowly turned.

He bowed to his teacher, keeping his swollen eyes downcast. "My apologies, sir, for my unseemly behavior. I thank you for your kind care."

Babbage sputtered and choked on his bit of egg, sending fragments across the table. On another day Ali would have found it difficult not to laugh.

"You apologize?!" His teacher scowled. "Don't be ridiculous. There is no shame in grief."

"To Allah belongs what He took, and to Him belongs what He gave. My father was a strong man, a righteous man. Non-submission to the will of the Almighty is an act of ingratitude, of *kufr*. I would not shame him, or you, *Ustad*."

Babbage held up his hand.

"I would have had much greater concern had you not grieved so, lad. It is to be expected at the passing of one much beloved."

Ali flinched at the understanding in his teacher's gaze. He dug his nails into his palms.

Babbage's voice was gruff, yet barely above a whisper. "Come, let us speak."

In silence, Ali followed his teacher back into the parlor, squinting as he did so. Babbage had opened the drapes and chilled autumn sunlight shone through the sheers. The room's comfort did not penetrate the numbness that had wrapped Ali from top to toe. He sat perched on the edge of the wingback chair across from his teacher, clasping and unclasping his hands as he waited for the man to speak.

And waited.

Then waited more as Babbage watched him as closely as he would the test of a new design. Ali shifted and the muscle beneath his eye twitched. He willed his features still, his expression neutral, until it felt as if he rested within a pocket of air in the midst of a sandstorm, aware of the fury of the wind, but as yet untouched.

From this stillness he spoke, "*Ustad?*"

Babbage narrowed his gaze in something other than a scowl for the first time in Ali's remembrance, as if deep in thought. He nodded, either coming to a decision or confirming one as he drew a sheaf of papers from a small table beside him.

"You do know you have a place here, if you wish it, yes?" Babbage tapped the papers against the palm of his other hand. "No matter your finances or your standing in society… Please, tell me you understand this."

Ali nodded, but did not speak. Would that wishing were enough…

A faint scowl pinched *Ustad* Babbage's brow at Ali's silence.

"Well…what do you wish?"

"I thank you," Ali began, respect requiring he answer a direct address, "but I have been summoned home by the head of my household."

Ustad Babbage's head bobbed in a slow nod. "I feared as much. That is why I procured this," he said as he held up the papers. Ali took them from his hand, his movements slow. The sheaf quivered as he brought it close.

It was Ali's turn to frown. He looked from the papers to his teacher…his *friend*. "Passage home?" The words came out tight. In one breath his teacher offered him to stay, with the next he seemed eager enough to be rid of Ali.

Babbage nodded, melancholy dimming his gaze. "You depart in two weeks' time."

Perhaps not eager, then.

"You will need to cover your meals and other incidental expenses," his teacher continued, "but this is at least one burden I can take from you."

Ali blew a sharp breath as he leafed through the papers. He gasped as he noted the details of the voucher. "Return passage?"

Babbage grunted, as if this were an inconsequential thing. "If you wish to come back at any time, you have the means in your hand, no matter the situation you find yourself." The man would not meet his eye. He leaned to the side of his chair and pulled up something from the floor. When he straightened he settled a pouch across his lap. "These were left with me by your—" he paused, his tongue moistening his lips as if they'd gone suddenly dry. "—your father." From the pouch he drew a book hand-bound in leather. The tome looked ancient, Persian in style. "I had the loan of this until you were ready for it. To be frank, I should have turned it over months ago. I beg your forgiveness…"

Ali felt the ghost of a smile tug his lips. "Granted."

Babbage handed him the book.

The feel of the soft leather tickled Ali's palms. Eyes wide with wonder, he ran fingers over the embossed title, written in Persian: *The Book of Knowledge of Ingenious Mechanical Devices*. The name scribed beneath was Al-Jazari. The parchment—crackling with age—had seen both obvious handling and the passage of time, but was clearly not the original, cited as written in 1206.

"I was told," Babbage said, "that it is a transcription of an exceedingly old text…written over six-hundred years gone past. Astounding really, how very much I have learned from just the images on those pages. The wonders of engineering that mankind was capable of, even then… I regret not having the knowledge to read the words."

Before the comment cleared his teacher's lips Ali sat forward, holding out the text on hands that trembled. "I could delay my journey, to read it to you before I go, perhaps even transcribe it… such would be little enough to repay your kindness to me."

Babbage waved him back with a familiar *phfft*. "I am an old man, too old for bedtime stories. The wonders in that book are for you to learn…to build on. Your father's legacy to you as surely as that box…"

"The box?" The priceless book dropped to the floor, forgotten, as Ali lunged forward to clutch at *Ustad* Babbage's chair. "You knew? Why did you not tell me?" There was hurt and the faintest reproach in his voice.

Babbage winced.

"Your father showed it to me once, before you came here. He said it contained his greatest secret and his second greatest treasure, after his children. Massoud told me then that it would find its way to you, should anything…happen to him." His teacher laughed, a sharp, humorless bark as he bent to retrieve the book, handing it back to Ali. "I had not expected he meant that literally.

"I am sorry…" he went on. "I did not want to believe, and I did not want to cause you such pain. I'd hoped to be proved wrong."

Taking the book, Ali sat back into his chair, betrayal and understanding battling within him. He started to rise, needing the comfort that only prayer and meditation could bring, but he held his seat at a halting gesture from his mentor.

"Just a moment more, if you please," Babbage said. "There is one final thing I must pass on to you." This time he held out the pouch itself. Ali took it and peered inside, stunned to find it heavy with coin. Not enough to make him a rich man, but sufficient to grant him options when he returned home, if he guarded it well, and spent frugally on his journey.

"I thank you for holding this in trust." Ali bowed respectfully to his teacher.

"I am sorry for the necessity," Babbage replied, his gaze turned inward, as if on memories of his own. "I fear that you have difficult times ahead of you, lad."

The next evening, as Ali struggled with a fractious set of gears and pistons destined for a special commission, there was a tapping at the door of the workroom. Normally, Ali would hurry to answer, but he barely noticed the knock, so caught up was he in frustration. *Ustad* Babbage set his own tools down and went to the door. After an exchange of quiet murmurs with the new maid, Millie, he cleared his throat.

"Enough, lad, the contraption seems to be winning. Best come at it fresh in the morning."

Ali scowled at the metalworking. He did not like that his teacher had cause to note his current failing. Bad enough the infernal thing was uncooperative, worse that Ali appeared a fumble-fingered tinkerer before *Ustad* Babbage. Ali began to suspect several components tooled by the blacksmith were not measured precisely to the specifications they had requested. He would have to grind them down. Almost without thought, Ali's hand reached for the first offending piece.

His teacher's expression deepened into stern lines. "Now, Ali."

Ali jerked his arm back, and his cheeks burned. He nodded as he wiped his tools clean and put them away. He then covered his work with a protective cloth and stepped away from the table. The corners of his mouth turned down as his gaze remained on the shrouded automaton. This commission was important. Not just for the funds it would bring in for their own projects, but because the client was a close friend of *Ustad* Babbage. It was to be a delicate clockwork doll for the man's young daughter. When complete, it would dance and jump rope and even giggle past steam-warmed lips of satin-smooth red gold. If only Ali could get the blasted clockwork elements properly engaged and ensconced in their pretty shell.

Barely did he realize his hand had crept out again until *Ustad* Babbage grabbed it and tugged him away.

"There are visitors waiting in the parlor, lad. It is rude to keep them waiting."

At that comment, Ali's head whipped around. Other than the servants and occasional visits from his teacher's remaining family, theirs had been a solitary existence. Upon occasion, a colleague might stop by to consult on some engineering matter, but never was Ali included in such visits. Nervous, he straightened his *besht* and followed *Ustad* Babbage without one more glance back.

They moved through the kitchen, pausing to wash their hands before continuing to the hallway that led to the parlor. Curiosity darted through Ali like a desert mouse scenting fresh water. *Who could be waiting? What did they want? Ustad* Babbage rarely bothered with social niceties…at least not since Ali had taken up residence. And yet a tray waited beside the parlor door, filled with a tea more sumptuous than Ali was used to seeing. His eyes widened at the delicacies even as his mouth moistened. Hunger tickled his gut, reminding him how long ago he had eaten breakfast. That hunger soured, then died, however, as his teacher stopped beside the door and shooed Ali on toward the stairs, his mouth opened to speak. Though he did not allow it to shape his features, Ali felt a deep hurt at being sent away. His eyes, however, must have betrayed him.

Babbage *humph*ed and shook his head. "Enough of that foolishness, lad, I merely wish you to fetch your book. Our guests are quite interested in seeing such a rare treasure."

Ali flushed with embarrassment. He bobbed his head, eyes lowered. *Ustad* Babbage again waved him toward the stairs. With a grin on his face and hunger again rumbling in his belly, Ali nearly flew up the stairs to do as *Ustad* Babbage bid.

When Ali entered the parlor he found that *Ustad* Babbage and his guests had already drawn seats around the fire and set out the tea on a low table usually crowded with various books. The three of them were in the midst of a conversation so Ali quietly lowered himself into the only empty chair, beside the divan and slid the book out of the way beneath it for the time being. As he settled in and clasped his hands on top of his thighs *Ustad* Babbage noticed his return.

"Shall I pour the tea?" Ali asked his teacher. Not waiting for an answer, he leaned forward, reaching for the service.

"Thank you, lad." *Ustad* Babbage wore a faint, proud smile as he nodded, then turned to his guests. "Lady Claramina, Fritz Langstrom, this is my apprentice, Ali bin-Massoud. He then turned to Ali. "My boy, these are the Langstroms, for whom you are making the construct."

"Clara, Charles. Or Lady Clara, if you must," the dark-haired woman said from where she sat on the far end of the divan. She dressed in a deep burgundy riding habit and half-boots, and spoke in formal, British tones. "Lovely to meet you, Ali."

"Likewise, Lady Claramina," Ali responded with a slight bow as he filled each of their cups. She gave him an admonishing stare at which he cleared his throat and corrected himself, "Lady Clara." It felt odd to address her so, but he would respect her preference. He still found it strange to sit and converse with a woman not related to him. It would never have been allowed in his homeland. These English were so, informal. However, his time in England had taught him there could be merit in the customs of others.

"I have seen your work, young man, very impressive," the gentleman added, his words strangely accented. Ali recalled *Ustad* Babbage mentioning Mister Langstrom was American. It was an effort not to stare. Everything about the man was unusual, from his extreme height to his clothing, a soft cotton shirt and loose, woolen trousers.

As the comment sank in, Ali's face warmed in a flush and he could not help but smile. "Thank you, sir."

"Yes," *Ustad* Babbage said. "I shall be disappointed to see him go."

"Go?" Lady Clara's dark gaze returned to Ali.

At her question, Ali's smile vanished like a mirage. "I have been summoned home by the head of my household," he answered softly, his spirit weighed down. "I leave in less than two weeks' time. But do not worry, I will not leave before your commission is complete."

"How unfortunate you must leave at all," Lady Clara responded, waving away his concern regarding the commission. "Though how splendid that you will see your family after so long."

The room fell silent, uncomfortably so. Ali struggled to keep a neutral expression as he focused on laying out the rest of the tea, gesturing the others to partake of the bounty. He lifted his own teacup and made an effort to savor the floral aroma, listening as his teacher and their guests continued their earlier conversation.

"Fritz would have to explain the details," Lady Clara said, "but I can assure you that the principle is sound…"

Ustad Babbage set his cup down sharply. "You can hardly expect me to believe any manner of machine is capable of extracting objects from the future."

"The Futuraositor can…" Fritz said. "Or it could before my lovely wife insisted I dismantle it. We drew something called a televisor…a broadsheet from many decades hence…even a man…briefly. It was all quite exciting while it lasted. I can't wait to see what else the future holds, though Clara insists I wait for it to take place, rather than find another way to 'peek'."

"Impossible." The word exploded from Babbage. "More foolishness and daydreams."

"Honored *Ustad*, forgive me, but you are wrong."

Ali cringed at the sound of his own voice. He had not meant to intrude on the conversation and while diverse opinions for discussion was all well and good, directly contradicting one's teacher and host was rude. All of them turned their gazes on him. His skin heated once more, but Ali forced himself to continue.

"The future has not happened yet, but Allah, and those he has blessed may know what is to come. Our destiny lies before us as a road. All that awaits is for us to set our own feet upon the path." Lady Clara turned more fully toward him as he spoke. Conviction burned in the depth of her gaze as well as intent consideration.

Ali lowered his eyes. He would not be so bold as to stare at a woman. But his heart lifted. This English woman considered him as an equal and seemed to give the same value to his thoughts. "If 'Impossible' is part of your journey, then Allah's will be done."

"Exactly, Ali. Impossible is a limit we place upon ourselves based on 'reason' and what can only be an imperfect understanding," Lady Clara added.

Rather than argue with his guests, Babbage picked up his teacup and sipped silently, disagreement clear on his face. They responded with wry amusement.

"Charles, do not limit yourself so. Attempt the impossible at every opportunity and let experience determine the truth of the matter."

Ali considered Lady Clara's words and felt her fervor echoing in his own heart. Part of him most definitely wished to accomplish 'impossible' things. "In truth, that of which you speak is not much different than faith."

All movement in the room stopped. Even the clock on the mantel seemed to pause between beats.

"What an interesting concept," Lady Clara said after moment, her voice thoughtful.

"And it would seem to coincide with the theoretical underpinnings of the ways of magic," Fritz added. "Too often, these two schools of thought have conflicted."

Babbage snorted, "Artificers are workers in mechanics and measurable results, clockwork and steam. The real and tangible world. What you speak of is brownies at the end of the garden."

"I think your apprentice may have the stronger argument, Charles," Lady Clara persisted.

Ali offered a half-smile but his thoughts had turned inward. Yes, his faith and his artificing worked together. He had been gifted by the Almighty and to use his skills would serve Allah best. He had no doubt his brother had other plans for him that did not involve the skills of an artificer. With all enjoyment fled, Ali braced to rise with the intent of excusing himself. Perhaps he might sneak back out to the workshop, and lose himself in the pleasure of mechanical things for what little time remained to him.

Ustad Babbage caught his eye and gave a subtle shake of his head. "Come, come, lad. Convince me. I am an old man. I believe in caution and good sense," his teacher added, as if he did not well know where Ali's thoughts lay, "and a good strong spanner. Explain to me this intersection. Faith and impossibilities. God knows, Clara and Fritz here have tried to convert me. Perhaps you will have better luck, eh?"

"Now, Charles," Lady Clara interjected. "Ali is clearly tired, this is not the time to drag him into one of your heated debates."

The warmth of the room brightened as everyone laughed and turned their attention to simpler conversation. Ali settled back and sipped his tea. Despite his sorrow about returning him, he found he rather enjoyed the animated discussion that resumed around him. It ebbed and flowed, topics changing from mundane to obscure, but always fascinating. He was not familiar with diurnalscopes or aether lenses, but the talk of invention and theory, carried mostly by Mister Langstrom and *Ustad* Babbage, held Ali's attention completely, as a dancing cobra would.

"I'm not much for the technical aspects myself," Lady Clara murmured to Ali from the divan. "But I do find my husband's enthusiasm contagious, if at times exasperating."

Ali nodded and smiled, though he was not quite sure he understood her. He heard her laugh behind him as the gentlemen's conversation again drew him and he could not help but edge closer. Some of the concepts were familiar, but the theories being bandied about were more advanced than anything Ali had yet learned. They bordered on the magical, an association distinctly at odds with matters of science. He soaked in everything anyway, certain the day would come when his practical knowledge would catch up. He wondered, perhaps, if he were frugal, might he be able to spend a small portion of the coin his father had left him on a book or two before he departed. They were much more common here, and easier to attain. With the right book he could study on his own...

The thought served as a jarring reminder, they had not yet examined the book. Carefully Ali drew it from beneath the divan, where he had tucked it out of the way.

He cleared his throat gently, but enough that the animated conversation trailed off as both men turned toward Ali. "Excuse me, but I had forgotten Mister Langstrom desired to see this..."

As Ali brought it out even Lady Clara sat forward.

Langstrom rose from his seat and came forward so swiftly Ali nearly jerked back.

"Fritz!" his wife admonished him in a low, but firm tone, almost like a mother reminding a child of his manners.

"Sorry...very sorry, may I?" The man flushed slightly as he stepped back and held out his hand, his eyes bright.

"By all means." Ali held out the ancient tome. Even as a copy, it was older than any book he had heard of, other than religious texts. With reverence, Mister Langstrom accepted the book and returned to his seat, placing the volume in his lap with care before turning back the cover to reveal masterpieces of ancient engineering.

As *Ustad* Babbage pointed out his favorite diagrams to Langstrom, Ali sat back and found pleasure in the American's excitement. Ali could not yet bring himself to look at the book. The manner in which he came to possess it was too deeply rooted in sorrow. That eased some now, however, to see the book bring such joy to another.

"Thank you," Lady Clara addressed him again, this time from much closer than she had been before. "This chance to see your treasure up close means much to my husband."

Ali nodded in acknowledgement of her thanks, but kept his gaze respectfully averted. This did not seem to offend or discourage her.

"Charles mentioned that you are from Arabia...perhaps we will see you there...after you have returned home. We are traveling our way east on invitation from the Artificers' Guild, giving lectures for their regional guildhalls."

Impressed did not begin to describe Ali's reaction. He had heard of the Artificers' Guild. It was small, but growing. In his homeland, magic was still considered the preferred tool as compared to mechanics, yet already there were several guild halls in the region. There was even talk of building one in Jerusalem, the Holy City and home of many sorcerer madrassas for teaching the magical arts. At one time, not long ago, Ali had dreamed of his eventual acceptance into the Artificers' Guild. Now...now he was not certain he would even be allowed to continue his learning *or* his craft, knowing his brother's prejudice against all things mechanical. Still, that was none of Lady Clara's concern.

"I would enjoy a visit very much, if it is the Almighty's will that our paths come together at a future time. You and your husband are welcome guests, should your journey carry you to my threshold."

Ali prayed his brother would not make a liar of him should the unlikely occurrence of a visit arise.

Chapter Four

A FAINT PROMISE OF DAWN LIGHTENED THE BEDCHAMBER. Ali lay half-uncovered by his blankets. It was an hour yet before he must wake but in truth he had not slept at all. He groaned and dropped his head back to the pillow, desperate to slumber before it was too late. Long into the night, conflicted thoughts on returning home had kept him awake. He feared they might well continue to do so if given the chance. Ruthlessly, he closed his eyes and cleared his mind.

Ali drifted at the edge of exhaustion, his body just beginning to warm and relax beneath his woolen blankets. *Scritch...scritch.* The faint sound came from outside the window. In an instant, he snapped wide awake once more.

Ali slowly rolled to his side and stared at the window through slitted eyes. All potential for sleep fled as he saw, improbable as it seemed, someone clinging to the roof outside his dormer window.

The blankets rustled as Ali's fingers clamped down on their edge. The furnishings of his room were sparse, with no visible weapon at hand: the bed, a small table beside it, the shelf for his candle next to the door, and another behind it, where his rolled-up prayer rug resided. His own belongings were even fewer. The puzzle box rested on his bedside table,

gleaming in the faint light coming through the window. His clothing hung from pegs behind the door: two *thobes*, a heavy *besht*, and his *chafiye*, with sandals and a pair of English-style boots below them. However, stored beneath the bed was his *khanjar*. By tradition, the blade was worn openly in the desert of his homeland. Such was not permissible in English society…at least not for him.

Reaching one arm under the bed for the sheath, Ali's hand instead came down on polished wood. His grandfather's staff, carved of sacred cypress wood, which was said to have properties of protection. Ali drew it out into the open rather than keep searching for his dagger.

He tightened his grip on the thick, strong length, then rose up, a cry of warning on his lips.

Before Ali could release the cry, a piercing shriek disturbed the pre-dawn quiet. The dark figure outside the window flinched, then a hand reached out to shove at the sash, the intruder clearly forsaking stealth to get in. Clothed to blend with shadow and darkness, the intruder was difficult to make out. Brandishing the staff, Ali lunged for the window. Two eyes stared at him past a tight-wrapped scarf. They flicked away from Ali to the puzzle box.

Ali backed away as the man drew from the folds of his clothing what looked like a large-bore pistol. Before he could fire, another angry cry pierced the silence. The man fumbled and nearly dropped the gun as something large and unnatural dove on him from the sky.

This time the man cried out. Ali watched as the intruder tried to duck away, his limbs scrabbling at the shingles as razor-sharp talons of polished bronze raked across his scalp.

Taking advantage of the man's distraction, Ali brought the staff crashing down on the hand that clung to the window sash.

A second scream trailed off as both man and gun fell from two storeys above the ground. A glint of metal caught the first rays of the sun as the clockwork falcon winged away across the sky.

Behind Ali, the bedroom door slammed open. He pivoted around, the staff gripped in both hands, the end raised.

Babbage stood there in a striped cotton nightshirt, his expression incredulous. "What the devil?"

"Thief!" was all Ali called out as he darted past and scrambled down the stairs. As he dashed through the back door, he heard a thud outside, then stumbling footsteps running down the path toward the back garden.

Ali gritted his teeth and increased his pace, fighting to close the distance between him and the thief before the man reached the back gate and escaped to the street beyond. In the early light, he could barely make out the fleeing figure dressed in all black.

"Thief!" he shouted to draw attention, and sped up. "The dawn will not protect you."

Rounding a stone outbuilding, Ali drew up short. Barely ten meters ahead, the thief stood by the garden gate, his chest heaving and blood glistening through a tear in his head scarf. The man glared over what Ali now recognized as a *howdah* pistol, a weapon popular in his homeland.

"*Ma'a Salaama.*"

Ali ducked as the gun fired. Stone fragments exploded from the corner of the garden shed as the lead ball crashed into it. Slivers cut into Ali's exposed face and neck. He shielded his face but kept moving.

In a crouching run, he overtook the thief in a heartbeat and leapt, swinging his staff. The thief fired again. This time Ali heard the whine of the lead ball as it flew past his face. Overhead, he would swear he heard an answering falcon's cry.

Ali brought the cypress wood down across the thief's hand. The gun dropped to the hard-packed ground, still smoking from its recent use. As the man drew back in reflex Ali spied an engraved silver band around his wrist. The design was of a coiled viper backed by crossed *khanjars*, but he could not tell for certain in the low light. Dropping his staff behind him, out of the thief's reach, Ali leapt upon the man. They crashed to the ground, each struggling for the advantage. The thief's scarf slipped low on his face and Ali went stiff with shock. He could not say he knew this man, but without a doubt his face was familiar.

Overhead sounded the ringing cry of the falcon. Both Ali and the thief jerked their gazes upward to the dark shape diving through the sky. The thief twisted and struck, desperate to get away. Ali grimly hung on until a well-placed blow connected with his temple hard enough to make his vision swirl. His grip loosened and the thief slipped free, disappearing out the gate. Again the falcon screamed, but drew no closer, banking away toward where the thief had fled.

Ali attempted to stand but found his legs unsteady beneath him. He stretched out to grip the end of his staff and draw it close. Using it to steady himself, he gained his feet. *Ustad* Babbage came running toward him, still in his nightshirt.

"A man tried to creep in through my window," Ali told him, gasping for breath, his head still reeling, "but the falcon returned and attacked him."

Babbage scowled his fiercest scowl yet. "Preposterous! How would they even reach your window that far up? You have surely confused a dream with reality." They both turned toward the house. Ali, at least, saw the path the thief had followed. The trellis of ivy and English tea roses hung in tatters from where the thief used them to reach the flat top of the covered walkway. From there it was an easy reach to the small ledge overhanging the lower level of the house, where the thief had likely used the sturdy window boxes to pull himself up the building. Turning to his teacher, Ali solemnly shook his head.

"I too would have thought it a dream, *Ustad*," Ali said. "Save dreams, I believe, do not bleed." He gestured toward a bloody hand-print overhead on one of the white columns holding up the covered walkway.

Babbage paled, then grudgingly nodded.

His next words were abrupt. "Inside. Now. As we're both awake, we might as well begin the day." He then looked at Ali, taking note of his condition. "Some toast and tea, I think, with sugar for the shock."

In minutes, Ali found himself once more ensconced in the parlor, a blanket wrapped around him and a cup of hot tea in his hands. As he warmed and the adrenaline receded Ali could already feel the pain beginning in his bare feet—which had taken the brunt of the abuse from the dash down the stairs and across the garden—and climbing to every bruised muscle and strained limb.

Babbage jerked on the bell pull. In seconds, Millie appeared.

"Sir?" she asked.

"Millie, we need to tend to Mister bin-Massoud's injuries. Fetch warm water, towels, bandages, and the healing unguent." At her pause, he added, "Ask Cook."

"Yes, sir," she said with a half-bob. Shortly, she returned with every-thing requested, including a tin of an oily substance that smelled foul.

Ali's nose wrinkled at the bitter scent.

Noting his expression, Babbage spoke, "Can't let any of those cuts fester."

The maid handed the items to Ali who gazed upon them as if in a daze. "That was very brave," she said before retreating back to the kitchen, her voice audible only to Ali.

Ali nodded but said nothing as he stared at the tin and bandages but made no move to dress his wounds.

Babbage sighed. "Let me. I've had to do it often enough."

"He was not just an intruder," Ali said.

"What?" Babbage's tone was distracted, his attention on applying the unguent to Ali's face. "Quit moving, lad."

"The man. I believe he was after the box."

Ali flinched as Babbage's hands worked more vigorously.

"How could he know it was here?"

"I do not know, but he spoke to me. In Arabic."

"What did he say?" Babbage asked, his tone light as he finished dabbing at the cuts and began to bandage them.

"Goodbye."

His teacher's hands stilled. "Nothing more?"

"He said that when he fired his gun at me," Ali answered. "But there is something else…I recognized his face. He is from Wadi Al-Nejd."

Silence fell between them as they both contemplated exactly what that meant.

The tension of recent events faded along with autumn's colors. *Ustad* Babbage chose not to summon the Metropolitan Police as explaining the particulars of the occurrence would have been met with incredulity at best. He merely moved Ali to the room beside his own for the fortnight that remained before Ali departed, set a lock on the back gate, and hired a pugilist to spend the night in the garden keeping watch.

With so little time left to him, Ali did not question his teacher's decisions. Instead he sketched the intruder's face and what he could remember of the silver band in his journal, then spent every waking moment finishing the clockwork doll and learning as much as he could from his mentor.

Two weeks passed swiftly. Too swiftly. Ali had finished the Langstroms' special commission—they were well pleased with the delicate work—and *Ustad* Babbage had assisted him in procuring a number of engineering texts Ali would have had trouble obtaining in his homeland. The puzzle box and Ali's meager belongings, along with a few simple gifts for Kassim and his wife, Malakeh, were packed in a satchel slung across his shoulder. Ali had strapped his grandfather's staff across his back, and secreted the bulk of his father's coin beneath his *thobe*.

Now he and *Ustad* Babbage stood before the gate of the airfield and Ali hesitated. As if in reflection of his spirit, a light mist left everything slick and wet as London fog settled over the landscape like a sodden shroud. Faint patches of sunlight occasionally broke through, but offered little warmth. Ali's reluctance deepened. Perhaps returning home was not Allah's will for him. Perhaps he was not meant to spurn a place where he did good work, to return to a household that held only rancor for him.

Ali knew a moment's shame. Family was a cornerstone of his faith. His doubts were selfish and unfounded. And there was no question that there was need for him to return beyond his family obligations. The box, the book. There was so much he still did not understand. Truths he could not learn in a townhouse on Dorset Street.

Ali shook himself, forcing his thoughts back to the present and his upcoming journey. He did wonder for a moment if returning home via aerostat was inappropriate. A sea voyage would be less wasteful. He knew *Ustad* Babbage had little coin to spare.

As if reading his mind, his teacher spoke, his voice filled with more than its usual gruffness. "All will be fine, lad."

Ali felt the corners of his lips quirk up at the affirmation. It was unclear if *Ustad* Babbage tried to convince Ali, or himself.

"Yes," Ali responded as he returned his gaze to the gently drifting aerostat. This conveyance would cut his journey in half. Of course, there was no reason for such speed, but he thrilled at the prospect of the rare experience. He had a boundless fascination for the physics of the great airships. Already, half-formed plans for convincing the crew to show him the mechanical workings tugged at his thoughts.

As if in response, the wing-engines engaged with a faint hum, causing the *Thaddeus Lowe* to strain against its moorings. The aluminum coating of the airbag shone in the cold October light and even though it was well-tethered the gondola swayed gently, like a ship at dock.

Babbage followed Ali's gaze and his lip curled in disdain. His teacher had a strong preference for machines of more erudite design and esoteric function. As a man of thought, philosophy, and engineering, he had been eminently clear that he preferred to build machines

that increased human capacity for greatness, rather than merely transport them from place to place. "Rudders and propellers, and boilers and thrust mechanisms. If man were intended to fly—"

"Then the Almighty would grant him the mental faculties to discover the means to do so," Ali quipped. "*Ustad,*" he added.

Babbage snorted and nearly laughed. "Don't be cheeky, lad." He paused and held out a hand. "Good journey."

Ali reached out and clasped Babbage's hand in return. "May Allah grace you with His Benevolence."

Grimacing as if something pained him, *Ustad* Babbage hauled Ali against his chest and clasped him briefly, but tightly. "I will miss you, son."

Ali gasped to be addressed so, he knew of his teacher's affection but the expression of it surprised and pleased him immensely. He had not been hugged since he was a small child in his mother's arms. It warmed his soul even as it inspired a thin blade of sadness. Silently, he said a prayer for his father's spirit. Before Ali could back away, Babbage released him. He drew a letter from his pocket and pressed it into Ali's hand.

"Give that to the engineer aboard the vessel. It will smooth your way."

Ali's expression was one of surprise.

"What? You did not think I would know that half your thoughts dwell on the journey while the other half scheme to worm your way into the engine room so you can explore the mechanics of these machines?" Babbage sounded particularly smug.

A second later, as quickly as a shadow passes over the sun, Babbage's lips pressed together as his eyes grew bright. "Go on... enough dawdling."

Bowing deeply, Ali slipped the letter into the satchel holding his possessions. He then turned away quickly lest his own tears embarrass the man who had become more than a teacher to him. Ali stepped onto the gangway leading up to the gondola. A crewman in a dark blue uniform with brass buttons down the front and gold braid on his shoulders stopped Ali with a suspicious look and a hand to his chest. "Passengers only."

A heavy accent cloaked the man's words. He sounded like he spoke through his nose. Another American, Ali guessed, though clearly from a different region than Mister Langstrom. Ali drew out his paperwork.

"Peace be upon you, brother. I am bound for Arabia." He kept his voice low and pleasant.

The crewman grunted as he scrutinized first the papers and then Ali himself. Ali waited several long minutes, the respectful smile never leaving his face. Eventually, the crewman seemed satisfied and waved him up the gangway.

Ali offered a half bow and walked with dignity up the planks toward the opening leading into the gondola. At the entrance he stopped a moment and glanced back toward his teacher, loath to leave him now that the time was irrevocably here. He scanned the crowd in search of *Ustad* Babbage, locating him to the left, heading for the gate to exit the airfield. Another onlooker caught Ali's eye in passing, causing him to lose sight of his teacher. The distance was too far for Ali to make out the man's features, but he had dark skin and bore what seemed a fierce expression. He glanced at Ali briefly before turning away to follow *Ustad* Babbage's path. What disturbed Ali most was the bandage wrapped around the man's temple. *It couldn't be the same man, could it?*

Before he realized it, Ali had retreated halfway back to the ground. He lost track of the man as the American who'd checked his voucher blocked his way. Ali tried to duck past him, but the crewman had already closed and locked the gate at the end of the walkway.

"You're holding up the flight," he said, interrupting Ali's thoughts. Turning away, the man raised his voice, "All ABOARD!" He then herded Ali back up the walkway.

As Ali reluctantly entered the gondola, the rumble of the engines increased in pitch. At his back the cold winds of the English lands pushed him forward, while from within the airship warm, dry air reminiscent of his desert homeland brushed against his face. Worry dimmed his pleasure as he followed a porter through the gondola and up into the passenger compartment to find his cabin. He did not know what weighed on him more, his concern for his teacher, or what he would find at home. The book and box buried deep within his satchel only added to the mystery of his future.

Kassim's new household was a prosperous one. He knew this, and some small kernel of piety acknowledged he should be satisfied. The finest of horses bedded in his stables, gold coin filled his coffers, and precious gems his chests. Treasures more befitting a sultan than a merchant of even his high stature appointed his rooms. As he moved through the household toward his chambers, he ran an appreciative hand over rare wood panels that decorated each doorway and window. His gaze moved from decorations of carved ivory to the fine mosaics that tiled the floors and around the costly glass mirrors on his walls. His wealth was such that any who might see it would feel envy in their hearts and any who were in his place would praise Allah for His blessings.

Kassim could not be so content.

On his desk lay a parchment scribed in his father's hand. Leaning forward Kassim again read the decree: *All of the wealth I, Massoud bin-Farzeen, have amassed, I hereby leave to my eldest son, Kassim bin-Massoud; my household, my business, and all valuables encompassed therein… with the sole exception of the legacy left to me by my father — one transcript of an ancient text on engineering and a pair of matched black diamonds, which go to my second son, Ali bin-Massoud, may Allah bless both my children.*

In that moment, Kassim's feelings for his brother moved from disdain to malice. The tendons stood out on his hands as he reached for the parchment. As if a living thing, it shivered in his grip. Cursing his father and brother equally, Kassim shredded the document, tearing, then tearing yet again until the pieces rained down upon his desk like flower petals falling from the trees during high wind.

The act should have held satisfaction, the fragments proof of the power he wielded, but bitterness rose like the morning mists off an oasis pool. His position as eldest son would in itself ensure his inheritance without need of written confirmation, but was this act of defiance futile? On the matter of the diamonds, he could not be certain his brother had not already been made aware of his inheritance.

Kassim's teeth ground against each other at the thought.

He found no more pleasure in the riches displayed to perfection around him or his success in the jewel market. Always at the back of his mind festered the knowledge that possession of those black diamonds still eluded him, and always would…unless he found them before his brother's return. It had all started with that long-ago night in the garden when he had spied on his parents. Never until that moment had he felt lacking. Never until his unborn brother usurped his parents' love. Their father's black diamonds were symbols of that betrayal. Ali was to be their legacy, not him. Knowing that, all of the treasures were as dust to him.

With each day that passed his brother's return drew nearer. Kassim wanted the matter resolved well before Ali arrived, the gems secreted away as if they had never been. Lines etched into his forehead and drew deep grooves beside his mouth. He sighed and rubbed a hand over his face. It seemed he could scarcely eat for the weight of this concern, and his nights had long been filled with thoughts of the black diamonds that taunted him. And to what effect? Most in his household avoided his presence, unless summoned. Even Malakeh moved about as meek and quiet as one of the servants, lest she awaken his ire. If not for his torment, such might please Kassim greatly.

If only he had the leisure to search undisturbed, he felt certain the diamonds would soon be in his possession. But how to ensure none spied his efforts? Or worse, took to searching themselves, though they knew not the prize? He growled and tore at the scraps of parchment again until even they resisted his further efforts.

What he would not give for solitude!

Kassim stilled. Considered the thought. Weighed it.

His lips lifted in a subtle smile that held not pleasure, but satisfaction, as a plan formed. He summoned Malakeh. Seated at his desk, he ran his fingers back and forth on the dark wood, barely disguising his elation.

Malakeh crept into the room, her steps hesitant. Kassim allowed his expression to go blank and his lids to lower halfway just to see her tense, thrilling at his power over even the one closest to him. For several long moments he remained silent. Only once she started to bob in agitation did he draw breath to speak.

"Wife," he said, schooling his expression as unyielding as stone. "You are going on a visit to your parents' household. You and the servants leave in two days." He chafed at the time he would lose, but he knew such a journey to Jeddah would require preparation. He could afford to be generous when two days of waiting would gain him weeks in which to search undisturbed.

Malakeh gasped but quickly quelled the dismay in her gaze. He knew she did not care for travel and had not done so since she'd come to Wadi Al-Nejd as his bride. Her failure to completely hide her alarm pleased him.

"And what, will I tell my parents, is the reason for this journey?"

Kassim thought on this, knowing his father-in-law would indeed wonder. "I shall send you with some rare jade that your father might sell for great profit, as a gift to show him I am well pleased with you." He could tell by her expression that this would placate her father, who was likewise a merchant.

"But, husband, surely my place is here, seeing to your ne…"

Kassim brought the flat of his hand down hard upon the desktop, rising from his seat. "Your place is where I deem it, wife. You dare defy me?"

Malakeh cowered, her head lowered and her shoulders hunched. "No, my husband, no…which servants shall journey with me?" Her tone was the meeker than it had ever been.

"All of them."

Malakeh's eyes went wide and her face pale at the undertaking, until Kassim half wondered if she thought he meant to banish her. Taking pity, he softened his expression. "Ali returns soon. I would have peace to meditate on Allah's will before my brother's shadow crosses our doorstep. Plan your travel to arrive back home in one month's time, that you might ready the household for his arrival."

She nodded, her eyes sparkling with a cunning gleam. She, no doubt perceived there was more to Kassim's demand than he explained. "As you wish," she murmured, and backed out of the room with a bow.

Kassim sat back and, for the first time since he'd found his father's will, a true smile graced his lips.

Before his wife's caravan left for Jeddah, Kassim carefully checked every bundle and cask packed for the journey, professing the need to ensure they'd forgotten no vital supply. As he bid travel mercies upon one and all, he searched each gaze for any signs the servants hid some secret that might tell him if any had already found his prize. Even Malakeh was not spared his scrutiny. Content in observing only carefully neutral expressions, with confusion buried beneath, he waved off his entire household from the oldest *hadji* to the youngest babe. His wife he clasped to his chest and briefly pressed his lips to her forehead in blessing before shooing her on her way. He was pleased at her obedience, but impatient to begin his search.

In their absence, Kassim methodically examined every room and courtyard, from his own chambers to the least servant's. He combed the gardens and the rooftop. He pressed upon bricks and pried at costly wood panels. He ran fingertips along rafters and across the floors. He went so far as to sift the grain stores in both the kitchen and the stables. Every conceivable place bore his scrutiny, no matter how improbable.

He would not fail due to lack of effort.

Even so, his search bore no fruit. Each day of his solitude, he repeated his inspection, cursing and railing against his father's soul as he did so. He uncovered no evidence but his memory that the jewels had ever been there.

His feelings for his brother hardened, as deep in his gut Kassim feared that perhaps Ali had already gained his inheritance. By the time his wife and their servants returned, he was half-crazed with his failure. The household bore the signs of his poking and prying. Stored goods were in disarray and foodstuffs left open to vermin. Malakeh came upon him on his knees in his chamber, tapping his knuckles against the wall.

Her mouth dropped open, clearly aghast at the condition of her home. "Husband, what is this?" she asked her gaze trailing from one sign of disorder to the next. "Have we been beset by thieves?"

"Hush, wife," Kassim ordered, ignoring her question. He rose and drew close to her, gripping her shoulders. "He is not here yet...I still have time, but we must have warning before Ali comes upon us."

Malakeh did not speak. She stared at him with eyes gone wide, her body remaining very still. Kassim grimaced and gave her a shake. "Do you hear me, woman? Do you understand? Once Ali arrives we will have lost our chance at my father's most precious treasure!"

At that his wife clutched at his arms. She had no idea of what he spoke, but he was her husband and she would support him against all enemies, even those of his own family. "What are we to do, husband?"

"You will go into the marketplace and find the witch, *Sahhaar* Bundi. Give her this coin and tell her we must know of my brother's approach...tell her it would not be amiss if he were to be delayed that we might have time to properly prepare for his return."

Chapter Five

MALAKEH KNEW HER HUSBAND'S HEART AND COULD WELL imagine the treasure of which he spoke. She thought of all the fine oils and perfumes she might then buy, the delicacies to be purchased for their table, and how the business could grow. Kassim's avarice had seeped from where it found its home in his soul and now it populated her thoughts with all manner of ways she might gain her husband's favor and secure the bounty he sought.

Dressed in her best silks and jewels, with a gold-threaded *rusari* to drape her head, Malakeh made her way to the market in search of the *sahhaar*. For much of the day she wandered, offering a careful query here, listening to a whispered conversation there, until finally she learned where to find the woman she sought. Malakeh came upon the witch in the herb market, fingering the leaves of a plant, her eye critical.

"Peace be upon you, *Hadja*," Malakeh said in greeting.

"And with you, child."

"Might you take a walk with me, grandmother, and pass some time in conversation?" Malakeh asked, careful to couch her words lest any other hear and wonder at her business with the *sahhaar*, of which the elders would not approve.

"*Ayeee*…but my time is precious," the witch responded. "I do not know that I have any *free* to spare…"

Bowing, Malakeh passed the gold coin to Bundi.

Smiling broadly, the woman slid her arm through Malakeh's. "Perhaps a walk would soothe me, in good company."

Arm in arm, they wandered the market, heads close together talking of seemingly commonplace things. Eventually, Malakeh spoke of Ali's imminent return and how they could not know even the day of his arrival. *Sahhaar* Bundi nodded, her lips pursed, as if she considered their dilemma.

"Making it difficult for you to prepare to greet him?" the woman asked half-guessing Malakeh's intent.

Malakeh nodded. "Not knowing does make such preparations complicated." Then she dared to add her own thoughts. "The desert is a dangerous place…this very year his father fell victim to its unmerciful sands. It weighs heavily upon us to fear Ali might come to such a pass." She bowed her head and cast a glance at the witch from beneath her lashes, the slightest tilt of her lips giving lie to her words.

Sahhaar Bundi's dark eyes caught Malakeh's own and she found that she couldn't look away. It was as if the old woman looked through her, as if measuring her.

"Ah…you do well to worry, child…well indeed…"

The old woman laughed, a high-pitched sound that grated on the ear, and with a blue-veined hand, gently patted Malakeh's own hand where it rested on her arm. They continued to wander the marketplace chatting as if old friends, their spirits in complete agreement.

Charles Babbage remained lost in thought as the hired carriage stopped before the house on Dorset Street. He gazed out the window, as he had since they'd left the airfield, seeing nothing. A bang on the roof jerked him from his dour musings. He left the carriage and stepped forward to pay the man. The driver did not even wait for him to step back before sending the horses forward, eyes already scanning the street for his next fare as the wheels of his carriage spattered Babbage with mud from the rains that had fallen during the drive.

As he stumbled back, only the application of self-restraint prevented Babbage from thumping the carriage with his cane as it rattled past.

"Bloody hack!" he grumbled beneath his breath before turning to stare up at the stark façade of his home. His brow furrowed and he narrowed his gaze. The servants had been given the afternoon off, yet Babbage would swear he saw a glimmer of light in the room that had first housed his apprentice. Or perhaps not. There was no sign of it now, just blank, dark windows reflecting a household devoid of life.

Babbage shook off the uncharacteristic melancholy and stepped with purpose up the front walk. There was work to be done. More so now than ever. He did allow himself a brief, silent admission. He already missed Ali, and would for quite some time, he expected.

Entering the dark foyer, he wiped his feet dry on the mat and set his cane in the elephant-foot stand by the door, before removing his Inverness cloak and hat and hanging them from their pegs. Already, he regretted letting the servants go for the afternoon. He shivered at the damp chill pervading the house. Seeing a flash of white on the side table by the door, Babbage picked up a calling card that must have been left after he and Ali had departed for the airfield.

So much for an evening of solitude, Babbage thought with a sigh. The Langstroms apparently wished a final visit before they left for the East. From the card, they would return—Babbage checked his pocket watch—in an hour. He sighed again. They would find cold comfort if he did not get at least a fire going. If he hurried, he might even manage a half-decent tea.

He engaged the gas lamps lining the hallway then headed toward the parlor. Halfway there his foot slipped on a slick spot on the marble floor. Babbage caught himself, then looked down, spying a now-muddied puddle of water he had not noticed previously. He scowled. Really, the maid should have dealt with the mess before leaving...

Babbage's scowl deepened, and his lips pressed tight as realization cut the thought short.

The storm had not begun until he'd been on his way home. The maid and the cook were to have departed soon after he and Ali had left for the airfield. From the looks of it, the water came from the kitchen and, he presumed, the back door. He turned and saw the trail continued upstairs. Someone had been in his house. He froze as he heard movement above and cursed under his breath as he recognized the sound of splintering wood. Bastards. Someone was *still* in his house.

Quietly moving back toward the front door, Babbage retrieved his cane from the stand. With a quick twist of the ornate handle, he released a catch and a slender blade slid out of its sheath. Holding it in front of him with a steady hand, Babbage moved with caution toward the stairs. He was no Metropolitan Police, nor one of the young men who practiced secret dueling techniques in London's *salles*, but he did believe in knowing how to defend oneself and his home.

Taking the stairs two at a time he charged up to the second floor. A moment later he turned in to the master bedroom. Across the room, pulling the down out of an oversize pillow, was a man in a dark frock coat and trousers wearing a bowler. Babbage raised an eyebrow at the hat. So he was not a man of the gentry, though from the design of his coat he sought to emulate one.

The blighter's back was to him, so Babbage stepped softly until he was directly behind the man. "Turn around if you please, *sir*." For emphasis Babbage let the tip of the thin blade prick the back of the intruder's neck. "I assure you, I have no compunction about putting this through your throat."

The man turned slowly, his expression contemptuous.

Babbage tightened his grip. This was not the reaction he'd expected. Also of note was the color of the man's skin. Even in the grey afternoon light slipping in through the far window it was clear the pigment was the color of strong tea.

"The teacher," the foreigner said with curled lip. It was not a question.

This situation made Babbage more and more unsettled. "What do you want?"

"The box, you fool. Give us the box."

Babbage jerked and started to pivot around, not expecting the response to come from behind him. Before he could shift from between the two threats something hard collided with the side of his head. It was a glancing blow, but enough to send his vision swimming with dark motes. He went to his knees, blade clattering to the floor. He was barely aware as the intruders dragged him from the room and down the stairs.

They spoke among themselves and Babbage struggled to listen. Only once he closed his eyes could he focus enough to make out their words, if just barely.

"It is not here," one of them said, his tone low and sullen.

"Maybe yes, maybe no," the other answered. "But we must be certain. When we are done with this one, I will take my carpet and catch up to the flying vessel at the next port, in case the apprentice has taken the box. I will deal with him. You must stay here and continue the search on this soil until there is no question."

"But Khizr has gone after the other one."

"Khizr is a dog! He knows nothing of finesse. Do you wish to risk the master's wrath on Khizr's competence?"

As they bickered, Babbage wondered were his brains more rattled than he feared. Carpet? What nonsense was that? He could not imagine how one would catch a flying machine with a carpet. This was no fairytale, though decidedly the whole affair did have an air of the fantastic about it. Then it struck him. The import of what the villain had said: *I will take care of him.* There could be no doubt this was not intended in the nurturing sense.

Gasping, Babbage tried to jerk from their grip, his fear for Ali lending him both focus and strength. For his effort he received another clout to the head. By the time he could again bring his eyes to focus or command any movement of his limbs it was too late. The intruders had bound him across his chest to one of the parlor chairs, but did not bother with his legs. He struggled but they were too strong. He couldn't help but groan at the sharp pain in his head from the motion. There was a flash, followed by a waft of sulfur as the intruders lit a lamp.

The two men stood before him, one tall and dark, the other about Babbage's height and of a lighter complexion. Both wore an odd jumble of clothes in mismatched European styles and had rolled carpets strapped across their backs similar to Ali's prayer rug. Babbage felt his eyes slide away from them as if they were not worth his notice.

Gazing around the parlor he stifled a sharp intake of breath. The room hadn't been ransacked, it had been devastated: chairs overturned, the divan cut open and its stuffing pulled out, paintings torn from the wall and tossed aside, the canvasses ripped. His roll-top desk had been destroyed, the tambour ripped from its runners and the drawers little more than splinters scattered about the room. As were his pages of calculations and design modifications, discarded as so much garbage.

"You…you…*thugs!*" Babbage growled.

"Now, now, Professor, you show your ignorance…wrong country." The words came from the taller man, clearly the leader of the two. Swarthy, with a full beard and dark eyes, there was no mistaking that he was from Near Eastern lands.

"My apologies," Babbage responded through gritted teeth. "I had not meant to insult India."

Rather than strike out at him, the foreigner laughed, as if at a great wit. It ended abruptly.

"Enough chatter. I believe it is time we get down to business."

"I have no business with the likes of you, unless it involves the constables." Babbage's voice felt as if it came from a distance. He shook his head to clear it and regretted the action immediately.

"You had a visitor recently," the man continued smoothly, ignoring Babbage's statement as one hand tugged at his beard. "A falcon of brass and iron. We know it flew on golden wings from the Rub-Al Khali to here. This falcon brought with it a mystical box. You will give that box to me." On his right wrist was what appeared to be a thick silver bracelet, but Babbage could not make it out.

"I don't know what you are talking about, foreigner," he snarled, praying nothing in his demeanor betrayed him.

"He lies," the smaller man said. Babbage noted the fading wound on his forehead and realized this was the same intruder who had tried to break in weeks ago.

The leader smiled. "Of course," he responded as he considered what he held in his hands, turning it over and over.

Babbage squinted to make it out. He caught his breath at a sudden gleam as the object caught the light. His cane sword.

"A beautiful piece, Professor. It is a shame to use it so," the man said.

"Use it h—" Babbage had not even finished the last word before he felt a slicing pain in his arm. He yelped. Glancing down he saw a small cut, only a couple of centimeters long, shallow, but painful.

"I learned *lingchi* early in my service. The skill has proven useful at finding information for me," the leader said as he expertly brought the blade to bear, opening another cut, this time along Babbage's jaw. Blood welled in the wound and trickled slowly down his neck to stain his collar. "My master desires the box, you will tell me where to find it."

Babbage winced but didn't cry out. He refused to add to the sick satisfaction in the other man's gaze.

"You waste your time," he said through gritted teeth. "I have no such box as you describe, and I never have." What secrets did the blasted thing hold, to bring these men to another land to retrieve it? How had they even known to come *here*? He was glad that Ali and the box were safely away.

Babbage paled as it occurred to him that might not be so. If these two were here, what if others trailed his young friend? Remembering the snatches of conversation from earlier, he could not suppress a groan.

With a pleased smirk at the sound, his attacker turned toward to his colleague. "Tell me, Abdul Asad, how many cuts, do you think, before the respected *Ustad* Babbage reveals where the box is? Two hundred? Three hundred?" His gaze flickered back to Babbage, as he continued, "I once knew a man who lived through two thousand cuts. I wonder if you shall be so lucky..."

His tone was mild, unhurried, as if he commented on the weather. Babbage shuddered.

Before the man could begin cutting him again there came a knock at the front door.

*Fritz and Clara…*it had to be them. Dear Lord, what if they brought their daughter, Sadie Rae, with them? Babbage was torn between calling out for assistance and remaining silent in the hopes they would leave in safety. But the thought of Ali out in the world, unwarned, decided him.

As blood continued to trickle a sticky path down his neck, he could not squander the possibility of assistance. He opened his mouth to shout for help only to shut it again as his own sword rose level with his throat.

The leader stared down the blade at him. Babbage narrowed his eyes and glared back. He needed another way to alert them. Staring up at this vile man, Babbage realized he'd moved closer when he'd brought the sword to bear. Careful not to telegraph his intent, he delivered a swift, hard kick to the man's shin, while at the same time throwing his weight backward, sending the chair and himself to the floor. Even so, the point of his sword took another solid nick out of his chin.

Babbage let himself cry out with the pain this time, as loudly as he could manage, having knocked the breath from himself with the fall. The friendly knocking outside turned into frantic pounding.

"Fritz! Hurry!"

A *crack* sounded as the wood around the locks began to give. Babbage wondered if it was too late for him as the leader lunged forward, the sword raised high and poised to strike.

"You can kill me," Babbage wheezed, yet still managed a sneer. "Or you can run."

The fury on the man's face woke some satisfaction in Babbage's bruised chest. The foreigner tossed down the blade and fled, footsteps pounding on the marble tile as he and his companion ran through the kitchen and out the back door. Trembling and dripping blood onto his antique Persian carpet, Babbage shouted as he heard the doorjamb give.

"In here! Hurry! They're getting away!"

More clattering in the hall as Fritz dashed by in pursuit of the intruders. In his wake, Clara hurried to Babbage's side. Her hands struggled with the bindings to no good effect, then she spied the sword. Taking it up, she carefully wedged it inside the rope with the edge pointed away from Babbage. His eyes went wide and he started to protest, when she braced a foot against the toppled chair and jerked up with the blade, parting his bindings.

"Annoy one of the professors at the University again, dear friend?" she quipped, though Babbage heard the concern underlying her words.

Before he could respond, Fritz returned, breath coming heavy and his brow drawing hard lines down his forehead. "What the hell's going on, Charles?"

"They're after Ali…or something he possesses, anyway," Babbage answered as he tried to rub feeling back into his arms while Clara dabbed carefully at his cuts with her handkerchief. "We must find a way to warn him."

"This is a splendid conveyance," Ali said as the porter, a friendly young American by the name of Tommy Giffard, led him through the gondola and up a steep wooden stair that took them into the passenger section. The crewman turned to speak, only to be interrupted by a series of clanging bells. The sound climbed above the low rumble of crew and passengers moving about the aerostat. Giffard swore beneath his breath and waved for Ali to move faster. "That's the high-wind warning. I have to get you to your cabin quick and report to duty."

Ali's joy at his first flight diminished somewhat, his gaze darting around as Giffard hurried him past many fascinating things Ali longed to examine more closely. He did not complain, though, understanding the need to be safe in uncertain weather, most particularly when suspended in the air. Still, at the door of his small cabin he turned and placed a staying hand on the young man's arm. "Please…might it be possible to have a tour of the vessel once the danger is no more?"

"I can't promise nothing, but maybe," Giffard answered with a rueful grin. "Assuming I'm not in trouble for being late."

Ali hastily dropped his hand and backed into his cabin. He looked around the close space noting two bunks made secure to the wall with rods and bolts and two lockers likewise attached. The room held nothing else, not even a window. Ali had known to expect this given the passenger compartments were situated within the hull. There were, he was told, locations where one could look out upon the heavens and down upon the earth, but he had not yet seen them for himself. Ali sighed. His grand adventure was not what he would wish it to be so far.

The chamber felt close around him, but blissfully warm. For the first time in three years, it seemed, the chill had left his bones. The cabins were heated using forced-air warmed by water from the cooling systems of the forward engines. He knew this because *Ustad* Babbage had recently obtained a schematic of the aerostat and they had spent their remaining evenings exploring the vessel on paper. Ali had wondered whether such a system was in use for all American aerostats or only those travelling across the Atlantic. He could not wait to ask. Settling on the lower bunk, he opened his satchel and drew out the letter *Ustad* Babbage had given him at the airfield. Written across the front was the name H. Giffard.

Ali read the name with a start. No…it could not be. In his studies, he had read of the great engineer from Faransa—France, Ali corrected mentally—Henri Giffard. Surely such a man as he did not crew a common transport—an American one, at that—no matter how innovative. And yet there was the porter that brought him to his cabin, Tommy Giffard. A relative? Ali could not contain his thoughts. No matter how he told himself not to be foolish, excitement kindled in his breast. Now more than ever he hoped he had not caused Tommy trouble. Not knowing what else to do, Ali laid back and closed his eyes. He did not expect to truly rest, but within moments sleep drew him down.

A low, piercing whistle woke Ali. He jerked upward with a start, nearly smacking his head on the bunk above him. Looking around he had to remind himself where he was. Again the whistle sounded. What did it mean? Climbing to his feet and straightening his *besht*, Ali slipped the letter into his pocket and moved to the door, cautiously opening it to peer into the corridor. All around him cabin doors opened and people dressed in fancy garb trailed out, moving at a leisurely pace.

Perhaps the whistle was meant to indicate that all was clear? Ali watched as the flow of passengers all headed in the same direction. Where did they go? Was he meant to follow? Uncertainty held Ali in place. Before he could decide, a hand came down upon his shoulder.

He jerked around with a start.

"Easy…easy," Tommy Giffard said, grinning once more. "You wanted a tour?"

"Oh! Yes, thank you very much."

Tommy just shook his head and his grin widened. He jerked his head the way he had come and started walking.

"Wait!" Ali ducked into his cabin to grab his satchel and slung it across his shoulder. The contents were too important to leave unattended. As they headed back down to the gondola where the primary controls were located, Ali's new friend pointed out a grand map showing the full route of the *Thaddeus Lowe*. Ali was suitably impressed. Not only had the aerostat crossed the Atlantic, but it was to circle around the world before it returned to its home port. Stopping a moment, Ali traced the route from England to Jerusalem, where he was to disembark. The only word to describe what he felt was awe.

"Hey, come on." When Tommy tugged on his sleeve to get his attention, Ali had to wonder if all Americans were so informal. "My father's waiting."

That got Ali's attention more than anything could. His hand slid into his pocket to touch *Ustad* Babbage's letter. He hurried after his guide without another glance sideways though much along the way tempted him. They traveled the length of the gondola in silence, the mechanical sounds making conversation difficult. Along the way Ali's shoulders twitched, as if under the weight of another's gaze. He tried to look around without seeming to, but he spied no one watching them. He frowned and turned back, hurrying to catch up to his companion.

As they neared the engineering compartment, the walkway vibrated with the steady rumble of the engines. Ali's heart stuttered like a stuck gear. He had to wipe his hands along his *besht* to clear them of sweat. Again it felt as if someone stared. Tommy glanced back and shook his head.

"Relax, I got permission."

Ali nodded.

Tommy just shook his head some more and stepped up to the door leading to engineering. He gave three brief knocks, then stepped back, his chin up, his feet a foot apart, and his arms folded behind his straightened back.

Ali gulped and awkwardly mimicked Tommy's stance.

The door opened and an older, brawnier version of Tommy stepped out. The edges of his dark hair had begun to silver and subtle lines creased his face, but otherwise there was no mistaking the familial relationship. The man's brow dipped as he glanced from one to the other of them, then he chuckled.

"At ease," he said as he waved them in to the compartment. Even the voice was similar to Tommy's. Though gruffer, it was just as American. Ali had no idea what the man meant, but relaxed as Tommy did. He hurried to follow, eager for the wonders about to be revealed, only to stop suddenly in the doorway. Never had he seen such a concentration of machinery in one place. Steam and the scent of hot oil made his head swim and the sheer cacophony of sound made thought nigh impossible. It took a moment before he became acclimated.

"Come along, young man," the older Giffard said, beckoning him forward.

Ali unstuck his feet from the floor and approached. "Thank you, sir."

"My name's Hugh Giffard," the man answered with a good-natured smile. "Not sir."

Ah…not Henri, then. But then the lack of a French accent had already told Ali that.

"And I am Ali bin-Massoud, your humble servant," Ali replied in return. Then, belatedly remembering the letter in his pocket, he drew it out. "For you, sir…Mister Giffard, from *Ustad* Charles Babbage."

"Ah, thank you," Giffard said, tucking the letter away without even reading it.

Ali's shock must have shown plainly on his face, though he had not intended it to. Where he was from letters were respected for the effort taken to produce them. One did not receive one and then treat it with such disregard.

The senior Giffard gave Ali a puzzled look. "No worries, lad. I knew to expect you. I'll read my friend's letter later. No need for it now when I have only an hour free for you to explore."

"Please, forgive my rudeness," Ali bowed, his eyes downcast, embarrassed at his lapsed manners.

"Nonsense, nothing to forgive," the man answered. "Now hurry… an hour, I said."

Tommy had to return to his duties, but his father was true to his word, devoting his full attention to all of Ali's many questions. For that hour, Ali was in bliss. They climbed up to one of the wing cars to explore the engine room in detail, from the turbines that propelled the aerostat forward to the vents that filled the bladder overhead with steam. At one point Ali was even able to point out a gear that had shifted and threatened to seize the works. Of everything he had seen he was particularly enthralled by the engines that provided propulsion.

As their time ended, Ali bowed deeply to the engineer, "I thank you again for your generosity. Long will I remember what I have seen."

The American grinned. "Any time, young man. You have a sharp eye and good head for all of this. I'm always glad to encourage the mechanically minded."

Ali could tell Engineer Giffard's attention had already shifted to his responsibilities, as was proper, and realized it would not be polite to interrupt further. Ali would have to content himself with the wonders he had seen this day. With another bow, he turned and traced his way back to his cabin, desiring a time of quiet solitude after his stimulating tour.

Again his shoulders prickled and Ali had to resist the urge to hunch, but this time he did not search out whoever watched. Such could be a dangerous thing. Instead he hurried to his cabin.

As he closed the door behind him his hand clutched the strap of his satchel.

While there was no sign of disturbance in his quarters, a faint aroma, the barest ghost of a scent that had not been there before, told him someone had entered the cabin.

Chapter Six

WITHIN DAYS, BABBAGE ONCE MORE STOOD AT THE GATE to the airfield with a satchel at his feet and worry in his gaze. He would have left sooner, restoring order to his house be damned, only the Langstroms had not been free to depart immediately. Now that the day was here, Babbage chafed at any further delay. Across the field, great cables tethered the *Earl of Chadsworth* to steel anchor points sunk into Portland cement. His gut clenched to see the compact vessel bob in the breeze. It was so much smaller than the aerostat that had borne Ali away. Never had Babbage thought to ever step foot upon such a conveyance. He did not trust this radical engineering where failure of the simplest element might mean plummeting hundreds of feet to the ground below. Still, when needs must...

Almost without notice his hands flexed. He gave in to the impulse for yet another glance at his watch, drawing it from his waistcoat. Half an hour he'd been waiting for the Langstroms. Half an hour and two days he had been waiting to leave, his tension ratcheted up with each second that passed. Who knew what harm might have already befallen his apprentice? Unconscionable, really, that they were not already on their way. What did he care about lectures and Society

meetings when Ali might already have been beset by more thieves, thieves who had already proven themselves willing to do violence? "Blast!" he cursed, jamming his watch into its pocket and kicking his satchel in frustration.

"Practicing, are we?"

Babbage pivoted about to find Lady Clara just behind him, her young daughter, Sadie Rae, standing properly at her side, lovingly clutching the hand of the doll Ali had constructed before leaving. The clockwork doll was nearly as tall as the child and walked all on its own.

"Pardon?"

Clara lifted an elegant brow and canted her head toward his bag. "Practicing…for the ruffians?" Babbage pressed his lips tight and disregarded the jibe.

"Where is Fritz?" he asked, though his tone spoke more of a demand.

The look she gave him was both chiding and understanding. "He's been aboard for hours checking the system before our flight."

Babbage lowered his gaze beneath his signature scowl and fought back a flush. He had not thought to check the airship. "Lovely to see you, Lady Clara, Miss Sadie Rae," he said, bowing briefly to each of them before bending down to retrieve his bag. He offered his arm to Lady Clara. "Shall we?"

She grimaced at his continued use of her title but gave a nod and placed her hand lightly in the crook of his elbow, with her other hand she reached down to grasp her daughter's.

"Don't worry, Charles," she murmured. "The *Thaddeus Lowe* must stop at many ports between here and Jerusalem. There is plenty of opportunity for us to catch up before then."

As they boarded the private airship, Babbage sighed. He did not refute her theory, but neither did he trust it.

Ali rolled over in his bunk and shifted, trying to get more comfortable. But no matter what he did, sleep eluded him. He reached a hand out to touch the bunk above his. He couldn't see it, but his fingers assured him it was there. He ran them up and down the rough wood panel, touching the imperfections and joints as if to memorize them. The nights on the aerostat were the most difficult. During the day Ali could explore, or visit with one of the Giffards, but when the sun set, there was very little to occupy him. After just a few days on board, the confinement left Ali longing for the wide-open horizon of the desert… or even the closed-in warren that was England. Despite the novelty of sailing through the clouds in silence, but for the low growl of engines, Ali found he missed the comfort of familiar things: working side by side with *Ustad* Babbage, deep discussions with his father, laughing and racing horses across the desert with his friends, even his brother. So much was different than it had been three years ago; or perhaps it was Ali that had changed.

The closeness of the cabin weighed on him. Perhaps a visit to the lounge would soothe his thoughts, with the heavens spread wide beyond those large glass panes. Sliding out of the lower bunk, Ali gathered up his puzzle box. He glanced at his grandfather's staff, but could not imagine he would need it.

There was a faint click as he opened the door. There was no one in the hall. He wandered down the starboard promenade to the lounge, where one wall was nothing but windows framed in polished teak. He moved to one of the well-stuffed chairs in the corner by the furthest window. Beside it stood a free-standing ashtray shaped like a nude woman with a glass dish held above her head. Ali blushed and averted his eyes, instead gazing at the night sky. A flutter outside drew his attention. For a second he swore he saw a flash of metal in the moonlight and a silhouette that looked too much like a falcon. *By Allah's mercy, it couldn't be, could it?* He rubbed his eyes and it was gone.

Ali sat down in the chair and pulled out the puzzle box, determined to solve it before the end of the journey. The sky gradually lightened and the box remained an obstinate square, revealing not even one seam or shifting element, despite Ali's experience with such things. Were this a conventional boat he might have been tempted to toss the *Himitsu-Bako* overboard and content himself with a place in his brother's household. Instead, he sat there in the twilight, the box in his lap and a frown weighing his lips. His eyes grew heavy, then his head slumped forward. Lulled by the rumble of the engines, sleep began to take him. He might have drifted off into true slumber, but for the squeak of a footstep at the door of the lounge.

Ali blinked furiously and pushed himself upright, his hands automatically closing around the *Himitsu-Bako*. Though he squinted he could not see who stood there. Something glimmered, though, sharp and bright. By the curve of the blade it looked like a dagger.

"There is nothing of value here, my friend," Ali called out, making an effort to keep his words light and his mind off of the puzzle box in his lap or the pouches of coin strapped beneath his clothing.

"Then you will not care if I relieve you of what I want, will you?" a hard voice spoke from across the way, slowly drawing closer. Though unfamiliar, the man spoke in the cadence of home. There was nothing pleasant in the realization. Ali was no fool. Whoever this was, he surely had something to do with the thief who had tried to break in to his room back in England. He cursed himself for not bringing the staff, or even keeping his own dagger at hand. It had not occurred to him there would be a risk once he departed.

Ali slid the box into his pocket and rose to his feet. With the man before him, he had nowhere to go. "I am afraid you are mistaken. The Almighty abhors a thief. I cannot allow you to damn yourself so."

"Brave words from a cornered mouse," the man scoffed, the steadily growing light glittering off his bared teeth. As he advanced, Ali grabbed the ashtray beside him, flushing as the carved figure's cool, metal posterior rested in his palm. As he hefted it up the dish fell to the ground, sending a cloud of ash into the air before the glass shattered loudly in the early-morning silence.

His assailant cursed and lunged forward, swiping at Ali with his dagger, the long blade barely missing Ali's side as the man attempted to slice his pocket. Ali countered with the heavy metal base of the ashtray. Before the man could attack again an angry shriek from outside the aerostat caused the combatants to flinch. They both pivoted toward the nearest floor-to-ceiling window, ducking as an enraged falcon dove right for it, metal feathers tucked against its sides.

Ali's breath caught in his chest at the sight. Behind him, his attacker screamed as if faced with all the demons of Hell. The sounds of a commotion in the hallway barely registered with Ali's ears as he dropped to the deck. Shattered glass rained down and the man's screaming cut off abruptly with a squeal. Ali could not help but look up as the falcon caught his assailant in razor-sharp talons and dragged him back out through the shattered window. The Security and crew of the Thaddeus Lowe tumbled through the open doorway of the lounge barely resisting the wind that tugged them toward the gaping hole.

"Quick! Get that breach boarded up before we lose more than just a few fripperies," the elder Giffard called out. "And someone get the lad out of the way!"

Strong fingers wrapped around Ali's arm, drawing him toward the corridor. He followed without complaint. The entire time his eyes remained locked on the falcon as it flew off. Ali gasped as the dark speck split in two. He shuddered as he imagined he heard the man's fading scream as he plummeted toward to the ground.

After what felt like an interminable time on the Langstroms' airship, Babbage had determined two things: that Lady Clara's optimism that they would overtake the *Thaddeus Lowe* had been misplaced, and that he had no choice but to journey to Ali's village to assure himself that his apprentice was well and, if need be, deliver his warning. He rubbed the scar the ruffians had left on his chin and prayed he was not too late. Massoud had warned Babbage that some risk accompanied taking Ali as his apprentice. Not from the lad himself, but born of dangers lurking in the father's past. Babbage had taken the warning too lightly. Hell, he had not taken it at all.

No more. He stood at the porthole in his cabin looking out across the clouds, but he did not see them. His mind tormented him with the memory of Ali with cuts on his face and blood dripping from the head wound garnered in his twilight encounter with the thief. From there, his mind built upon that actual misfortune to speculate more detailed horrors he could only hope were nothing but worry-induced fancies. Babbage shuddered and forced the imaginings away, staring hard at the clouds outside the porthole.

In his solitude he allowed himself the luxury of a heartfelt curse.

"I cannot apologize enough," Fritz spoke from the hatch behind him. "I didn't realize the pneumatic actuator was faulty."

Babbage gritted his teeth at being caught yet again in a usually rare moment of profanity and waved off the apology. "How could you have known?"

"Still..." Fritz trailed off at Babbage's scowl, his fingers uncon-sciously playing with the hatch's lift-ring. "Anyway, my crewman and I have replaced the unit and gone over both engines to ensure there are no further complications. We should arrive in Jerusalem tomorrow."

Tomorrow. "How far are we behind the *Thaddeus Lowe*?" Babbage asked.

"Hard to say, they were scheduled to arrive in the city two weeks ago," Fritz said, his expression thoughtful. "There's no knowing if they've had their own technical issues, though."

Damned if part of Babbage did not hope that was so. He turned back to the porthole glaring at the vibrant shades of sunset. Though such was not his habit, he prayed his apprentice fared well. Ali would have no doubt celebrated Babbage's use of prayer, an attestation that there was a place for faith in his world after all. Babbage *humph*ed. Next he'd be believing in Lady Clara's impossibilities, monsters in the shadows, and fairies sipping milk in the moonlight.

Behind him, Fritz cleared his throat. "So... Sadie dearly hopes you might join us for dinner..."

Babbage *humph*ed again. "Sadie, you say?" He turned a pointed stare on the younger man. It was doubtful the three-year-old even knew who Babbage was. She had seen him all of two minutes when they boarded the airship. He had kept to himself since then, not being particularly good company.

Fritz grinned shamelessly. "She wants to show you her doll."

That startled an unexpected laugh from Babbage. The doll he was already intimately familiar with, having overseen its construction. Still, it touched him that the little one took such pride in the toy he and Ali had worked so diligently upon.

"Dinner it is, then," he said still smiling faintly as he followed his host through the hatch.

Ali looked out from the observation deck as the aerostat descended toward Jerusalem. He was eager to disembark in such an historic city. Perhaps he could take some time to reacquaint himself with the place before beginning his trek across the desert. Or perhaps not... Kassim expected him. They were already a day late in their arrival, thanks to the window that needed to be replaced after the impact with the falcon. It would be unwise to delay further.

Unfortunate, but Ali could not begrudge the time spent in Madrid. They had lain over there to make the repair and Ali had gained a cabin-mate at the same time. He had been pleased to discover that the passenger assigned to share his cabin was a Moor making his *Hajj*, his pilgrimage. When Rashid had boarded in Madrid the two of them discovered a mutual rapport as Muslims far from home among people who looked down on them, equating different with lesser. Time had passed more comfortably for Ali after that, spent in conversation.

Rashid rested now as the turbulence of the airship's slow descent unsettled his constitution. Ali had left the cabin so as to not disturb his friend. He found himself in the lounge for the first time since the attack. The broken glass had been replaced, but the teak frame still bore faint scars of the encounter. The ghost of his assailant's scream still haunted him.

Ali put those thoughts from his head and focused instead on the city below. The view was breathtaking and Jerusalem itself was a marvel, home to the three great faiths and their attendant *medreses* of magic. In the early dawn light he could see as far as the great walls of the Old City. Built by Suleiman the Magnificent, it was said that he infused magic into the very stones. For all its history and culture, this was not a great venue of trade. Jerusalem was, however, close to home. In the market, Ali would obtain a donkey and — if Allah saw fit to bless him — join a caravan travelling in the direction of Wadi Al-Nejd, far into the Arabian Desert. If not, Ali would brave the sands alone to complete the last leg of his journey.

From the calls of the aerostat's crew, they would soon land north of the walls just after full dawn, as planned. No sense in arriving before then. All of the residents of Jerusalem lived within the walls of the Old City, and the gates were locked from sunset to sunrise. Ali sighed at this reminder of home. He blinked back tears. Soon.

The landing was quicker and smoother than Ali anticipated. In minutes, he and several other passengers disembarked, as well as a few crates and bags of post. The Thaddeus Lowe would not stay but continue on, turning north toward Damascus and then Istanbul. Ali would miss the Giffards, many an hour he'd passed with them companionably during the long journey. He'd wished Rashid well on his journey and with one last look at their shared cabin had quietly closed the door and headed to the exit with the rest of the passengers.

Shouldering his satchel, Ali joined the general traffic on the road. It felt exceedingly good to be among people who would not stare at him and his manner of dress. His traditional garb was unremarkable here, as was the *chafiye* draped loosely around his head and neck. He luxuriated in the feel of sand…blessed sand beneath his leather sandals as he moved with the flow of the crowd.

This early in the morning, the road leading to the city was filled with men and their heavily-laden donkeys, camels bearing jars of oil and bags of fruit, men in striped shirts, women with red caps and yellow kerchiefs, the Fellahin with their goats and sheep — Ali found the experience overwhelming after so long away.

These people headed to the bazaar, the thought of which stirred Ali's heart. An English market could not compare with the passion of its Eastern cousin. Ali did not know whether to cry or shout praises to the Almighty. Part of him felt the need to squeeze his eyes shut tight. Part of him wanted to never close them again lest he miss some familiar sight. He did neither, but he did drop his gaze, realizing that his heart searched for his father in the crowd. Ali had only traveled with his father to Jerusalem twice but he remembered the journey with the exquisite pain that only a beloved memory can draw. Massoud bin-Farzeen had loved the energy of the bazaar, particularly this one, and had been known to wander the stalls for hours with his friend Hiram, a Jewish merchant here in Jerusalem, specializing in crafted goods including puzzle boxes. Ali's father had ever searched for simple treasures to bring home to his son, reveling in the more zealous, informal dealings than he himself experienced in his own trade.

Ali sighed and pressed his grief deep into its private place in his heart. Father would admonish him for dwelling on it so, particularly if he were its object. Such memories should bring joy, not sorrow, lest he begin to question the Almighty's will. It was not Ali's place to do so.

"Thanks be to Allah, I have dreamt long of this journey."

The unexpected comment shook Ali from his thoughts. He turned, surprised to see, Rashid, had come up beside him. The Moor smiled. "It is truly a beautiful sight," he said, with a nod toward Jerusalem.

Ali drew a deep breath, allowed his eyes to scan the ancient city before him, and had to agree. Their destination, the great gate, Bab El Amud, stood embedded in the stone walls that ringed the city. Towers, battlements, and parapets gave the entrance an appearance that was both beautiful and imposing. Beyond its portal lay the morning bazaar. Ali prayed he would find what he needed there: both a sturdy, serviceable animal and a caravan to join.

"How long will you remain in Jerusalem?" Ali asked, turning his gaze back toward Rashid, a hope he dare not voice glimmering within.

"I am to be here a fortnight," the Moor answered his face glowing with joy and religious fervor. "There is so much to see in this holy city, Al-Aqsa Mosque…The Dome of the Rock…"

Rashid went on, but Ali only half listened, trying not to show his disappointment. If only he could have continued his journey beside his new friend, but two weeks was too long. Their paths must diverge here.

As his friend went on about his pilgrimage, Ali guided him toward the gate. When they passed through and found themselves in the bazaar, Rashid was for a moment struck silent, his eyes wide and his gaze darting from one delight to another.

The bazaar quickly became crowded as others shoved through the gate behind them. Ali pulled Rashid to the side and let him watch his fill as vendors raised their canopies and laid out their wares. Voices called out offers and discounts in a variety of tongues as haggling, the very language of the bazaar, began. All around, there were foodstuffs that tempted the eyes as much as the palate—figs, olives, pomegranates, pistachios, walnuts, and apricots. The rich, dark aroma of roasted coffee beans teased his nose, holding dominion over the bazaar in this early hour, before the sun baked the wares below into a stew of scents. Ali's stomach grumbled, reminding him that he had not broken his fast. He traded a few copper coins to a one-legged man selling oranges from a cart.

"What is that?" Rashid asked, nodding to a building ahead of them.

"The Hospice of the Knights of St. John," Ali replied as he deftly peeled the orange and separated the fruit in half. "It marks the line between the Muslim quarter of the city and the Christian." He offered half the orange to his companion, who grinned and nodded his thanks at what was to him a rare treat. Ali popped a segment into his mouth and closed his eyes as a sigh slipped past his smiling lips. Sweet and tangy.

"Water from Bir Eyub! May God be compassionate to me!" called out a young boy, his bare feet and his skin browned by the sun until he was as dark as an English chestnut. He wandered the bazaar nearby, rattling brass cups in one hand while the other carried a full goatskin, its battered sides rounded with what was likely cool, crisp water from the local well. The child had just enough dust about him to inspire pity, when paired with his thin face and arms that spoke of enough food to subsist, but not enough to thrive. True plight or calculated effect? Hard to say, with one so young. Veiled women sided-stepped the boy without giving him a glance, giggling together as they perused the stalls.

Ali continued on, drawing Rashid behind him, dodging baskets of rice from Jordan and Egypt as they were unloaded in front of a nearby stall. He had been barely ten when he had first visited with his father, not much older than the boy. *Father would have fed him and cleaned him up.* Ali's heart pinched at the thought. He would like to honor his father's memory by allowing it to guide his own actions, but he did not have means to do so. Until he secured his donkey and travel supplies, he could not spare any more of his dwindling coin. With that in mind, he sniffed the air, trying to catch the scent of livestock that would tell him the way he must go. It had been almost five years since Ali had last trod upon the stones of the Holy City and time had worn away the edges of his memories. A faint scent of dung seemed to come from his left, along with a calf's low bawling. Guiding Rashid in that direction, Ali could not help but spare a final glance at the water boy. From across the way, the boy watched back, something unsettling in his gaze, haunting and undecipherable.

Ali frowned and turned away. He could not allow the boy's woes to distract him from his task. He must get to the livestock pens before the good quality beasts had been claimed or he would face a hard journey across the desert. Still, Ali vowed at least to come back for a drink if any coin remained.

As he and Rashid made their way toward the other side of the bazaar Ali ignored those hawking their wares with a practiced ease. Most were respectful, but he had to wave away a vendor of magical amulets who seemed to believe that sheer volume would encourage a sale, and that grabbing would ensure one. The man desisted when Ali brandished his staff, but as Ali turned away the merchant dangled glass beads to catch Rashid's eye. The Moor seemed mesmerized, though the beads were nothing special. Ali grabbed his friend's arm and drew him away from the charlatan's temptation.

As he did so, Ali again spied the water boy watching nearby.

No longer enchanted by the bazaar or memories of his father, Ali tugged Rashid's arm and moved into the flow of traffic, just barely avoiding a string of camels being led in the direction Ali headed.

"What is wrong, my friend? Why do you rush so when there are so many wonders to see?" Disappointment and confusion infused Rashid's words.

Ali turned to him wondering if he should mention the boy's presence. *A thief perhaps?* Ali was a merchant's son and had received many cautions from his father on the ways of thieves and beggars in the large cities, many who targeted travelers, seeing them as easy, and often rich, prey. "I am sorry, my friend. It is important that I secure a beast of burden swiftly. Do you wish to part ways for now and we can meet after?"

"Please, if you do not mind," Rashid answered. "Where should I meet you?"

Ali calculated in his mind how long it might take to bargain for his animal. As he formulated his answer, the bells of the Christian cathedral rang the hour. Good. Good, surely an hour would be enough time. He glanced at the Moor. "Shall we meet before the Hospice at the next ringing of the hour?"

Nodding agreement, Rashid went off to explore the wonders of the bazaar, may Allah have mercy on him. Ali hurried on toward his goal, moving much faster unimpeded by his friend.

Wandering the pens, Ali mostly kept his expression neutral, allowing only the occasional shade of disappointment to darken his eyes accompanied by the faintest frown. Not enough to insult the merchants, but sufficient to send the message that their offerings could be better, thus putting Ali in a superior position to negotiate. Inwardly though, he sighed. The beasts on offer were limited and mostly of good quality. Silently, Ali lifted a prayer to Allah and his Prophet that he had sufficient coin for his needs.

"Finest horse flesh anywhere," one merchant called out, running a hand down the flank of an Arabian mare. "Fit for kings and swifter than the wind, Baba. I make a special deal just for you." Others called out half-heartedly, but did not make much effort, noting Ali's modest dress, and the lack of a heavy money-pouch at his waist.

Ali nodded respectfully to the horse merchant but did not allow the man to draw him in. A horse of such quality would not do for his needs, requiring too much pampering far out in the desert. Instead, he turned his gaze to the next pen, which held more pedestrian beasts of burden: camels, mules, and a lone donkey, a jenny whose ears were laid back as she menaced her pen-mates. She jostled and shoved mercilessly, keeping them away from the manger. The beast was small, but stout of heart.

Approaching the pen, Ali settled in to haggle.

Weary, but with the donkey trailing behind, making only occasional efforts to bite, Ali made his way back through the bazaar toward the Hospice of St. John. Bargaining had taken half an hour and too much of his coin. He gnawed the inside of his lip as he considered how much more he needed to buy and how little money he had to do so.

As he dwelled among his worries, Ali felt a bump from behind. Again. The donkey apparently had a preference for chewing cypress and kept trying to latch her teeth on the staff strapped to Ali's back. Her efforts had not all been successful, several attempts resulting in her biting down on Ali instead.

"Enough, you obstinate beast!" Ali growled. The donkey, incongruously named Jasmine, merely blinked and flicked a long white ear in his direction. Sighing, Ali unslung his grandfather's staff and with it in his free hand, continued forward. The bazaar had grown more crowded as the morning aged. By noon, the entire square would be empty, but now was when the market was at its height. Ali found himself jostled and shoved as he made his way to the far side of the square. The muscles across his shoulders bunched and the impulse to drop his hand to his satchel, to check the complex knot was secure, became an obsession. He resisted the urge, though, as it would require that he stop and free a hand to do so, all of which would draw notice to the fact that the pouch held something he valued. Never wise. If his merchant father had taught him anything it had been how to safeguard against theft.

Ali continued on, only to feel another brush from behind, then something tug lightly at his satchel.

The damned donkey grew more ornery with each step of their mutual journey. Ali spun at a second bump, a rare glower upon his countenance that surely echoed those bestowed upon him by *Ustad* Babbage. The glower slipped, then deepened. It was not the donkey, but the water carrier. The boy's eyes were edged white in panic as he snatched at the satchel he had been unable to pilfer with stealth. Ali would have grabbed his wrist, if not that his hands were both engaged. All he could do was pivot his torso to remove the satchel from the boy's reach and bring the staff around to block his desperate grasping, tapping the boy's knuckles smartly with it.

The boy paled and his gaze went wide with terror. Ali noted how he trembled and shrank in on himself before he dashed away. Something told Ali to follow. The boy's reaction and the fear in his expression was far from normal but Ali could scarcely do so encumbered as he was with Jasmine. He followed the fleeing young thief with his eyes. No, not thief…. The lad had not the practiced skill. He had not done this on his own initiative. Ali's expression darkened at the thought of the scoundrel who clearly had taken advantage of the boy's desperation.

As he watched where the boy had vanished into the crowd, a hand gripped Ali's shoulder. On instinct, he spun and brought up his staff. Behind him, Rashid raised a calm hand to intercept the strike.

"Peace, my friend. What troubles you so?"

Embracing providence, Ali thrust the donkey's lead rope into the Moor's hand and dashed after the boy, calling over his shoulder as he ran, "Please, wait for me at the *caravanserai*."

Not waiting for acknowledgment or agreement, Ali wove his way through the bazaar. Partly by luck and partly through stubbornness, Ali eventually caught sight of the ragged boy. Once he did, he did not take his eye from his quarry, nor did he draw closer. His intent was not to capture the lad, not yet, but to see where he fled: to safety or to the handler who sent him. Ali would know why the world suddenly coveted his modest possessions.

The boy scurried like a mouse, casting fearful glances around him, huddling in shadows, taking paths where few might follow. He crawled across the rooftops and skulked through vacant gardens, crept through alleyways, but never entered a structure where he might find himself with no escape.

Ali's luck left him, if he had ever had any, near the Mount of the Rock. The boy skirted the crowd and then suddenly darted within their midst.

Ali cursed and was about to move forward with haste, only to fall back into the shadow of the building he hid beside. A large man clothed in a striped *djellaba* came shoving out of the crowd. The loose robe hung off of broad shoulders and the man kept the hood pulled low making it impossible to see his face. The boy stumbled after him, making a frantic effort to free his arm from the man's grip. "But I told you what happened!"

Aside from Ali, none in the crowd paid the pair any mind. Not even a glance. Such treatment was hardly of note when the most likely presumption was that the boy was a servant or offspring remiss in his duties.

Ali's hand tightened on his staff. Drawing his *chafiye* over his face, he followed at a discreet distance.

The man dragged the boy into a small vacant courtyard. Ali slid his staff into the strap that held it to his back and leapt to grab the awning of the building beside the courtyard where his quarry went. He drew himself up and crept across the low rooftop, flattening to the warm stone at the edge to peer over at those below.

"Where is it?!" the man hissed at the boy, shaking him. There was something familiar about the voice, but not its harshness. Ali could not place it.

"I could not get it. I tried!"

Ali spied just the barest swath of skin at the man's wrist. He scowled, noting it bore a familiar band. The man struck the boy, who cried out and fell to the ground, a spatter of blood speckling the stones around him. The sight of such violence sparked Ali's righteous anger. Perversely, part of him felt guilty for foiling the boy's attempt. It took great restraint to remain where he was and listen.

"Did I not tell you how important the box was?" the man said towering over the slight boy. "Did I not say you would regret any failure?"

The boy cringed and tried to scramble backward. Blood trickled down his face and his gaze darted to find some path of escape. But walls rose to all sides of him and the man blocked the way out.

"You have wasted my time," the man repeated in a low, lethal tone. "Do you even know where the man who carries the box is?"

A whimper was his only answer.

Without another word, the man drew a dagger from within his robe. It was wicked and curved and showed signs of frequent use. The air went still and the bustle of the street beyond the courtyard faded into nothing, at least to Ali's ears. He watched, his muscles bunching and his jaw grinding, as the man wove the blade through the air with practiced ease, slowly sliding closer to the boy, taunting him.

Bad enough the cur threatened the boy, Ali could not stomach that he now toyed with him as well. Without realizing he did so, Ali rose up into a crouch with the staff gripped tight in both hands a shoulder-width apart like a fighting staff. A faint tremor traveled up his arm from the wood. His brow puckered as the staff seemed to warm within his grip. Below, the whimpers grew more frantic and the boy's efforts to scramble away did no more than churn up dust. Ali reached up to ensure his face remained covered by his *chafiye* and then leapt to the cobbles, landing between the boy and his attacker. The impact sent a jolt from his ankles clear to his skull. He brandished the staff trying to recall what his maternal grandfather had taught him of *tahtib*, Egyptian stick-fighting. It had been long ago…nearly half of his life.

Ali suppressed a shiver. As the cypress warmed in his grip, he felt cold suffuse his body.

He swung the staff in a large, defensive figure-eight pattern. It was a basic *tahtib* pattern and the wind whistled audibly at the speed with which he wielded the cypress wood.

The man cursed and stepped in with a lightning-quick slash. Ali called a challenge as he struck outward with the length of the staff. At the movement, the heat beneath Ali's hands intensified and the staff flashed with a mystical light. He missed, but forced the man back with his swing. As the end of the staff brushed past the man's *djellaba*, heat radiated from the cypress wood in Ali's hands and the golden glow flared like a thousand suns. The man hissed as his *djellaba* began to smolder.

"Sorcery?" the man sputtered, patting at the front of his clothing, his eyes dark with hate, "You are a coward."

Ali's gaze narrowed but he said nothing.

Rather than retreat, the man came at him again. The staff flashed, but this time, Ali's opponent deftly sidestepped the blow. Each time the man drew too close another flash of magical light lit the courtyard. With every burst, Ali felt a bit more energy drain away from him.

The man chuckled, noting Ali's trembling limbs. His eyes followed the *tahtib* patterns and then, seeing a gap in Ali's defenses, stepped inside the staff's swing and lashed out with his dagger. Ali stumbled back, almost treading on the boy.

Weariness dragged upon Ali's limbs. Even with the greater reach of the staff, he was not a seasoned fighter, unlike his opponent. The man slipped in and out, Ali's staff barely missing him; the tip of his blade left fine tracings of blood on Ali's hands and cheek below his eye, small slits in his sleeve. At each engagement Ali tired, and his meager skills became more evident, until he began to fear for both himself and the boy.

Suddenly, a familiar piercing scream sounded above, conveying frustration and rage. A great raptor circled overhead, casting its shadow on the ground. Heartened, Ali pressed forward, jabbing with the length of the staff, forcing the villain back and to the side, away from the archway that led back to the street. The magical light flared and Ali heard a pain-filled cry as the staff connected, setting the man's arm alight. Ali called out to the boy behind him, "Run, and reflect on the Almighty's mercy!"

The boy fled, as expected, and — to Ali's surprise — so did the man, slapping the flames out as he ran. Ali was left with nothing but dazzled vision, the stench of scorched cloth, and the memory of the man's anger-steeped eyes…eyes that like the voice were strangely familiar.

Chapter Seven

ALI HAD TIME TO THINK BEFORE HE TOO FLED FROM THE courtyard and made his way to rendezvous with Rashid. He swapped out the *besht* he wore for the one in his satchel, despite the heavier weight of the fabric. He slung his satchel beneath the vest. He then removed his *chafiye* and wound it around the staff as a grip, thus further altering both of their appearances. Even so, he kept to the alleys and side streets as he made his way to the *caravanserai* where he could find rest and a meal. He moved with slow, weary steps even with the aid of the staff.

Ali could no longer deny that the attacks he'd endured of late were calculated and deliberate. Someone…that *man*… desired Ali's puzzle box to such a degree that he had pursued it across several countries. Such effort could in no way be described as casual or opportunistic. It seemed laughable that the box might hold anything worthy of such obsession, all evidence to the contrary.

Ali's frown went so deep his head ached. What had his father bequeathed him? What secrets did the cursed box hold? Nothing Ali could think of would be worth such effort. And yet, clearly there were those of another mind on the matter.

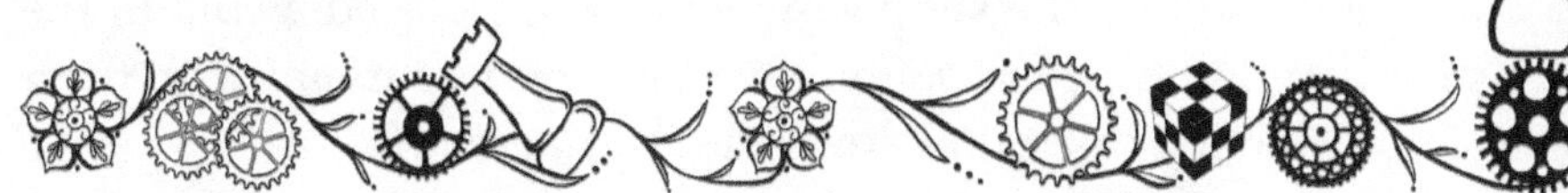

Sighing, he wended his way through the dark, cluttered back streets of the city.

And what of the staff? It had never responded with such magics before. A magic that targeted the man who sought the box. All the mysteries were connected. He just did not understand how. It occurred to Ali that right here in Jerusalem resided one who might have knowledge of the box or, at the very least, Ali's father's intent. Hiram, whose very trade dealt with puzzle boxes every day. Ali would seek out his father's friend, who had a proper shop in the artisans' quarter. Surely he, of anyone, could help. In fact, it occurred to Ali that Hiram had likely provided the box to begin with. But first, Ali must return to Rashid and reclaim his donkey.

The journey to the *caravanserai* was uneventful. From time to time, Ali's neck muscles tightened as if beneath the weight of another's gaze, but such moments were fleeting. The weariness persisted, as did the ache in his legs and back. As he arrived at the squat, low buildings that made up the *caravanserai*, Ali moved as if the last of his energy had drained away, the staff bearing most of his weight.

He found Rashid waiting at the neighboring outdoor coffee shop. Men, old and young, were settled around several tables, sipping tea or coffee, smoking *shisha*, and playing backgammon or *shah-mat*. Ali stared longingly at the teacup that sat in front of his friend. The scent of sweet honey and steeped herbs taunted him from the interior of the building. The Moor shoved to his feet on seeing Ali, his expression deepening with concern and a glimmer of something darker for a moment before he schooled his features.

"I am sorry, my friend," Ali said by way of greeting. "It is unconscionable that I have robbed you of this day and all it might have held for you."

Rashid waved off the apology as he hurried forward, gently taking Ali by the arm. "Come, I have secured a room." His gaze cautioned silence and obedience. Ali readily complied. He would have wavered on his feet if not for his friend's grip. The Moor reached to take Ali's satchel for him, but Ali tightened his grip, unwilling to be parted from it. He thought he heard his friend sigh, but couldn't be sure.

As they passed by the shop's owner, Rashid placed a coin in the man's hand and said, "Please, if you would, send a servant with fresh tea and some honey cakes. We are at the *caravanserai*."

Ali groaned as Rashid guided him to one of the low whitewashed buildings. The sight of a simple bed across the room filled Ali's vision until he could not say what else furnished their accommodations. Nor could he claim to care. His grip on the staff loosened without intent. The staff would have fallen to the tiled floor if not for Rashid's quick reach. His friend flinched and nearly dropped the staff himself before tightening his hold.

"Lay down, Baba Ali," Rashid said, while ensuring he did so. The Moor tried to set the staff aside by the door and again claim the burden of the satchel, but Ali was oddly reluctant to be separated from either one.

"Please…no," he said, his voice but a wisp, his hand reaching out. Rashid frowned, but dropped his hand from the satchel and laid the staff on Ali's palm. Ali pulled the length of cypress to his chest. Then, as weary as he was, he tried to explain about the thieves and Hiram. His efforts came out garbled and the room swam.

"Hush, now," Rashid commanded, tugging his sleeves down where they had ridden up, until the edge covered the back of his hand. "Rest, refresh yourself with food and tea, then we can discuss what has beset you." Ali nodded…or attempted too, and settled back against the bedding as Rashid moved to answer a knock at the door. When he returned he bore a platter with a simple tea set and a plate of cakes. The aroma borne by the steam alone revived Ali, if only momentarily. Rashid propped him up and held the tea cup to his lips.

Ali could scarce believe the afternoon's events had left him so weary.

"It is the *bâton*…the staff," Rashid said as he broke off a piece of honey cake and brought it to Ali's lips. Though it pained him to be served so, he could not summon the energy to feed himself. "I have seen such things before. The artifact beside you is quite old and powerful. Unless one knows to guard against the effect, the magical nature of the thing draws energy from around it each time the spell upon it is triggered."

The warmth and the chills, Ali thought as Rashid continued to feed him. *The way the man fled. This makes sense.* Ali would have jerked his hand away from the staff, only some of its current warmth leeched into him and he could not stand to be parted from it.

"How…" The words caught in Ali's throat until Rashid again lifted the teacup to his lips. Ali tried again. "How do I guard against this?" he asked.

Rashid hesitated, as if loath to speak, the tension in his body in conflict with his serene expression.

"Please…" Ali said, reaching out with a shaking hand. He did not know the nature of the battle he witnessed but eventually words forced their way past Rashid's lips.

"Claim your energy," Rashid answered, glaring at the staff as if he would break it in two. "Focus on your core, then expand your awareness until you reach the border of your outermost skin. Feel that energy…that essence of you, and lay claim to it. Once you are aware you will never lose that and your energy cannot be drawn off."

Rashid's lips pressed tight a moment and his eyes dimmed.

"By an artifact, anyway," he added, his voice curiously flat. "You must take care around practitioners of magic. If they are strong enough, knowledgeable enough…they could rob you of your essence."

Ali—somewhat restored by the sustenance and rest—reached out to lay a hand on his friend's arm. "You have lost someone thus?"

Looking away, Rashid nodded sharply, but made no further comment.

"I am sorry, my friend. Thank you for sharing your knowledge, despite the pain it must have caused you."

Silence reigned a moment before Rashid sat forward and met Ali's gaze once more. "So, tell me what has transpired."

Ali told him of following the boy and then the encounter with the man.

"But why did this one not attempt to rob me himself?" Ali wondered aloud, his gaze hooded.

A frown compressed Rashid's lips but he offered no suggestion.

Ali thought back. The break-in at the house on Dorset Street. The attack on the airship. Excepting this last occurrence, in so public a place, each time the clockwork falcon had appeared and come to his defense. At least one of those other times it had not ended well for the thief. Thinking back to the blood he'd discovered in *Ustad* Babbage's garden, Ali suspected there had been other attempts. In fact, who knew how many there were that he had no knowledge of?

"I believe," Ali answered his own question, his words drawn out as his thoughts raced, "that I have a protector and knowing this, the thief had rather risk another than himself."

Rashid's gaze glimmered with anger. "What is so important that they pursue it so?"

How much to share? Ali wondered. He had not known Rashid for long. How certain was he that he could count the Moor friend and not foe? Friendship was simple enough to mimic. Faith as well. Though, if Rashid were among those after the box he would have had ample time to try for it before they had left the airship. There were moments where Ali was certain his belongings had been disturbed, but nothing had ever gone missing and he had seen no sign that Rashid was anything but honest and caring. Of course, Ali had been careful never to leave the puzzle box unattended. Suspicion rose like bitter bile from his gut. Still, Ali raised a silent prayer to the Almighty that he was not about to be most foolish. Calm descended upon him. Slowly, Ali drew the *Himitsu-Bako* from his satchel.

"Magnificent," his friend said, wonder lighting his gaze once more. Rashid reached out and ran a finger across the surface of the box but did not attempt to take it in his hand. Ali relaxed enough to wonder why the magical responses remained dormant, no glow or sparkling lights, even though Rashid had traced one of the trigger points for the effect. "Have you discovered the secret?"

Huffing, Ali shook his head. "This is more complex than any box I have ever seen. I have tried every method known to me, and the box protects it secrets. Every error results in a painful correction. There is a chance, though…" Ali fell silent, doubt weighing heavy on his chest.

"A chance?"

Ali met his friend's gaze. Searched it. Narrowed his own in an effort to peer into the other man's soul. He found nothing but openness and friendship, care and concern.

"Nearby, in Mamilla, the artisans' quarter," Ali finally answered. "A man named Hiram owns a shop where such boxes as these are sold. I must go to him and see if he can help me."

This time Rashid frowned, his already swarthy face darkening. "You are not fit to go anywhere, my friend."

"I must," Ali said. "Besides, I am feeling much restored."

Rashid nodded slowly and did not argue, but there was a knowing look in his gaze as he said in quiet tones, "Stand."

Ali hesitated a moment before gathering his determination around him. Slowly he drew himself up and swung his legs off of the bed. His knees shook and his vision blurred a moment before coming clear again. He dropped his head forward, his shoulders slumping as the energy ran out of him. He did not even attempt to push to his feet. When Rashid came forward to help him recline again, Ali did not resist.

"Rest, my friend," the Moor murmured over him. "I will bring this Hiram to you."

As the door clicked closed, Ali embraced sleep.

"You did what?!" Kassim swept his arm outward and struck Malakeh with the back of his hand. She cried out and dropped to her knees, cradling her cheek against her shoulder.

"Stupid woman! Did I say to you 'I wish my brother dead'? Did I charge you to cast his soul upon the desert until his body and *all* he carries might be *lost* to us for all time, as with my father?"

Malakeh cringed from him and would not meet his gaze. "I beg forgiveness, husband. I had thought to please you…to ensure your brother could never take from you your heart's desire…"

Kassim gripped her chin, forcing her to look up, "And if he possesses it already, wife?" he hissed. "What if even now it rests on his person? Will you search the sands for his remains to reclaim my prize?" His grip increased in pressure. "And would you deny me Paradise? You spoke in my name, you purchased this favor with my wealth, woman. I may not enter with my brother's blood on my hands. Allah forgive you." Kassim all but snarled the last three words.

"As you will, it shall be so," Malakeh murmured, tears coursing down her cheeks, confusion in her voice.

For a long moment, Kassim remained silent. "Should my brother survive your scheming, you will find a way to claim his things that I may search them before he has had a chance to hide anything away."

Malakeh bobbed her head, "Yes, my husband, it shall be as you decree."

"And should my brother precede me to the Prophet's side in Paradise…" he let the words fade into silence, his displeasure clear.

Kassim considered striking Malakeh again, before deciding it would be unwise, lest in his anger he go too far. "Absent yourself from my presence, woman, else you may find my will bodes ill for you."

She scurried from the room, nearly scrambling on all fours in her haste.

Words twisted in a sardonic smile, Kassim called out after her. "Best you should pray Allah's blessing upon my brother…that what you have wrought might fail and your life be preserved."

Ali woke to find that beneath his blankets he had huddled around the puzzle box as if even in his sleep he feared it would be snatched away. He lay there and tried to get a sense of the room surrounding him. Foremost was the sound of deep, even breathing, punctuated by the occasional resonant snore. Ali relaxed at sounds familiar to him from their weeks sharing a cabin on the aerostat. He rolled over and opened his eyes expecting to see Rashid stretched out on a pallet on the floor.

Likely, he was, but Ali could not see him past the man who sat in a chair beside Ali's bed. By the dim flicker of a brazier in the corner, he noted that the man wore a full beard and a fez above a striped robe and dark coat, in the fashion of those of the Jewish faith. He sat there with his hands clutching a small book and his lips moved silently, as if in prayer. Ali saw fresh sorrow writ upon his brow. Rashid must have told the man the fate of Ali's father.

"Honored Hiram," Ali said in soft tones, that Rashid's rest not be disturbed. "I thank you for coming."

Hiram nodded in acknowledgement, but continued his prayer aloud, likewise keeping his voice low. Ali waited in silence for the prayer to end, slowly sliding himself upright, this time without the room spinning. He kept the box beneath the blankets, nestled in his lap.

After the final "Amen" Hiram leaned forward and took Ali's hand. He smiled and his eyes nearly disappeared into the wrinkles mapping his face.

"It is, I think, as if I am looking into the past," the man said in Yiddish, "and seeing the face of my good friend Massoud—may God rest his soul—as a young man."

It was an effort for Ali not to pull his hand away.

"My father spoke well of you, sir," he answered in the same tongue.

"Thank you, Ali." Hiram's eyes misted over. "Now, what is it I may do for my good friend's son?"

Ali took a deep, steadying breath before drawing down the blanket to reveal the box.

"It is my hope, perhaps…" he said, struggling with the words, "that perhaps you are familiar with this box. That perhaps you are the one from whom my father purchased it."

Hiram sat back heavily in his chair, his expression even sadder. The woven reeds and wood frame creaked under the man's bulk. Rashid's snores stopped at the sound. The Moor sat up, as if assessing the threat, but Ali never shifted his gaze from Hiram's. After a moment, Rashid lay down again.

"I know this box," Hiram murmured, his voice barely reaching Ali's ears. "But I did not sell it to your father. It came to him as an inheritance, or so he told me. He brought it to me to have your name engraved, though why he came so far for that I cannot say. He showed me the workings knowing how honored I would be to see such ancient craftsmanship. He thought, perhaps, that I might learn from its complexity and thus further my craft."

"And did you?" Ali asked unable to keep his excitement from his voice.

"I was enriched by the experience," Hiram answered, with soulful eyes and a shake of his head, "but alas, the maker of that box was as much sorcerer as master craftsman. The skills that made it were beyond me."

Ali felt his expression fall in pace with his heart. A weary sigh slid from his lips.

"Now, now," Hiram said, once more reaching out. "What is this? Have you not opened the box? Massoud spoke often of your skill at such things."

Cheeks burning, Ali shook his head. "I have tried everything. Every trick I have ever learned from the many boxes my father brought me over the years and nothing works."

Realization dawned on the old man's face.

"Ah!" he said, holding out his hand. "Then perhaps I may help you after all…if you will allow it?"

Ali frowned, his brow furrowing. "How?"

"Why, I have never in my life forgotten a sequence, once seen," Hiram answered.

Ali must have looked perplexed because the artisan smiled and leaned forward to claim the box. When Ali pulled, the man merely shook his head and bid him come closer. Ali complied but he also noticed that Rashid had drawn himself up to a sitting position, watching the two of them with a glittering gaze. Ali did not know why, but the look made him uneasy. He shivered, feeling the overwhelming urge to whisper a prayer to the Almighty for protection.

"Wait," Ali murmured in Yiddish, before turning toward the Moor. "Rashid, please, could you procure some more tea for us?" Did the Moor hesitate? Did he tense? Ali could not say if he imagined so in the dim light of the brazier.

"By all means," Rashid answered, his tone genial as he rose and left the room.

When the door closed Ali leaned forward, "We must be quick."

The sorrow returned to Hiram's gaze as he complied. He took the puzzle box between both hands, palms flat against its sides, then allowed his fingers to trace the whorls of filigree marking the front of the box, pressing at key points along the way. Ali watched closely, mimicking the motions. It took him a moment to notice that the corners of Hiram's lips had tugged down, as if the box did not response as it ought.

"What?" Ali asked. "What is wrong?"

A full frown blossomed on the artisan's face. He repeated the actions, then followed them by pressing on other points upon the box, his brow bunched in concentration. He then turned the box around and tried again.

"I do not understand…" Hiram murmured.

Ali's heart ached to see the man's disappointment, to see his confidence shaken after being so certain.

"If it is Allah's will, it will happen in the Almighty's chosen time," Ali said in an effort to reassure his father's friend. "I thank you for your efforts."

Hiram rose. "I must return to my family."

Ali struggled to his feet, and embraced the man, kissing him once on each cheek. "Then I bid you good night and good fortune." Ali tried to press a coin on his father's friend, in thanks, but the man refused it.

By the time Rashid returned with the tea, Ali was alone and the box tucked away.

In the morning, Ali woke to a hard, smooth surface under his cheek. And his hand. And cradled against his belly. At some time in the night he had drawn the staff onto the bed. He should have been concerned with the sudden propensity for odd bed fellows, but he found he could not care at the moment as heat radiated from the staff, flowing into him to curl deep beneath his skin like a flickering warmth. Ali sighed and curled closer, the precursor of a smile tugging the corners of his lips. He felt as if he could race across the desert with swift strides to rival his father's stallion, Biaban Govad. As he lay there, though, his body recalled him to needs other than for rest. Ali drew down the blanket under which he nestled, blinking with the brightness of the morning light pouring through the unshuttered window.

"What did you learn?"

Ali jerked at the sudden, abrupt question. He turned to find Rashid kneeling upon a prayer rug beside the bed. Though the Moor appeared in meditation Ali could not but wonder at the faint lines of tension about his eyes. Had Ali caused his friend such worry?

And what a curious question with which to greet the day. Ali was uncertain how he wished to reply.

"Allah's blessing upon you this glorious day, my friend," he greeted the Moor before answering. "Nothing, I am afraid, save that Hiram is as enamored of *Himitsu-Bako* as I am, but likewise just as thwarted by this one."

Rashid's eyes narrowed. "You seek to deceive me."

Ali's shoulders jerked back at the accusation and concern furrowed his brow.

Rashid continued. "He told you the sequence, did he not? He showed you how to open that cursed box."

"No," Ali said, his words heated as confusion and hurt tightened his heart. "He was wrong, he did not know the secret."

"I do not believe you, *Baba* Ali," the Moor answered, a hard expression twisting his features. "And I cannot wait any longer. You will give me the box and you will show me how to open it."

"You could have stolen the box at any time." Ali could not help pointing out.

"A wise man considers before he acts," Rashid answered, his expression set in harsh lines that seemed foreign to Ali. "I have watched you, given you time to solve that *thing*. After all, what good is the box without the secret? I need both if I am to preserve my life."

A sense of betrayal robbed Ali of breath. He did not know what grieved him more: that Rashid would steal from him, or that the Moor's life was in danger over a simple box …or the secret it held.

But the Moor went on. "I lost patience. Foolish of me, but not so now… You will give me your secrets and I will give you a swift death."

Ali could not help but gasp as deepest betrayal robbed him of breath.

"You were my friend, Rashid."

"It is true…I like you, Ali," Rashid said, his expression drawn. "More than I should, but I would preserve my own soul."

"You do not have to do this."

The Moor turned a furious gaze on Ali. With the sight of those angry eyes Ali came to realize Rashid was the man who'd attacked the boy. His heart broke at the treachery.

"I have no choice. I swore an oath to my master long ago. He demands the box, and I must obey, though it pain me to do so."

Slowly, Ali edged back trying to gain distance.

Rashid rose from his kneeling position, his demeanor completely transformed from the gentle, devout man that had been Ali's near-constant companion for weeks. This was a man whose eyes carried a lifetime of pain and desperation.

"I am sorry, Ali. Truly."

Rashid did sound regretful. But it was clear to Ali that nothing he said would steer Rashid's course.

Ali's eyes flickered from Rashid down to the mattress, gauging the position of the staff, his only means of defense. As he grabbed it up the Moor tried to snatch it away. Ali felt the warmth inside him, the one linking him to the staff, unfurl and flow back to whence it came.

"No!" Ali cried out, but it was too late.

Rashid first snarled, then gasped as golden light flared from the wood, creeping up his arm and wrapping him in a blaze of pure white flame too quickly for him to scream. For an instant, a silver band gleamed in the unnatural light, the stark lines of the familiar engraving stood out on his wrist before the silver melted and the skin blackened, then crisped.

Ali gasped and fell back against the wall, burying his face in his arms.

He could feel the heat and smell the stench of burning flesh. He expected to be smothered by smoke until robbed, first of breath, then life. Ali remained huddled, his gaze averted and his lips moving in fervent prayer as guilt and relief battled within him.

Rather than searing heat, he felt the stirrings of a cool breeze coming through the slats of the window. In disbelief, he peered over his arm at the room beyond, startled to see no signs of flame at all. Glancing down at where Rashid had stood, Ali noticed the cypress staff lay unharmed across the rug on which the pretender had been kneeling. The carpet itself, stained by a blackened residue; was the only evidence of the Moor's presence and of his ending. As Ali watched, a glow like the deepest embers of a coal limned the carpet. He snatched the staff away as the carpet lifted into the air with a loud snap and zipped away through the window. *Magic.*

More weary than angered or fearful, Ali gathered his things and went to claim his donkey, anxious to return home and be away from this deception and thievery.

Ali gazed out over the desert past the fabric of his *chafiye*. A sigh seeped across his lips and lost itself in the folds. If he had but realized that Allah would answer his many prayers all at once, Ali would never have prayed so fervently to be both dry and warm through three years of English spring times and bitter winters. Now he stood on desert sands and the heat weighed on him, heavy and still.

He had traveled long weeks alone, in the air and on the desert, and wished only to be home. He had told himself if he hurried he would reach Wadi Al-Nejd before dark, but there was little hope of that now. The sun had nearly completed its descent from the sky.

Ali frowned, squinting against a sudden, abrasive gust. It was not the season for the *shamal*, the north winds that at the height of their strength could tear the skin from a man and scour the very metal on mechanicals. Yet he would swear such a wind brewed in the cauldron of the sky. Long ago, in his father's company, Ali experienced such a storm. His neck bore scars from where his *chafiye* had been poorly wrapped. The air felt much as it had then, heavy and lashing, scented with heat and dust. Unease crawled across Ali's skin. Only good luck, Allah's mercy, or sorcery could protect a man caught out in such winds.

By the landmarks, Ali estimated that his home lay only a few hours south, but already grit stung his eyes and Jasmine, his poor donkey, had hung her head to lean into the growing wind, her coarse hair bristling protectively around her. For both their sakes, he had no choice but to seek shelter now if he hoped to see his home on the morrow. Ali blinked away the grit and hunched his body. He pulled on leather gloves to protect his hands and drew his outer clothing into place, ensuring it did not gape nor leave any skin exposed. Satisfied that he was shielded, Ali searched from horizon to horizon for any place that might shelter them from the wind.

He spied nothing.

"Allah, I place my soul into Your keeping. Your will be done."

As the prayer left his lips, Ali shivered, certain he heard the wind bellow, despite the muffling folds of his chafiye. The sound held unnatural notes, unlike any Ali had ever heard from the wind upon the desert. Squealing, his donkey jerked beneath him, her hooves scrabbling in the loose sand. Jasmine tossed her head and Ali tightened his legs on her barrel. As the wind increased in intensity, so did her agitation until, with a panicked bray, Jasmine bucked, once…twice…three times, finally throwing Ali to the ground. She then galloped away with a speed uncommon in a donkey. Even she had sensed something unnatural in the wind.

As his satchel with his father's precious gifts remained over his own shoulder, Ali did not chase the beast. Already the air grew thick with dust. He searched desperately for a boulder or some brush to shelter against. To his right, at last, he spied a small outcrop. Fighting the wind, he made his way to the meager shelter. If he crouched at the base with his spare clothing wrapped about him, he might see the storm through, Allah willing. Focused on his goal, Ali barely noticed the growing violence of the wind until it raked him with hot claws, tearing at his clothes and jerking him this way and that against his will. He lost track of the outcrop he strove for, barely able to see for the wind-driven sand. His eyes burned and dust tickled his throat as he fought the urge to cough.

To his ears it sounded like the air breathed a malevolent chuckle around him. Ali wiped the burning sand from his eyes and nose and hunched lower, still fighting his way toward where he prayed his shelter lay. He stumbled and nearly fell as the wind abruptly stopped. Catching himself, he looked up, blinking furiously to clear the grit from his lashes.

"In the name of Allah, the All-Merciful!" he cried out.

Before Ali towered a man-like form. There the resemblance ended. Muscles bunched in a manner never seen upon a mortal. Muscles that were skinned in blackest pitch, flexing and flowing like the wind itself, echoing the force and violence of the *shamal*.

Ali clutched his satchel and braced his legs, chin trembling, but raised.

"He cannot help you…" purred an infernal voice, like the low rumble of shifting stone. "But, little Ins, you may seek Allah's blessing when you meet Him."

The *ghul* drew back its arms and took a step forward. Its eyes glowed with a green flame as its lips pulled back and away into a grin that bared teeth like rows of wrought-iron spikes.

Ali swallowed hard but refused to flinch. The Almighty was merciful to the faithful and if he were to meet the Almighty it would not be crouched and cowering.

"There is no God but Allah, and Mohammed is His messenger," Ali said as he waited for the blow that would speed him to *Jannah*. Then, something flew by overhead, laying a shadow upon the sands that dipped and glided and circled around the *ghul*, a shadow that Ali recognized. He took a breath, slow and deep, willing himself calm. And then the cry came…the scream of a hunting raptor radiated across the desert, ringing like a struck bell. As the *ghul* jerked and looked toward the sound, Ali turned and dashed for the nearest *saif*, praying to lose himself from the sight of the *ghul*. The *ghul* roared and lunged for him, shaking the sand. Ali dodged and twisted over the churning ground. He used hands and feet both as he struggled, a tiny mote of dust in a swirling storm. The ghul's powers tumbled and turned Ali within the choking cloud until finally he lay still, eyes closed, coughing sand, his body stunned. Half buried in the saif, Ali closed his eyes and made his peace with Allah, only to gasp as something grabbed him by the shoulders and tangled in his thick robes, jerking him upward until his body left the ground.

"Ayeee!" he cried, his head straining up and back in an effort to see what gripped him. His body went lax as over his shoulder he spied a great bronze wing much larger than was usual for a hunting bird were it flesh and blood. He had lost his fear of the clockwork falcon, having benefited from its presence and protection too many times to doubt its benevolence.

Ali heard a muted roar from below, the *ghul*. A blast of hot air burst upward, snatching at Ali once more, causing the falcon to tighten its grip. Ali winced and resisted the urge to thrash. To do so would only make the falcon's flight more difficult. The sand tore at Ali's clothing and it grated against his bare skin, leaving it raw. He swallowed against the pain.

He heard sand pinging off the metal surface of the falcon. Ali glanced upward only to squint against both the harsh sand and the falcon's bright gleam.

"Close your eyes, young Ins," a voice said from above, ringing like steel on steel.

Without question, Ali squeezed them tight and ducked his head within his *chafiye* for good measure. Even so, he cried out when a light like a thousand and one suns radiated around him, emanating from the falcon.

The *ghul* howled. The cry sharply cut off, as did the wind, leaving the smell of sulfur and scorched rock hanging in the air. In the stillness the light faded, but Ali was not so foolish as to open his eyes. A gentler breeze tugged his *thobe* and *chafiye* as the falcon descended. With a slight bump, Ali returned to the ground to find he could not stand, though the metal talons carefully withdrew from his robes. He spread himself across the sand and waited for the tranquility of the earth to settle him.

The falcon coughed a peculiar clang that might have been a laugh.

Ali lifted his head and forgot himself so much as to glare at his mechanical savior. His ire quickly faded as he met those gem-bright eyes and in the sunlight spied the smoke whirling in their depth.

Ali fought the urge to let his mouth hang open in astonishment. "Are you Ins or are you Djinn?" he breathed. It was an old phrase, one that most children learned along with tales of magic and wonder at their mother's breasts.

The falcon coughed the same peculiar clang again. This time Ali had no doubt it laughed at him.

"Is it not obvious, Baba Ali, son of Massoud?"

Ali gazed into the smoke-filled eyes and his heart beat faster. For the first time in his life, he beheld a djinni, but one that did not mirror the creatures of his childhood tales. This one reminded him of his *Himitsu-Bako*: a mingling of magic and mechanical.

"Who…who is your master?" Ali asked on a whisper.

"I serve no master," the djinni answered, his metal brow furrowing. "I honor the memory of a friend."

"Your friend…was it his box you brought to me?"

The clockwork falcon bobbed but did not answer.

"Please… I can find no way to open it, but I must."

At this the falcon mantled and fidgeted.

"I can tell you nothing more but this: The secret to your puzzle box is in your grandfather's blood. When you understand this secret, the words 'Open, Sesame' will open this box."

"Now…If you have need, young Ali, call out to Shahin, for I am the guardian of the guardian and that is now you. I am connected to your box. When it is near your person I will know if all is well with you, or not, so keep it close. If I am able, I will come to your aid, but know I cannot come to you in a public place. This is why you must be wary, son of Massoud. Others move against you."

The djinni's words left Ali confused but he had no chance to ask for explanation.

With that final warning, the falcon launched into the sky, leaving Ali sprawled in the sand an arm's length from his donkey. Jasmine promptly bit him in greeting.

Ali yelped and pushed her away. "*Bas…enough,* Jasmine. Enough." But his words weren't unkind. He was pleased that no ill had come to her.

Ali stood and dusted the sand from him, wincing at the patches of skin the *ghul's* wind had left raw and oozing. Painful, but not dangerous to his health. Wrapping them as best he could, Ali mounted the little donkey.

"The *ghul,*" he said to himself as he rode toward Wadi Al-Nejd, deep in thought. *Ghul* were malicious and powerful, but like other creatures of magic and myth, they did not act irrationally. Like men, djinn and their cousins—the ghuls, ifrits, divs—were free to choose or not choose the Righteous path, as written by the Prophet, peace be upon him. For the ghul to have attacked Ali, that meant that someone had sent it. This was no thief in the night. This was someone who meant him dead.

What had he done to displease the Almighty, that he was so beset? What brought so many attacks on his person, starting with the thief in England? Why was all of this happening now? And more, what did it have to do with *him*? Ali drew his satchel into his arms, one hand brushing against the square shape of the puzzle box within, while the other cradled it protectively. His father's last gift to him…how could a single object bring both blessing and adversity?

Chapter Eight

Rassul was a great leader. A great man. He led the largest, most successful band of raiders in Arabia for more than one hundred years. He was powerful, the keeper of great mystical secrets. And yet, the leader of the desert thieves stood impotent in the center of his lair filled with a cold fury and frustration. His expression alone urged every one of the thirty-seven men who stood around him, to complete silence.

It was a silence that reverberated off the stone cavern walls. The light in the cave was a yellow glow coming from glass tubes that crisscrossed the room. The cavern was fully two thousand cubits in length. And everywhere, riches glittered in the pale light. Gemstones the size of a man's fist, large sacks of gold coin from a myriad of nations, delicate machines of copper and brass that danced and sang when wound by a key, silks and thick rugs and treasures well beyond what a single man could enjoy in a thousand lifetimes. But Rassul saw none of that.

He brought a hand up to stroke his trim beard. His lips pressed flat as he looked upon the man who cowered before him. He was a small man, with skin the color of weak tea, Abdul Asad.

"One of you? Three of my...*best*...men go out and *one* of you returns?" he said, his voice level as though the matter were of no import. The men did not dare whisper. They stood mute, their eyes on Rassul and Abdul Asad, their expressions tense. Rassul took a step closer to Abdul Asad. "What befell the others?"

Silence.

Their lair had been discovered once and though the intruder had been dealt with it might well be again, unless the box was retrieved. Such risk was not acceptable. Great was their amassed treasure and no effort was to be spared in keeping it secure.

"You have one hope of preserving your life, my friend."

Abdul Asad whimpered. The sound brought a smile to Rassul's lips. It was pleasant-seeming, but empty. He moved forward and placed a hand on Abdul Asad's shoulder as he leaned closer yet. The scent of fear rose from the thief's robes, faint, but enticing. Any other time, Rassul would have taken pleasure in the man's quaking. Today, he tightened his grip and narrowed his gaze, exerting just enough will to tug life essence from the man's soul. Rassul felt the man's spirit, like a sliver of warm sunlight as it flowed between his fingers. Abdul Asad moaned, this time high and tight with pain.

"Tell me," Rassul whispered beside the man's ear, "What is the name of the one who eluded you all?"

"There...there were two," Abdul Asad stammered. "An Englishman by the name of Charles Babbage..."

Rassul frowned as the man fell silent. "And?"

"His apprentice," Abdul mumbled. "We could not learn the other's name. We tried, master, but none could tell us. He is Arab returning home on one of the sky ships. Perhaps Khizr or Rashid..."

"They are dead." Rassul growled. He held up the flying carpets that had returned to him upon their users' deaths. He was disturbed. Both Khizr and Rashid had sworn themselves to him decades ago. They shouldn't have been so easy to dispatch. "Tell me...why should you be spared?"

A bright glimmer of cunning sparked in Abdul Asad's gaze.

"I have seen his face."

With a faint curl to his lip, Rassul nodded. He let go of Abdul Asad's shoulder and selected one of the carpets, its weave scorched black. He then spoke a *ruqa* incantation upon the carpet until it glowed and handed it to the thief. "Return to Jerusalem to find this apprentice's trail, Abdul Asad. Bring me the box…or you will wish you had died this day."

Despite his weariness and the late hour, Ali's spirits lifted as his donkey trotted into the courtyard of his father's…no, his *brother's* home. That fact became quite clear to him at the sight of the simple braziers lighting the courtyard. Kassim had apparently wasted no time destroying the self-filling lanterns. Ali had engineered them as a gift for their father before he'd left for England. Ugly scars marred the walls of the courtyard where they had been torn away.

Ali sighed. He could not understand his brother's hatred for the mechanical works that Ali so loved. He tucked away his heartache at this, though, as a sudden mass of bodies flowed through the door led by his kinsman.

"Ah, my brother!" Kassim greeted him, his manner effusive and jovial, in stark contrast with his hard, flat gaze.

Ali almost stepped backward, startled by the conflicting emotions. His shock grew even greater when Kassim embraced him and kissed him on each cheek. "You have returned," his brother said, with no indication if this were good or bad, despite that his own missive had summoned Ali home. Before Ali could respond, Kassim raised his hand and those waiting surged forward in a festive display.

The entire household and more laughed and cried in welcome as they surrounded Ali. So many people… yet he frowned at how few were familiar to him. Scarcely four years had passed and his father's faithful servants had been none too old. He searched the crowd looking for his favorites: Old Hamza, who had worked in his family's gardens since he himself was a boy, and the kitchen servant, Paknoush, whose leg was twisted from a fall, but whose hands were swift and sure when preparing a meal. Or bestowing a treat. These and many others were missing from Ali's sight.

The greeters tugged at him and showed great joy at his return, but they knew him not at all. Their many questions about England — most of them absurd — set an ache pulsing at Ali's temples. *Did ice truly fall from the sky? Was it true that their great cities were grey and smoked and steamed and walked across the land like those in the Eastern provinces? And* did *these* English *eat human flesh at the bidding of their false god?*

Ali suppressed a laugh at the last one. If he were honest, he would admit that he himself had wondered, particularly after a rather confusing and heated discussion with a cleric from their Anglican Church. After that one argument, *Ustad* Babbage had thrown the man out of his home and forbid Ali from conversing over such foolishness. Ali had thought that a shame as he would have enjoyed further discourse. Then again, his teacher did not appreciate talk of gods or demons, calling himself a materialist and spurning all other faiths. The matter had not caused Ali much concern and his teacher's faith or lack thereof did not impact Ali's own willingness to train as an artificer. He sobered as fresh heartache welled within his breast. He stared again at the scarred walls of the courtyard and held no hope he would be able to continue with his craft as he had under *Ustad* Babbage's tutelage.

"Stand straight and wipe the frown from your face, brother. We have guests. Would you have them wonder at your unhappiness when your homecoming should be joyous?" Kassim said, waving toward three wealthy men standing to the side, their expressions growing impatient. "Do not shame me. It is critical to maintain good relationships with those necessary to keep father's business and trade flowing."

Ali swallowed hard at the reminder of his father's death.

"Your odor offends, Ali. Take care of it." Kassim added dismissively. "We must return to our negotiations."

Anger drew the muscles of Ali's neck tight as he pressed his mouth closed to avoid protesting his brother's insult. He fumed as Kassim turned toward his guests, a broad smile on his face that still didn't quite reach his eyes. "Please forgive the stench. My brother's journey was long and wearying. Let us withdraw. I'm sure we have more important matters to attend."

Ali watched Kassim cajole and entice the others back to the sitting room with promises of coffee and sweets. With the departure of the head of the household and his esteemed guests, those gathered to welcome Ali abruptly lost interest. He found himself in an almost empty courtyard. None remained save his brother's wife and a young servant boy. Malakeh's expression appeared sullen at being left the chore of seeing to his needs.

"I will take your things," she said abruptly, grabbing Ali's satchel.

Feeling distinctly uncomfortable, Ali resisted, clutching his bag close to him. "I am grateful, wife of my brother, but that is not necessary."

"The odor pinches my nose from here, *Baba* Ali." From her lips the honorific twisted in mockery. "You will give me the bag that I may have your clothing laundered…or more likely burned," she murmured that last beneath her breath.

Ali scowled and yanked the strap of his satchel out of her grip, shaking his head. Under no circumstance would he let the bag out of his sight. It contained too many things precious to him. He could well imagine it would come back with its treasures damaged or gone. He let his eyes speak his defiance rather than disrespect his sister-in-law's… *hospitality* aloud.

Malakeh withdrew her hand, a look of frustration quickly masked. "As you wish, I will send this one with you to bring away your clothes," she answered, her words tight and clipped.

"You will stay in the gardener's room." She pointed to one of the smaller sandstone outbuildings. "I suggest you retire there now. I will have a bath brought to you immediately."

Ali frowned, ignoring her slur, in favor of his primary concern. "Is there something amiss with my own room?"

Her chin lifted and she sneered at him, her eyes cold. "You would do well to recall this is no longer your father's household. Kassim is master here and has repurposed the rooms as he has seen fit. If the gardener's room is not too your liking there is always the stable…"

Ali felt his teeth grind. "And what of Old Hamza? It is hardly respectful for me to displace him."

Malakeh arched her brow. "Who?"

"The gardener…"

"We have none at present. The old man was let go. He could not complete his work to my satisfaction."

"Let go?" Ali said, his voice rising, aghast. Hamza had been with his family since before his father's birth. In Ali's own youth, the gardener had plucked figs from the trees for him and had shown the wonder of how nature's engineering worked in all living things as Ali followed him about his duties. Often, Hamza would hide little surprises for him beneath a flagstone in the garden or tell Ali stories as he worked. That the man had been let go in his later years was a grave injustice.

Malakeh shrugged, then looked Ali up and down, her lip curling.

"Do you want the room or would you rather sleep with your donkey?"

Ali's chest tightened and acid stung his throat as he recognized the same disdain from her that he had received from certain of the English. He had a small ungenerous hope that Jasmine might bite Malakeh. The donkey had already snapped a couple of the guests before their departure. Blocking the white donkey, who had a mutinous look in her eye, he bowed respectfully. "I thank you for your hospitality."

Malakeh shook her head. "You can thank me by bathing. Kassim will require your presence later," she snapped before turning on her heel and returning to the main house.

Ali patted Jasmine between the ears as he led her into the stable. The servant boy followed in silence.

"Welcome to your new home, little one. It would seem that sentiments have not changed overmuch since I left." At the thought, Ali felt a deep sadness. He had hoped his absence would allow the rift between Kassim and himself to heal. It was time to accept that perhaps healing would never come.

His spirit heavy, Ali trudged to what had been the gardener's room.

Ali's banishment from the main household proved to be a blessing from the Almighty. After a bath in tepid water, Ali donned his brother's cast-off clothing, which the servant had left when he took Ali's soiled garments away. He took up his satchel, still containing his treasures and his simple gifts, and exited the gardener's shack. Ali knew the perfect place to safeguard his things: beneath Hamza's flagstone. Presuming, that is, that his brother had not changed too much in his effort to claim their father's domain.

To Ali's left a path led through the garden toward the household. He could not help but notice the sad state of the greenery and the absence of his mother's beloved ring-necked parakeets. Ali frowned and looked more closely at how much lush growth had been hacked away. Large, garish statues and ill-suited topiaries had been installed in its place. His steps slowed as he approached the heart of the garden, where of an evening his parents would lounge to enjoy the perfumed air in the night's breeze. Every evidence of their bower had been removed.

Ali's throat tightened and angry tears gathered in his eyes. A denial clawed at his throat. Though the sight devastated him, he slowly circled what had been his parents' bower. Did nothing remain? As his eyes catalogued the multitude of changes, in his mind he summoned image after image from his memory, mourning the loss.

Bitterness toward his brother for allowing this burned in Ali.

He rounded the monstrosity of a fountain, the Greek statuary watching him with dead eyes, and saw that one thing remained—the true heart of the garden. A large granite boulder that sank deep into the earth. Behind the stone, but not blocked by the fountain—Allah be praised!—was the special flagstone. It was sealed as tightly as its brothers, but if one pressed the correct corner just so the stone lifted from its place, revealing a compartment beneath.

Ali glanced around, eyes narrowed, as he looked for any movement in the surrounding darkness. Content that he alone wandered the garden this night, he knelt in the shadow of the boulder. His grandfather, Farzeen, had placed the rock, though Father had not said how. Ali leaned his weight upon the proper place to release the flagstone. A faint click sounded, followed by the earthy scent of disturbed soil, then the stone lifted enough for him to grip the edge and draw it aside. The tension across Ali's shoulders eased. He thanked the Almighty for this blessing and quickly drew his books, the pouch of remaining coin, and the puzzle box from his satchel, leaving only the trinkets. Placing his precious items in the secret compartment, Ali then pressed the flagstone back into place.

Satisfied that his treasures were secure he rose and continued on his way to the house. Perhaps it was not wise to meet with his brother when his spirit remained so unsettled, but Kassim, as head of the household, had summoned him and Ali must go.

Stopping before the door that opened to the garden, he closed his eyes and expelled a forceful breath, then slowly drew air deep into his lungs, striving for the Almighty's peace that he and his brother might speak without quarreling. He did not hold much hope, however, given his ill-favored status in the household.

He moved to push through the door and his efforts at calm disappeared as swiftly as tears shed in the depths of the desert. The door had been secured. Ali schooled his expression with a skill honed against the whetstone of English bigotry. When he'd attained some semblance of indifference, he raised his hand and rapped upon the door in three measured blows.

Then he waited. And waited.

Just as his grip upon his anger began to slip once more, the latch rattled and the door swung in. The sullen servant boy from earlier said nothing, but waved Ali forward before turning and walking off into the household. Pride tempted Ali to slam the door. Common sense told him to reclaim his treasures and ride away upon his donkey. Heartache whispered, *this is the last of your family, do not shun them.*

Defiance kept Ali's pace measured and slow, though no amount of dawdling could stave off the unpleasantness he expected. Ali felt it in his bones like the chill of an English winter. His guide continued on unaware of the emotions that whirled within Ali. Rather than lead him to Kassim's chambers, the servant continued forward to what had been their father's rooms. Ali should have expected it, but this further evidence of the loss of their father pierced his heart anew.

As the boy ushered Ali into the room, Kassim sat behind his father's desk like a shah on his throne, disdain clear in the angle of his brows.

"Brother," Ali said. Mightily, he struggled to afford Kassim a respectful bow. He succeeded only by fixing his gaze upon the wall at his brother's back. "Allah's blessing upon your household," he forced through tight lips.

Kassim in no way acknowledged the nicety, let alone exchanged it.

"You will not shame this household as you did this evening," he said his tone sharp. "I will not have it said that we are accepting of slovenliness."

Ali did not bother to argue. "My apologies for any offense you or your guests found in my appearance, brother. What is it that you wish of me?"

Kassim stared at Ali with a hooded gaze. "I have a great responsibility both to the business and this household now. You will undertake your duty in assisting me with this."

Ali did not object to helping shoulder his brother's burden, but his knowledge of the business was rudimentary. Their father had fostered his youngest son's natural passion for all things mechanical, including numbers suitable for engineering, not bookkeeping. His only interest in luxuries and trade was learning which gems would serve well as refractors or which metals best suited the inner workings of delicate clockwork inventions. "I will do my duty and uphold the family honor to the best of my abilities."

Kassim looked him up and down. Cruelty colored his gaze. "We will work on rectifying your deficiencies. Until then, see Mateen in the morning, he will assign you your duties."

Ali went rigid at Kassim's words. Mateen was in charge of the servants.

"I will not drudge in my own family's household." he said quietly, the words as taut as his expression, though he did not allow his bitterness to flavor the words.

"You will respect the head of your household and serve as I have deemed appropriate at this time, Ali. Now leave me, I have important work to do."

The declaration and dismissal were a slap and the death of any hope Ali had held of reconciliation with his brother. Grappling for control, he turned without another word and stalked from the room. His chest heaved and his fists shook at his sides as he made his way back through the garden. It took even more effort, now, to resist reclaiming his treasures and leaving Wadi Al-Nejd forever. Ali had to remind himself of the importance of family. At the very least, he owed it to his father's memory, and—his gaze set lovingly on the place where the bower had once been—and the joy his parents had once shared in this home.

The domes and minarets, and the great walls of Jerusalem grew larger as the airship descended. Babbage sat by a viewing port in the passenger lounge, strapped securely to his chair against turbulent air currents. He trailed his gaze over the stone structures, both grand and modest, and could not help but wonder if he were too late. So many people. And Ali with no idea he should be cautious. Babbage worried for the lad.

A sound from behind him drew Babbage out of his musings.

Fritz stood in the hatch wearing trousers and a grease-marked cotton shirt with the sleeves rolled to his elbow. A frown drew down the corners of his mouth and his eyes darkened as Babbage watched.

"More troubles with the engine?" Babbage asked, forestalling whatever heartfelt conversation loomed.

"No, no…" Fritz said his gaze dropping to his shirt. "I was trying out a few ideas when Clara reminded me it was time to land."

Babbage nodded, more than familiar with his friend's propensity to get lost in his tinkering. He lifted a brow and waited for Fritz to go on.

"Um…so, it's time to land."

Again Babbage nodded, this time with a wry quirk to his lips. "I had noticed. Was there something you needed from me or are you merely here to warn me to make things right with the Lord?"

The sarcasm went clear over Fritz's head. "I'm sorry we can't take you further, old man. If we hadn't lost so much time…"

"Nonsense," Babbage interrupted. "You've more than gone out of your way for me already. Don't worry. I'm quite capable of getting myself from here to there, as it were. This isn't the first I've traveled, you know. Now…shouldn't you be at the helm or some such thing?"

Fritz's head cocked slightly to the side and his brow gathered in a faint look of confusion. "Well…no. I keep the engines running; Clara does the flying."

The world swayed as Babbage's blood pressure plummeted. "Clar…Clara flies this beast?"

"She sure does, and she's a—what is it you Brits say?—a dab hand at it too. Only crashed the once…"

Babbage stifled a groan and tugged at the strap across his lap.

"Relax," Fritz said. "That was ages ago, and it wasn't her fault."

"I am quite reassured," Babbage muttered through clenched teeth.

Fritz grinned. "Now, now, Charles, it is practically the 20th century!"

Charles shot Fritz a dark look that the other man blithely ignored.

"Anyway," Fritz continued, "what I came to tell you is that you can find a caravan to take you into the desert at the local *caravanserai*. It's a mix of an inn, merchants' trading stop, and way station. The largest should be just inside the Old City gates. Of course, there will be a fee to take you."

Babbage's lips quirked. "There is always a price."

The American held out a card printed with the name of the inn and the street where it could be found.

In the coolness of twilight, Ali and his brother sat at Abu Farid's teashop, on plump pillows nestled in fine wicker chairs. He'd suggested the outing in the hopes that a public place would keep their conversation civil, allowing them to discuss matters peaceably, outside of the hearing of the servants. The setting brought neither calm nor comfort. Ali barely noticed the beauty of the mosaic inlay table, meant to encourage patrons to relax and thank Allah for the blessings of tea and sweets and good company to share them with. They had the tea and sweets, but the company was lacking. Kassim did not have it in him to be soothed and Ali had all but reached an end to his patience as his brother yet again dictated the path of Ali's future.

Ali picked at the sweets, half-listening to his brother's lecture, waiting for a chance to speak. His gaze wandered across the narrow, dusty street to Baba Abdiesus's shop. The aroma of lubricants wafted from the open doorway, and just inside Ali could see casks of clockwork components and tooled metals. They reminded him of his time with *Ustad* Babbage, the long, pleasant hours spent in the workshop. It had been months since he had cleaned oil from beneath his nails or picked up a spanner. He splayed his hands and noted that dirt now creased his skin.

With each day that passed, he regretted more and more, leaving England.

His brother slapped his hand on the table to get Ali's attention.

Ali did not startle, but his gaze did move from Baba Abdiesus's shop to his brother's darkening visage. He thought of *Ustad* Babbage. *What would his mentor say?* "Forgive me, Kassim, but I cannot follow your path."

"You cannot?!" Kassim reared back, gesticulating wildly. "Cannot, or will not? Don't be foolish, this is for your own good."

"I would respect our father's wishes," Ali spoke with firm resolve. "And his wish for me was to follow the ways of the artificers."

"Father did not wish you to live as a pauper!"

Uncomfortable, Ali now regretted they had not kept this to the privacy of the household. He strove to remain calm and quiet, while giving no ground. "Nor did he wish me to act as servant in what was once my home."

Kassim huffed out a breath. "You haven't the knowledge to work in the family's trade. Would you have me ruin our *father's* business to soothe *your* pride?"

Ali shook his head. "No, but I would have you respect my path."

"You would live in my house, and eat of my food, yet toil only for yourself?" His brother's anger hovered like *shisha* smoke above their heads.

Ali sighed. "I would not abuse your hospitality so. When I have the means—"

Kassim cut him off, leaning across the table until less than a hand's breadth separated them. "But you do. Father gave you the black diamonds, did he not?"

His brother's claims, paired with the hunger in his gaze, startled Ali. "Diamonds? I have no diamonds…"

"Do not lie to me, *brother*," Kassim said. Ali recoiled from the venom in those words.

"As Allah is my witness, I speak no lie."

Kassim waved off Ali's assurance. Then his eyes grew cold until Ali despaired, knowing that his brother had closed his heart to him.

"You will do as I say, then," Kassim said, his words leaden.

Ali's gaze locked with his brother's. "I cannot."

"You will," Kassim repeated, his voice rumbling and imperious. "You have not the means to support yourself. You would insult our father's memory to become a beggar in the streets?"

"You are wrong," Ali answered, refusing to give way on this. "But even should your words bear truth, I cannot live a lifetime that is against my nature."

"If you would live in my house, then you *will* do as I bid."

"Then I shall seek another accommodation," Ali said softly, "though the necessity brings me great sorrow, brother." With that, he stood and, with a heavy step, left to make his own way.

At his back the sound of breaking glass made Ali cringe as the other patrons of the teashop gasped, but Kassim did not yell or come after him. Ali mourned the loss. Kassim was all he had; the last of his family. The thought brought a lump to his throat, but even the recognition that he was now alone in the world could not sway his conviction.

"Impossible things," he whispered to himself, finding strength in those words as he recalled the conversation with *Ustad* Babbage and the Langstroms not so long ago.

With long strides, he made his way back to his brother's household. Seeing his grim expression, the servants scurried out of his path as he entered the main gate and crossed the courtyard. As he neared the garden, Malakeh stalked toward him, her mouth in a petulant moue. She no doubt thought to harangue him regarding some chore or another. He stared at her and did not slow.

It was with more than a little surprise that Malakeh had to quickly step out of his path. The hurried slap of her steps followed him through the ill-maintained garden. Ali stopped and spun around suddenly grabbing her shoulders before she ran into him. "You will go into *your* household, woman, and leave me be. I have no ear for your complaints or demands."

Malakeh's mouth opened and closed but no sound came out.

Ali released her. "You *will* do me this one courtesy. Leave me in peace as I gather my things and remove myself from this place."

Malakeh's eyes widened to the whites and her head bobbed frantically, but she did not move. Hands clasped, she twisted her fingers, her gaze going from Ali to the house and back, undecided.

Ali lowered his brow and stared at her hard, bringing his face close to hers.

"*Now.*"

His brother's wife scurried away, her more-than-generous curves shaking.

Ali sighed and in the silence of his heart begged Allah's forgiveness, before turning and making his way to the center of the garden. Dropping beside the granite boulder he carefully pulled up the flagstone. His treasures remained safe within. Unwinding his *chafiye*, Ali wrapped it around his possessions before lowering the flagstone back into place. He then returned to his room to gather the rest of his things.

Not even half an hour had passed before Ali strolled through the city gates heading for the solace of the desert sands to find peace. Nearby there was an oasis, just a small stand of palm trees and a few arta bushes huddled around a trickling spring that pooled in a low rock basin. An outcrop of rocks formed a shallow cavern beyond the palm trees, high enough for three to sit in relative comfort, deep enough for them to stretch themselves in slumber.

His father used to bring Kassim and Ali here when they were young. They would lie beneath the starry sky or huddle together in the cavern, as the weather dictated, and share the missed moments of their lives. Father would tell them of his recent journeys and they would recount their adventures on the desert or in the market while he had been away. Those visits were rare and precious times, when Ali and Kassim had been at peace with one another, joined in their devotion to their father.

Sighing, Ali approached the oasis. After a draught of the crisp, cool water, he filled his goatskin and plucked a few ripe dates for later, then set his satchel as a pillow beneath the shade of the trees and lay down, his staff beneath his hand. For long moments he did nothing but breathe, slow and deep, with each exhale emptying his heart and his head of anger's poison until only grief remained. It took more effort to release that, to uncover the ember of love still nestled deep at the core of his being. Ali resigned himself to the divide between he and his brother, but bitterness had no place in the soul of a child of the Almighty. He would not find contentment until he relinquished the discord within. By the time his heart had settled, stars glittered in the sky. With a cool breeze rustling the palms overhead and a dove cooing from the branches, Ali embraced peace and found rest. Tomorrow would be soon enough for charting the course of his future.

Chapter Nine

ALI WOKE AT DAWN'S LIGHT TO DARK, DIAMOND-BRIGHT EYES peering down at him. He blinked, then slowly sat up, sliding back as he did so to gain some distance between him and the clockwork falcon…the djinni.

The construct gave its clanging laugh and launched upward, soaring until it was no more than a speck against the lightening sky. Shahin spoke into Ali's thoughts as he winged away.

It is not safe for you to slumber alone on open sands, Ali. Remember this for I will not continue to stand guard over a foolish Ins.

Ali scrambled to his feet with his staff ready in his hand as he looked out over the still sands, noticing signs that feral dogs had drawn close in the night. He shuddered. These beasts were known to be vicious, a danger to all, particularly lone travelers. Again that clanging laugh came from above, though the falcon had vanished from sight.

You might look to your box, Shahin said, echoing faintly, as if from a distance. Frowning, Ali scrambled for his satchel. Thinking on the djinni's warning, Ali drew the bag into the shallow cavern before delving within. As he undid the flap an azure light spilled out. It clung to Ali's hands and shimmered

on his skin. Warmth flooded him. Ali gasped at the sensation and nearly drew away, but already, he could see the scrollwork swirling. He placed his hands on the box, mimicking the grip Hiram had shown him. The glow flared until the cavern surrounding him became lit as bright as noonday. Ali gasped, and would have dropped the box only it would not let him. He found his hands locked tight to the surface.

Ali sank to the floor of the cavern, his arms trembling. Catching his lip between his teeth, he squeezed his eyes shut and began to trace the scrollwork with his fingertips, as Hiram had. Beneath his palms the surface of the box began to shift. Shocks travelled up his arms and the glow surrounding the *Himitsu-Bako* pulsed with his heartbeat. Ali opened his eyes and watched as the scrollwork curled away, drawing tight to the corners, leaving most of the surface bare. His fingers moved over the box more quickly, pressing and sliding and tugging as instinct told him, until he completed all seventy steps. He frowned as nothing happened. Then he remembered and breathed the words Shahin had told him: *Open, Sesame.*

"Shahin!" Ali cried out, but the falcon did not come. Before he could call out again, a sharp sensation like an adder's strike pierced his palms, burning and stinging fiercely, then fading away in soothing warmth. "Shahin! What is this?" The djinni did not answer, though Ali would swear he heard the falcon's strident cry beyond the horizon.

Awed, he set the box down on the cavern floor. When he drew his hands away each palm bore a smear of blood. His gaze returned to the box. The lid gave a sharp *click* and popped open. As it did so, the glow dimmed then faded away, leaving the interior of the cavern too dark to see the treasures revealed. Gingerly lifting the box again, Ali edged closer to the opening, sitting with the *Himitsu-Bako* in his lap. It was fitting, perhaps, that he did this here, in a place where a small piece of his father's spirit lived on in Ali's memory. With care, he reached into the box and drew out three objects: a letter, a book the size of his palm, and a small, silken pouch. As he removed each from the box he placed them on the sand before him. The letter glowed with the morning light, bright and clean and not so very old. The book, however, had clearly seen many years, if not decades, and much handling. The pouch gleamed with the sheen of fine silk and, by the feel of it, held gems.

He reached for the pouch first. Loosening the tie he spread the mouth of the bag and shook out the contents, gasping as two gems the size of large dates tumbled into his palm. Kassim's black diamonds. Ali knew enough to marvel at the size, brilliance, and clarity of the stones. A king's ransom rested in the cup of his hand. Instinctively, he closed his fingers over them, drawing the hand protectively close to his chest. Men committed murder over gems such as these. No wonder his brother's eyes had glistened with obsession when he'd demanded to know if Ali had them. Ali very well might have given them to Kassim if it would have healed the breach between them. With a solemn heart, he returned the gems to the pouch and tucked it back into the box still cradled in his lap.

The letter and the book remained. Ali sat in quiet contemplation, not taking up either one for several minutes. These would be the last of his father's legacy. The last time his father's words and deeds would be able to touch him directly.

"Foolish!" he admonished himself aloud. "You are being foolish, like a child."

Taking a deep, steadying breath, he reached for the letter, breaking the wax seal before he could second-guess himself. His hand shook as he unfolded the parchment.

To Ali, my beloved son,

The blessings of Allah and the Prophet be upon you.

Ali closed his eyes as sorrow swelled inside him until he thought it might rob him of his breath. When he had himself under control he opened his eyes and again began to read.

It is my great regret to have left you alone and at the mercy of the world.

Now that I am gone from it, I must tell you of our family's secret legacy and my personal shame in the hopes that you might restore our honor. You are descended from a great line, all artificers to Persia's ruling family of the Afsharid dynasty. Your grandfather, Farzeen, was the last of these. Before the dynasty fell, Prince Shahrokh sent your grandfather away in secret along with Nadar Shah's treasure to safeguard it for the descendants of the Shah. He journeyed to the Nejd and found a cavern deep in the desert where he hid these riches. With him he brought mystical wardens to help keep the treasure secure. None can move it without the wardens' aid.

At his passing, this charge fell to me, at the time a boy of only ten. To my shame I could not decipher the secret of the hidden treasure trove and it has been lost to me.

I rejoiced at your birth, my son, for your brother was like as unto me, where you…you were born with a fascination and natural skill for mechanical things. In you lies our hope.

With this letter I leave you your grandfather's safarnameh – his travel diary. Hidden within its pages you must find the knowledge that will lead you to the treasure trove. It now falls to you to honor this sacred duty and if Allah wills it, find a way to return it to the line of Afsharid. You will need the box to prove yourself, so guard it well. Tell no other soul of this sacred charge lest dishonor shadow your path forever more.

I also leave you a gift, two of the finest gems I have ever seen, left to me by my father. Should you choose to sell them, they will make you a rich man.

It is my hope that you will not need to; that my passing will bring you and your brother closer together and your future will be secure.

Tears blurred Ali's vision and he ran his fingertips over his father's letter, following the flowing script, knowing the love with which the words were written. Tension eased from his shoulders. He could not, of course, part with the gems — their value was of more than riches — but his father's words buoyed him. He would find a new home for himself. He was clever and had skills taught to him by *Ustad* Babbage. He would start a modest trade as an artificer. He would fulfill his destiny and chose the path that faith and duty crafted. Sniffling and wiping the tears from his eyes, he continued to read.

This is all I may leave you, to my earnest regret. I know that you will do great things. You have ever been the holder of my pride.

Have a good life, my son, and Allah keep you safe in this and all things.

With my deepest love,
Massoud bin-Farzeen

Flooded with warmth and peace at these unexpected words, Ali refolded the letter, reverently pressed it to his head, his lips, and his heart, then laid it back within the box. While he had never doubted his father's love for him, neither had he realized its true depth. It saddened Ali that he could not share any of this knowledge with his brother, but even had his father's letter not cautioned him against revealing the secret of the treasure to anyone, Ali knew he could not trust Kassim with the knowledge. Greed had burrowed into Kassim and now gripped his brother's heart.

Only one item remained. Drawing a deep breath, Ali took up the diary and began to read.

After weeks of shifting his weight for balance on the airship, Charles Babbage found it disconcerting to walk… nay…even stand upon firm ground without the sensation of a subtle swaying beneath his feet. As he moved through the Holy City, scarcely taking in its age-steeped splendor, he relied more heavily upon his cane than was his wont. The marketplace closed in around him with its exotic aromas and the tumult of merchants hawking their wares. Babbage kept his more-than-serviceable glower in place and strode ahead as if plowing through a throng of nattering students at the University. At the airfield, the flight manager had given him directions to the *caravanserai*. Babbage would not diverge from those until his purpose was met. Once he passed through the market his path cleared and he traveled with greater purpose until the *caravanserai* was in sight. He approached the collection of squat buildings. The closer he drew near, the more the air reeked of smoke and animals and sweat. Judging by the sacks and baskets of goods lining one wall and the curious beasts tethered in the courtyard, a caravan had recently arrived. Several men in dusty, travel-stained robes sat alone on plump cushions at the neighboring teashop. A larger group ate together in silence at a table next to the courtyard. Inwardly, Babbage groaned. If these had just arrived he could scarcely expect they would turn around and head across the desert soon. Skirting several sacks brimming with fruit and another from which rose the familiar aroma of Ali's favorite tea, he approached the shopkeeper.

"Do you speak English?" he asked hopeful, but not expectant.

The man frowned and continued about his business.

Huffing, Babbage dug in his pocket searching for the note the airfield manager had written out for him explaining his desire to travel to Wadi Al-Nejd. Before he could hand the paper to the man, a voice spoke from behind him.

"It is better that you should speak Arabic."

Babbage turned, his forehead crinkling as he looked down at a short, native man, his head swathed in an intricately wound scarf and his body clad in a simple, white robe similar to what Ali wore.

I am called Behnam, I speak this English. May I be of service to you?" His smile shown bright against his dark skin and his eyes were shuttered, though his expression remained eager to assist.

"I am called Charles Babbage and I am looking to join a caravan heading for Wadi Al-Nejd," Babbage answered, making an effort to keep impatience from his voice, something that grew difficult the more time passed. Perhaps he was a fool. Either Ali was fine and was never in peril, or Babbage's efforts were much too late.

The uncertainty robbed him of all reason.

Behnam gently bobbed his head, lips turned down in thought. "In two weeks these will return to the sands," he said, gesturing behind him. Babbage followed the direction of his wave, noting the six men and a boy eating at one table, but inwardly he groaned.

"Two weeks? Can they not leave sooner? Perhaps for more coin?"

The man shook his head with a regretful air. "These goods must be sold and supplies gathered."

"And there is no other caravan I can join?" Babbage asked, working to keep the desperate edge from his voice. "Or perhaps a guide I might hire?"

Behnam glance toward the shopkeeper, who slowly shook his head.

Babbage blew out a frustrated breath. The delay chaffed, but there was nothing for it. He could not make the journey on his own. "Please…" he said. "Will you ask them if I might travel with them? I have coin."

That blinding-white smile returned. "You have asked me. That is enough." Then he quoted a price Babbage expected qualified as bald-faced thievery. He countered with a figure more within his level of comfort. With a fierce, near gleeful grin, Behnam fired back another figure. Back and forth they went until the final figure landed near half between the original two. His new guide let his lips relax into a more natural smile and gave a brief, respectful nod.

"Onager will fetch you when we are ready to leave, Baba Charles Babbage," the man said, pointing at the young boy. "Be ready, at all times as we cannot wait when the hour comes to leave." With that admonition, Behnam returned to his fellows, speaking rapidly in his own tongue. Whatever he said, they greeted with laughter before settling back to their meal.

Babbage nodded as he turned back to the shopkeeper. "I have need of a room, if you please."

Then inwardly he groaned as the bartering began again. Only after, in the privacy of his simple room, did he it occur to him that the innkeeper spoke quite serviceable English.

In a shadowy corner of the teashop, a solitary figure raised his head and watched as the Englishman moved off toward the *caravanserai*. Satisfaction gleamed bright in his gaze.

Abdul Asad had come here looking for a trail to follow, never suspecting how fortune would favor him. There had been no trace of the apprentice, yet here came the master unwittingly leading the way.

After three days of solitude in the desert, Ali slowly approached the home he had just rented, which had taken most of his remaining coin. His eyes traveled the simple lines of the squat building and the courtyard, scarcely bigger than his room in England, to settle on the modest workshop. It appeared worn, but cared-for, and somehow expectant, as if eagerly awaiting him. Kissed by dawn's light, the buildings shone.

Ali leaned his staff beside the door of the house and drew out his key. His hand shook as he brought it to the lock. He drew a deep breath and held it until his hand steadied. As the key slid into the lock and turned with a firm *click* Ali laughed. Truly he had not dared believe his good fortune until that moment. Taking up the staff again, he entered his new home. Within were four rooms around a small, central garden with a modest wind tower for cooling: a main room for entertaining, two chambers for sleeping, and one for preparing meals. All were simply furnished with what appeared to be cast-offs from the widow woman who had rented him the building.

A solitary tear trailed down Ali's cheek at her unexpected kindness. He sank to a cushion and a broad smile stretched his lips as he looked around in wonder. Such a blessing he had not expected. In truth, it was too much for just him. He vowed at once to find Old Hamza and offer him a place, should he wish it. The man had no family and Ali would not have such a loyal servant cast upon fate's fickle mercy.

Ali settled in, putting away his few belongings, all but the travel diary. This he lay beside the threadbare cushion before going to prepare some tea. With a fresh pot at hand, he picked up his grandfather's journal. On the surface, it seemed a mere accounting of Farzeen's journey from Persia to the Rub-Al Khali leading a long train of 'ships of the desert,' — Ali chuckled at the poetic turn — mingled with entries of an engineering nature, several of them referencing Al-Jazari's book. Subtle inconsistencies in the details made Ali wonder, though, if this were not another sort of puzzle, akin to his *Himitsu-Bako*. Retrieving some ink and scraped parchment he had purchased earlier, Ali started a list. By the time he'd reached the last page of the *safarnameh* — a peculiar diagram marked with what appeared to be engineering symbols — Ali found himself thoroughly perplexed.

May Allah forgive him, but despite all the blessings bestowed upon him Ali could not help but find frustration in the final charge his father expected of him. How could Ali hope to find this treasure with so little knowledge to guide him and no one left to help uncloud his understanding?

He closed the small journal, wishing not for the first time his mentor was near at hand. *Ustad* Babbage had a gift for helping Ali focus his thoughts. Taking the diary to the room he'd selected as his own, he placed it on the shelf with his few books. His hand hovered over Al-Jazari's *The Book of Knowledge of Ingenious Mechanical Devices*. He had barely glanced at its pages, struggling to move past the heartache the book represented, but his grandfather's entries on invention had awakened Ali's curiosity. He drew the book down and returned to his cushion in the other room, pausing only to light one of his lanterns as the hour grew late.

Ali slowly relaxed as he delved into the book, closely reading and rereading the details of each engineering masterpiece diagrammed within. Al-Jazari had designed these works so many hundreds of years before; it humbled Ali to possess even a copy of the great book. He paged through once more, this time specifically in search of those diagrams his grandfather had noted in his diary. At first, Ali could not see past the intricacies of the designs, but by the time he reached the third diagram certain details snagged his gaze. The measurements were the key to his grandfather's diagram. Grinning as if he might never stop, Ali flipped from page to page. He had the key, the first step in unlocking the puzzle, but as with the *Himitsu-Bako* the solution was in the sequence.

Ali had little warning beyond an odd, metallic screech and a growing cloud of dust that moved across the sands. For weeks he had sought out the desert in an effort to decipher the cryptic diagram at the back of the travel diary. Not once in all that time had he spied another soul. To see a caravan now, traveling to the deep desert, far from any market or trade city, woke Ali's sense of caution. Scrambling atop the tallest dune at the edge of the oasis, he crouched down, half-concealed behind sand and arta bushes. He watched in silence as men riding sturdy desert horses led a train of heavy-laden camelids in his direction. At the sight of the great beasts towering above the riders, Ali's heart pounded in time with the hoof beats. True ships of the desert, these camelids were not flesh-and-blood, but constructs; dull brass machines smoking and whirring as their long, pistoned legs churned through the loose sand. He wished that he could share the sight with *Ustad* Babbage. One of the constructs lurched oddly in comparison to the others. As any good artificer would, Ali wondered why. Part of him—a very foolish part—longed to observe the camelids closer, to examine the workings of such a grand invention. The rest of him embraced the wisdom of remaining unnoticed.

Where are they bound? he wondered. *There are no villages nearby; Wadi Al-Nejd is two days travel in the other direction.* Wherever they headed, he wished they would move more swiftly. The delay in achieving his goal soured his belly. He longed to finish the journey begun nigh seven months earlier when the box containing his grandfather's *safarnameh,* with its hidden secrets, came into Ali's keeping. He clutched the satchel slung over his shoulder with those prized items inside. Instinct warned him that now was the time for patience.

Ali watched as the camelids' broad, shovel feet sank deep into the shifting terrain. He studied the men. He counted forty of them. Their garments were the same colors as the desert, as were their horses. As they drew closer he noticed two things. Their horses' hooves were wrapped in cloth, and the riders carried with them sharp *khanjars* and an air of menace.

These were not signs of honorable men.

As Ali realized the possible danger, he flattened himself against the dune and tucked his head. "Allah, preserve me," he said so softly it barely disturbed the fine grains of sand mere inches from his lips. His stomach twisted remembering his father's fate. Could these men have played any part in his death?

In all the weeks Ali had walked through the *saifs*, the corridors between dunes, he had never yet encountered trouble. In fact, since his return to Wadi Al-Nejd he had not experienced any of the mysterious attacks that had plagued him during his time in England and Jerusalem. Feeling more secure, he had recently begun venturing deeper into the Rub-Al Khali. When anyone asked, he claimed to search for the mysterious desert glass that could be found there. It brought better coin than could be had for the fuel he usually gathered, and hid well the fact that he searched for the shah's treasure. If Ali read the scant lines on the parchment properly he had all but reached his goal…and so had these men. Ali feared perhaps this was not by chance.

He wrapped his *chafiye* more tightly around his head and pressed himself deeper into the dune. As he waited, the sand grew cold beneath him. A shiver shook Ali's body. The first stars of night glittered against the darkening sky as the caravan slowly drew closer. Ali groaned as they entered the oasis rather than passing by. He hoped they merely stopped to drink and fill their goatskins.

The riders drew up directly below his hiding place. The leader raised his right arm to call a halt. In the moonlight, a too-familiar symbol, this time inked into the skin, stood out on his bared wrist. Ali gasped. This man was no follower of Islam. To disfigure one's self was *haram*…sinful.

At the sight of the tattoo, the impulse for vengeance heated Ali's blood. These men surely were the ones who killed his father, and now pursued him—though Rashid could not have passed knowledge of his name on to this group, or they would have found him quite easily by now.

These men had much to answer for.

Ali leaned forward as the leader dismounted and stepped toward the dune until he stood with a pile of stones to his right and an arta bush with a twisted trunk to his left. As if sensing someone watched, the man raised his head. His glanced over the darkened landscape, including Ali's hiding place. Ali dropped low among the brush, which was anchored to the rock, and sheltered beneath its sturdy branches.

After a moment, the man turned his narrowed gaze back to the dune before him and spoke, his voice rumbling in stentorian tones, "Open, Sesame!"

Ali gasped and could only pray the rumbling of the earth masked the sound as the dune beneath him shook and the sands flowed away to each side like a curtain. He waited for the outcry that would spell his doom, certain all eyes would spy him, but all he heard was a hiss, as of steam escaping, followed by rock grinding as it shifted. Slowly, the world around him settled. Ali heard the men below dismount, then walk the camelids forward into what he had no doubt was his grandfather's secret place, now den to what were clearly thieves and murderers.

As he waited, darkness filled the space around him. He did not move, barely breathing lest he be discovered. Gradually, the birds and tiny insects of the oasis once again sang their night songs. As the thieves lingered within, Ali's body tensed. There was nothing he could do from here, but to venture down to the cavern would be suicide. However, Ali could not withdraw. This was a matter of honor. And so he waited.

Chapter Ten

ALI WOKE FROM A SHIVERING DOZE TO FIND THE MOON HIGH above and sand digging into his cheek. Voices still drifted from the cavern. He sighed and thought longingly of the oasis below. He had been about to replenish his goatskin when he'd seen the dust. These many hours later his mouth was dryer than the desert while the water lay in sight, just out of reach. Resting his aching head against the rock, Ali strained to hear the thieves' conversation. He could not make out what they said, but the low, deep tones of the leader stood out. He issued orders, his words short and sharp. Ali prayed those instructions were not to set camp.

At long last, the unmistakable sounds of saddle leather creaking and anxious horses being led onto the sands rose to Ali's ears on the night air. He silently thanked Allah and the Prophet for preserving him.

Ali belly-crawled forward to watch them depart. The leader stood precisely where he had earlier, facing the dune. A strange, unwavering light poured from the mouth of the cavern. The thief's *chafiye* wrapped most of his features, leaving only his eyes revealed. The light reflected in their dark depths giving them a demonic cast. Ali shook at the sight and

once more tucked his head low. He listened intently as the lead thief spoke the words, "Close, Sesame."

Again the ground rumbled and shook and the sands flowed, this time back into place so swiftly that Ali found himself buried beneath the powdery grains. Instinct told him to thrash and fight his way free. Grim reason forced him to wait lest he be discovered. His chest squeezed tight and his body begged for air. He clenched his jaw against the urge to gasp. Instead he drew shallow breaths as he strained to hear if the thieves had gone.

With his senses muffled, only the tremble of the sands upon his skin told Ali when the had thieves departed, slowly lessening as they galloped away. He held his place until his flesh tingled and the darkness grew heavy behind his lids. Then Ali flung himself back, fighting to be free from the folds of suffocating sand. It clung to him and dragged on his limbs. He gulped too soon and drew in the desert along with sweet, fresh air. Coughing and choking on the fine grains, Ali lunged up and broke the surface, crouching on his hands and knees as he spat the sand from his body. When he could breathe without gagging, he collapsed. He lay there only briefly before dragging himself up. Clearly, the Almighty had decided now was not his time to die. He stared at the slope of the dune and nearly wept at the need to climb back down. Ali looked to the broom-like limbs of the arta bush he'd sheltered beneath and snapped off a low branch full of blossoms to sweep away his tracks.

The moon lit his way as he scurried down to the oasis. His first instinct was to fill his goatskin and flee back toward Wadi Al-Nejd before the night grew any older, but as he knelt beside the pool, he could not control his gaze. At first it merely darted toward the dune and back again. His eyes locked upon the slope a while longer, his mind furiously working on the puzzle of how the dune hid a cavern. He longed to go in, to explore. To know for once and certain that this was the place he sought.

The next he knew, Ali stood where the lead thief's footprints still shaped the sands, between the rock outcropping and the arta bush with the twisted trunk, his hand toying with one of the robust red blossoms from the branch in his hands as his teeth worried his lower lip.

He should not do it. Allah knew he should not do it.

"Open, Sesame."

The words were but a whisper across his lips, barely spoken before the sands again separated to reveal the rock outcrop. His eyes widened as next the stone facing slowly slid beneath the desert. Ali forgot once more to breathe. He had not believed it would work. He had been sure the sun had baked his brain. But there it was: the secret cavern, spilling its steady light upon the oasis.

The blossom snapped off in Ali's tightened grip. He barely noticed as he crept into the cave. As he passed the entrance he noted two divots in the chamber floor that mirrored where he'd stood outside. Ali stopped and turned toward the oasis. It would be best to not betray his presence. "Close, Sesame," he murmured, recalling the leader's words; hoping they would work from the inside.

And the earth swallowed Ali whole.

His first impulse was to pound upon the rock, to order it open once more. Instead he turned and allowed his gaze to sweep the cavern. He could see no sign of the guardians his father's letter had warned about. Perhaps they had been released by his grandfather's passing, for they were not here. Still, Ali's hand crept down to rest upon his satchel, which contained the puzzle box, the travel diary, and his father's letter. Reassured, he took in the wonders of the cave. The first thing he noticed were the camelids standing in ranks against the far wall, their curved brass flanks dully gleaming. He gasped as he realized *these* were the 'ships of the desert' mentioned in his grandfather's diary. The ache to explore their inner workings was so strong it was almost physical.

Knowing he could not, Ali dragged his gaze away to examine the rest of the treasures. What he saw dazzled his eyes. Without a doubt, this was Nader Shah's treasure. A jewel-encrusted platform stood in the center of the cavern. Twelve pillars—each capped by two peacocks with fanned tails—supported a canopy, the underside of which was covered in rubies and diamonds, emerald and pearls. The whole of it rested on four gold feet. Ali shivered in awe at that splendor alone. He had heard of the fabled Peacock Throne, but it had not occurred to him that it would be the centerpiece of his family's sacred charge. Closest to the platform rested elegant urns filled with chalices and golden platters, some plain, others likewise encrusted with gems. Stacked around these were chests made of precious metals and rare wood. Ali marveled at the finely carved cinnabar and ivory that filled them. Part of him had scarcely believed he would find the treasure of Nader Shah hidden in the heart of the Rub-Al Khali. It was evident that part of him had been wrong.

On the fringes of the shah's treasure, the thieves had piled canvas sacks and ceramic jars brimming with more pedestrian blessings: common-day coins and costly spices, aromatic perfumes and sparkling jewels, bolts of silk and casks of fine tea. There, shoved to the sides, blanketed in dust, he spied bundles of glass, copper, and brass piping that set his artificer's heart tripping. The things Ali could make with such supplies! He closed his eyes and turned from the sight, lest avarice take root in his soul. If he was meant for such wealth, Allah would provide.

In the corner beyond the camelids, Ali noticed a workbench the likes of which he'd only seen in his dreams. This, more than even the shah's treasure let him know that he had found the secret place his father had been searching for.

Charcoal sketches similar to those in Al-Jazari's book were pinned to a board that leaned against the cavern wall, their black marks softened by a thick layer of dust. Half-finished inventions resembling sketches from his grandfather's diary gathered dust on the work surface. He sighed, knowing he dare touch nothing, lest he betray himself in some way to the thieves.

His fingers hovered above delicate tools and sturdy spanners his meager coin could never afford. Even these were coated in fine dust and sand, as if long without use, though surely the camelids required maintenance. Glancing more closely, Ali could discern initials engraved on the handles. Were these his grandfather's tools? They looked to have been well-used at one time, but obviously, that time was long past.

With all his heart, he vowed to reclaim his family's legacy.

Beside the workbench stood a vat of oil and two barrels, one filled with copper gears, the other black tar for fuel. Beyond that, in the shadows, someone had piled a junk heap of scrap metal and defunct parts next to which stood one of the camelids, its body darkened by smoke residue along one side and the torso open on its hinges. He peered within and noticed a bent cog had twisted one of the shafts. A simple enough thing to fix, and yet it was clear by the coating of dust on the camelid's back that the thieves had neither interest nor skill for such things. Ali resisted the urge to make the repair himself, instead examining the mechanism with a careful eye. Even damaged, the inner workings of the construct enthralled him. The design was similar to some he had seen at *Ustad* Babbage's side, but this was more elegant; as much art as engineering. Inside, a compact copper boiler connected to narrow pipes that led from the tank to an intricate assembly of gears, rods, and pistons, two to each side, corresponding to where the legs attached. Another rose through the aperture where the construct's neck connected to the body. He could not identify what directed the locomotion, but what he did see gave him some understanding of how the smooth, league-spanning stride of the camelid's walk was achieved. Ali avidly studied the design, storing the knowledge for future use…assuming he ever had enough coin to do more than dream of crafting such complex engineering. Since Kassim had ordered Ali's return to Wadi Al-Nejd, there had been little opportunity — or coin — for true invention, only the tinkering that supplemented his dwindling reserve. Sighing, he turned away from the workbench, lest he be tempted to touch.

Oh, what Ali would give to linger in this place for the rest of his days, creating magnificent constructs. But no, he had already lingered too long. Even now, his shoulders tightened and he caught himself darting glances around the room.

It was as if eyes were upon him, causing the skin across his back to crawl. Ali turned to examine the cavern in its entirety, rather than just the riches it held. He spied no one, but for the first time he took note of the cave itself, marveling at the workmanship. This was no natural cavern but had been crafted by human hands. He could almost make out tool marks, likely from some rock-boring construct. The walls were only partially visible for the lattice of steam pipes crisscrossing overhead and down to the floor. Most of them were copper, but inter-mixed were glass tubes emitting a soft yellow light from no source Ali understood. Those pipes framing the entrance to the cavern were all glass, thick and gleaming, with brass fittings. To either side of them Ali saw a complex assembly of great-toothed gears in a variety of sizes, interlocked and showing signs of wear. They appeared to operate a pulley system as a massive metallic cable ran up to the ceiling and down into the ground. He recognized elements of the design from *The Book of Knowledge*. He would have examined these workings more closely as well, only a sudden movement distracted him.

Inside those pipes by the entrance swirled lavender mist too delicate to be mistaken for steam. For a brief instant Ali would have sworn there was a flutter, as of eyes blinking. Surely he was mistaken…and yet, the sensation of being watched increased.

Trying to ignore it, Ali continued wandering. Repeatedly, he had to remind himself not to touch each new thing he discovered. He told himself he was blessed just to be here in the secret place his grandfather had created and his father had long sought; it was enough to feel surrounded by their spirits, to see such glorious things, to smell the fragrance of the spices and costly perfumes that sweetened the chamber. Almost, Ali believed the lie. Thinking of the thieves, he fought the urge to lash out. This was his family's responsibility, his family's charge, his family's treasure to guard. That last bore remembering. These riches were not his and never would be, but he could not help but wish just once to hold such wealth in his hands, to know, however briefly, what it felt like to be a rich man. No. No good could come of such thoughts.

Ali sighed. The sound echoed in the chamber until he nearly overlooked the softer sigh that followed his own. And then the light brightened and Ali stiffened as a woman's voice filled the cavern.

"What have you in your hand, Child of Adam?" The voice was like the crackle of a fire, darker notes beneath light.

Ali spun. He saw no one.

"What have you in your hand?" the voice repeated. Sweeter than a nightingale, the surging power in that voice sent Ali to his knees, fervent supplication to Allah on his lips, though he had no breath to utter them. His gaze fell upon the glass pipes by the entrance where the roiling mist had taken on a darker, violet hue.

"Tell me!" All sweetness and light fled both the woman's voice and the chamber.

Ali thought desperately. He purposely had not touched even one piece of treasure. No, not even the bent cog. In the darkness, he focused, startled to realize he did, in fact, cup something in his right hand. Slowly, he reached over with his left and ran his fingers across the sturdy anthers of the arta blossom he had plucked from the bush outside the cavern.

He tried to speak and it was as if the desert itself once more filled his throat.

The darkness took on more weight at his continued silence, but the voice did not speak again. Ali frantically coughed and cleared his throat.

"A flower…" His voice sounded harsh and grating to his ear.

A gasp answered him. The longing in that single sound tightened his chest. Light once more flooded the chamber. Before him the mist swirled in agitation. Following instinct, Ali crept forward, still on his knees, and laid the flower beside the pipes, the small anthers only slightly bent for having been clutched in his hand.

When he looked up, a woman formed out of the swirling mist; perfect in all proportions, but no larger than a ferret, her body cloaked in smoky robes. The glass tube held a djinni. Her solid black gaze locked on the blossom. Here at last, one of the guardians of which his father wrote, though Ali wondered how well she could guard from within her encasement.

"He planted them for me," she whispered. "My master planted them for me. It has been so long since I have seen evidence of his gift. Not since his passage into Death's Garden."

The glass pipe rang as bolts of energy slammed into it, followed by the djinni herself. She lunged but could not cross the glass. As her body hit the surface, the surrounding air went bitter cold. The glass became opaque, like milky quartz…like ice on the Thames. Again and again she threw herself against the glass. Ali fell back. With a final shriek, the shadow of the djinni drew in upon itself, and the surface cleared, revealing her huddled form in the center, not one bit of skin touching her prison walls. She stared, eyes locked on the blossom, her face a mosaic of heartache so deep Ali felt the pain pierce his own breast.

She closed her eyes and her body went taut. The mists returned, swirling off the edges of her limbs. Violent static, in shades of dark crimson and purple that put Ali in mind of blood and bruises, shot through the vapor. The colors jarred the glass. A few even seemed to pass through. The djinni trembled and shook as if in great pain. One arm, more solid than the other, reached out toward the arta flower. But even as Ali watched, the blossom shimmered, then faded, and finally burst into flame leaving only ash.

The djinni cried out, then jerked as if struck, before vanishing into a heavy fog that swirled in agitation at the bottom of the glass tube.

Silence descended upon the cavern, a silence that carried pain and longing. Ali was loathe to disturb it. "Farzeen," he murmured. "Your master…he was called Farzeen."

At his statement, the djinni's eyes formed once more, blazing like violet embers out of the smoke.

"What know you of my master?"

Ali bowed his head as he drew the *Himitsu-Bako* from his pocket. "Not much, I fear, save he was my grandfather."

He held the box out for her to see only to flinch at a familiar jab on the palms of his hands. A faint trickle of blood trailed down his skin. As if in response, the light in the chamber flared.

"You are of my master's blood?" The djinni's voice held a note of panic as she swirled about her crystalline tube.

Ali winched as she brushed the sides triggering sparks through her mist form.

"You must leave…*now*. It is not safe."

Ali offered no argument. He slid the box back into his satchel, all the while vowing to end the thieves' dominion over the cavern and *all* it contained. Wiping his hands on his satchel, Ali backed away until he stood above the divots. There, he waited for long moments until the djinni's voice again filled the chamber.

"You must say the words...and you must say them correctly."

Ali nodded. "Open, Sesame." The djinni visibly calmed as he complied.

First, he heard the familiar rumble of a boiler firing, then the high-pitched hiss of steam, followed by the soft grind of gears that needed greasing, until finally, the ground shook beneath his feet. He jerked as the gear assembly by the cavern entrance began to turn and the massive cable scrolled upward and back down again. The rock before him lowered into the earth. Normally, he would watch in close fascination to observe the workings of such a marvel, but this time his gaze turned to the sullen fog that was the djinni.

"I am but the watchdog chained to the gate," she answered his unspoken question. "Now...smudge your forehead with the ash from my flower and be quick, or I will not be able to aid you on your way." Puzzled, Ali looked to the ash and for the first time noticed that it shimmered in shades of crimson and purple. With some trepidation he knelt and pressed his thumb to the ash. Something sparked and tingled, causing him to jump.

The djinni chuckled, but the sound held no joy.

"Now! Or do not bother at all."

Ali brought his thumb so swiftly to his forehead that he winced as the digit jammed against his skull. He felt the tingle transfer at the touch of dry ash against his brow.

"Go you, swift and sure across the sands, Farzeen's grandson." The djinni's blessing sounded more of farewell.

Ali frowned as he stepped toward the opening. Not caring for how final his leaving felt he turned back to her and bowed deep. "I would like to return, gracious lady."

She took her human seeming and turned to look at him with perplexity twisting her expression. "What foolishness is this, Child of Adam? This place holds a constant threat of death which you have cheated thrice this night alone. Are these treasures worth such a risk?"

"As Allah wills, but still I would return, not for the treasure, but for honor's sake. My grandfather's sacred duty falls to me. And," Ali hesitated, "I would speak with you."

She continued to stare, eyelids half lowered, then shook her head. "Tell me your name."

"Ali bin-Massoud."

He waited politely for her to offer her own name in return. She ignored the unasked question. "Then, Baba Ali, I shall await your return."

With dawn just lightening the sky, Ali entered his dwelling mere hours after leaving the thieves' cavern. His eyes and forehead both burned and he'd worn his sandal leather near through. Whatever magics the djinni worked had allowed him to pass a journey of days in less than one night. But he was now weary beyond measure.

Ali drank a full skin of water and ate some flatbread and hummus he did not taste before falling upon his bed, clothes yet covered in sand and ash.

He woke at dusk, still dwelling on all he'd seen in the cavern. His mind did not linger on the treasures, but upon the charge his father had bequeathed him, to find the treasure and safeguard it until it could be returned to the shah's descendants. Though he had accomplished the first half of this goal, Ali found it hard to fathom how to execute the remainder of his task. He was an artificer…or near enough…not a warrior. And yet he found his mind returning to the djinni in her mist of sorrow. It was difficult to say which fascinated him more, his grandfather's steamworks or the woman of smoke. To free her would be an honorable thing. And the inventions…he longed to spend time studying them without the threat of the thieves above his head. *Allah willing*, he told himself, as the djinni's warning and her welcome both whispered in his memory.

As he shifted on his bed, his father's letter crackled in his pouch, a tangible reminder of what awaited him.

Ali reached for a lever by his head, part of a simplified design based on the lanterns he had once built for him. A sharp pull released a measure of lamp oil into the lantern's reservoir. This, in turn, caused a bit of flint to strike against a small length of steel just above the oil, igniting it. In the warm glow from the lamp, Ali rolled over and sat on the edge of his bed.

"Surely I am both blessed and cursed." He must speak to the djinni, but how to do so without alerting the thieves…or wearing the skin from his feet? Slowly his lips quirked and his head tilted as Ali devised a plan.

He grabbed a sturdy pair of sandals from his chest, extinguished the lamp, then left the house, crossing the courtyard to his shop. There he placed the footwear upon his scarred and worn workbench. Lighting another lamp he laid out his simple tools. He then retrieved a bronze sheet and copper bands from his meager supplies. Tracing the sandals against the metal, he scored the bronze and popped out two metal soles, which he then scoured on one side, to allow him traction. He then took the copper bands and formed from them and the bronze a sheath for the sandals that would cushion his feet as he marched across the desert in his now metal–soled shoes. Once that was done, he added a framework of struts to each sandal to which he attached small, soft-bristled brooms to whisk away his prints as he strode across the sands. Pleased with the result, Ali again wished he might share the accomplishment with *Ustad* Babbage, though perhaps the man would not be impressed with a working so simple and pedestrian.

Loosing a sigh, Ali grabbed a water skin and more flatbread, wrapped his *chafiye* close about his head, and donned the modified sandals. He then carefully crept from his home, taking care not to be seen as he passed his brother's lavish house. Kassim and his wife surely slept. Ali prayed their servants had likewise retired for the night.

Upon reaching the edge of the city, he exited via a lesser gate. He then turned to the Rub Al-Khali and brought his thumb to his forehead. A little ash still remained. He closed his eyes and thought of the djinni. The familiar tingle began anew, slight, yet still palpable. The sensation traveled from his temple clear down to the soles of his feet. As it settled there, Ali opened his eyes and began to run. His feet carried him through shadowed dunes, and past oases bright with camel-dung fires where Bedouins sang the songs of their ancestors while they drank sweet tea. He moved in silence, his ensorcelled body winging away before any might notice him, the tinkered sandals leaving no tracks.

And thus it went, until mere hours later he entered the thieves' oasis. Panting, his body covered in a sheen of sweat, Ali dropped upon the cool sands beside the spring, sitting with his head braced against his knees as he drew shuddering breaths. Allah, forgive him. Was he mad to risk death at the hands of these thieves? And for what? Duty to a fallen dynasty and a measure of time with a woman that faded to mist?

Ali sighed, thinking perhaps he was a fool, but unable to care.

His home held cold comfort; out here in the desert, only darkness and silence. Three words granted him the warmth and light and companionship to ease his soul. Standing, Ali brushed the sand from his *thobe* and moved toward the standing place—between the pile of stones and the arta bush. As he did so, he noted the sweetness of night-blooming jasmine on the air. A memory surfaced of the glimmer of joy in the djinni's eyes on seeing the arta flower he'd laid before her.

By scent, he sought out the jasmine hidden among the low ferns skirting the oasis. He reached out and snapped off a sprig, beautiful in its simplicity, worthy of a sultan's daughter. Rising, he swiftly traced his path back to the cavern entrance.

"Open, Sesame," he said, and waited with both fear and elation sparking in his chest.

"I did not think you would return."

Surprise and pleasure flavored the djinni's words. She showed him no face, but the lavender mist swirled and danced through the glass tubes. Not sure how to respond, Ali only nodded and held out the jasmine. The tiny white flowers seem to shiver in his palm. Ali grimaced as he realized his hand shook, not the flower. He knelt and gently set the bloom down before the djinni then backed away.

"A gift. For your hospitality, gracious lady."

Ali let his gaze wander, not wanting to know if his offering displeased her. His interest in the exotic treasures he dare not touch had faded; his artificer's heart, however, still longed to delve into the glory of the workbench and all it held. Even more, his interest in the camelids could swiftly become obsession.

"They have been and gone this night and will not return," the djinni murmured, as if well aware of his longing. "There is some time."

Relief seeped through him. Ali nodded as he stepped closer to the camelids. His mind swam with visions of his hands dismantling one of them to learn all the secrets of its inner workings. The constructs were not a design from Al-Jazari's *Book of Knowledge*, which Ali had studied in great depth. The style was likewise different than that which he had learned in the land of the English. Were these the work of his grandfather, or had he merely brought them from the Shah's court? Hardly realizing he did so, Ali drifted even closer to the ranks of mechanical beasts. He could still see in his mind's eye the might and power evident in each stride as the caravan had trekked the desert. Fancifully, he imagined his grandfather walking beside them.

"Once there were hundreds." Ali jumped at the djinni's unexpected words. "Now only these few remain."

"How do these marvelous creatures work?" he wondered half aloud as he circled one of the constructs. *How had such a procession hid its tracks?* And then he realized the djinn must have played some part in masking the trail.

"Once the boiler is fired, you press down upon the tongue. This engages the engine. The construct then walks in the direction it faces until the operator of the lead beast tugs the reins to alter the course. If the traces are connected, all the constructs follow the same path."

"And to make one kneel?"

Unexpected laughter bubbled through the cavern like a spring from an oasis. "You tug its tail."

Delighted with her knowledge and her willingness to share, Ali posed question after question, absorbing the information as the desert drank rain. His eye traveled every inch of the camelid while the djinni explained what she knew.

Their conversation went long into the night, moving on to talk of life and dreams and cold-hearted fate, anything to continue talking. Ali told her of his modest tinker shop and showed her his sandals, of which he could not help but be proud. In return, the djinni astounded him with tales of his grandfather and the wondrous inventions he'd once made, the least of which were the camelids and the mechanism that opened the cave. Ali found himself dreaming that perhaps one day he too might build wonders such as these. This reminded him, of course, that he had not broached the matter of the thieves and how to oust them. He told himself that would be a conversation for another day.

Instead, Ali folded himself to the ground beside the entrance and leaned his head against the rock, eyes engaged with his companion as they spoke. Not since leaving England had he enjoyed a conversation so. Though she remained mist, Ali did not care. Finally, he gathered the courage to speak the one question he longed to ask.

"What keeps you here?"

He regretted asking, the moment the mists darkened.

"My djinn form is anchored to an onyx ring. When the thieves invaded this cavern they fell upon my master and slew him." Ali flinched, but said nothing as the djinni continued to speak. "Their leader, Rassul, well-versed in sorcerous ways, took my ring for his own. I fled from him within these pipes which were part of my master's last working, only to have them become my prison. Rassul trapped me here and placed a compulsion upon me to operate the mechanism that opens the door when the proper words are spoken." The djinni hissed. "As long as I am encased in glass, Rassul cannot summon me. As long as he possesses the ring I am not free to roam, lest he command me against my will."

"You were not always alone, were you?" Ali said, leaning toward her, expecting that Shahin had once shared guardianship of this place, given his connection to the box.

She shrank away without answering.

"Please…will you not tell me? I wish to know more of you."

Agitation swirled the mist.

"No…I was not always alone, only since my master's passing. Before that there was another…you might call him a brother, of sorts…another of my kind, but he is gone now." Bitterness and regret colored her words, edged with what Ali thought might be shame. He would have asked more but was not given the chance as the djinni spoke again.

"Night is near done, Ali, as is our time together. The cursed ones will soon return. You must away." Once again, the mist reached out, straining to send sparks through the glass. As before she cried out, but not before the jasmine flowers were reduced to ash. "Go you swift and sure across the sands."

Frowning, Ali rose as she bid. They had talked long this night, but not about such things as his grandfather or the treasure. No mention of duty or destiny. The lack of knowledge now weighed heavy upon him, yet he felt no regret for his time spent with the djinni. Touching the ash and bringing it to his forehead, his gaze still firm upon her, Ali spoke. "I would return again, gracious lady."

The djinni's smoke swirled in agitation.

"The cavern holds a constant threat of death, Ali—"

"Perhaps, but I would return again to visit with you."

"If you will, then I shall await your return," she answered, her voice threaded with warmth.

Chapter Eleven

A LI ARRIVED HOME AS THE ROOSTER GREETED THE DAWN. THIS time his sandals held, but the straps snapped with the weight of their metal-soles. Leaving them on his workbench to fix later, Ali went inside his house and fell upon his bed.

And thus the pattern of his fate was set; days spent in exhausted sleep while nights he spanned the desert of the Rub Al-Khali to converse with the captive djinni during the hours when the thieves were away on their vile business. He saw to his body's needs as he could between his journeys across the sands. For six nights, each visit continued much as before: a flower presented, talk of tinkering, hopes, and dreams, then a petition, reluctantly granted, to return.

He chided himself for these self-indulgences. Long had he been without simple companionship, but no matter how he'd grown to enjoy their talks, he could not forget his purpose, even knowing he would wake the djinni's sorrow. *Soon,* he told himself, *soon I will ask her council on the matter of my duty and banishing the thieves. But soon is not now…*

On the seventh night, when Ali prepared to take his leave, the djinni stayed him.

From the cloaking mists, her eyes glowed with a gentle light and her head tilted as she considered him. He thought perhaps a faint blush accompanied the smile that graced her mouth. He startled at the ethereal sensation of soft lips brushing his temple. Then she spoke, the words sounding close, as if whispered in his ear. "There is a leather-bound chest far back under the eaves of my cavern. Take you two sacks and fill them only with gold coin from that coffer. The treasure is mine and none may put hand to it that I do not give leave. You are welcome, for your kindness and the joy you bring to my heart, Ali bin-Massoud. Take nothing more, lest the cursed ones know."

The sorrow that wrapped around those words of blessing clutched Ali's heart. He could not care less about the gold. In that moment, he acknowledged in his heart of hearts it was she he'd rather carry away, if he only knew how to do so. Yet to refuse the gift would offer insult, so Ali acquiesced and moved to do as she bade him.

He found the chest where she indicated, deep in the shadows. Filling the sacks, he returned to stand before the closed mouth of the cave. Once more he touched the djinni's ash to his brow and let the magic suffuse his limbs. That night, he hesitated before leaving. "Please…what is your name?"

She seemed lost for a moment. "There is none I have any right to claim."

He frowned at this answer, but did not press her.

Ali could not say what passed between the oasis and Wadi Al-Nejd, nor if any had spied him along the way, so late had he returned. By the time he arrived home, he'd barely the energy to slide the sacks of gold beneath his bed, too tired to care when one of them toppled, sending a solitary coin rolling across the floor. He nudged the sacks further out of sight. Tonight he would bury them beneath the trough in his yard, where none would notice, but first he must sleep.

Ali woke to darkness. Night had fallen. He lay stretched out on his stomach with his arm half under his cot, his hand resting on the sack of coins. His feet ached. That brought his thoughts to his djinni and the night he'd passed conversing with her. Ali's stomach churned with guilt that another visit had passed without the matter of his duty discussed. What was worse, he realized he had not secured permission to return.

Ali prayed it would not matter, as he rolled over and left his bed. He would return to her regardless. But it was not safe to leave his new-gained wealth out in the open. Drawing out the sacks, Ali rested them by the door, then slipped out to stand in his small courtyard. A glance at the heavens confirmed it was the dark hour after moon set. Perfect. He reached inside and brought out the djinni's gift. Without magical aid, it took more effort than before, but Ali managed to heft both sacks and carry them to the stone trough behind his tinker's shop where he watered his donkey. By the time he shifted the trough and began to dig, sweat coated his face and the promise of dawn pinked the heavens. Ali dug faster.

At last the hole was deep enough. He grimaced as he reached for the first sack, every muscle knotting as he dragged the treasure to the hole, too worn to lift it. Making sure the neck of the sack remained tightly secured, he tumbled the treasure into his hiding place and returned for the other. A frown took his lips. The tie was loose on this one. He reached to tighten it only to find his fingers trailing through the gold. The memory of his daydreams came to him and despite the need for caution Ali pocketed two coins, telling himself he could explain such a bounty without too much suspicion falling upon him. After all, he'd made no secrets of his efforts to gain coin for his tinkering. Imagine the supplies he could afford with just these two.

Giving in to the smile tugging his lips, Ali finished his task and pushed the heavy trough back into place, hiding the newly mounded dirt just as the sun crested the horizon. The trough sat a little higher and no longer as flush to the workshop wall, but close enough to where it had been before that no one should notice. For good measure, he scuffed the dirt to blend it up to the edge of the cobbles. Satisfied, Ali crawled back to his bed and slept well past the noon meal.

On waking, he chuckled, his mind already dancing merrily with images of all the supplies his coin could buy: gears, pipes, bronze sheets, and—dare he hope?—a small copper boiler. Perhaps he had enough even for the fine set of tools Baba Abdiesus displayed in his shop; imported all the way from England, or so the merchant claimed. They were not as fine as those in the thieves' cavern, or even those

Ali had used in the workshop on Dorset Street, but, if he were honest, he had coveted them since his return. They would aid him much in creating his inventions.

No longer noticing his aching muscles, he cleaned himself up—all but the djinni's mark, which he could not bring himself to wipe away— then changed into fresh clothing before going down to his small shed to feed Jasmine, and lead the small donkey to the bazaar.

Ali's steps quickened as he approached Abdiesus's shop, eager to buy as he wished for once. But sudden concern crept into Ali's heart and would not give him peace. If he were to buy all he desired, talk would spread of his sudden wealth and others would wonder if there was more. He feared being made victim by ordinary thieves, but worse yet he feared word of his good fortune would come to the cursed ones' ears.

As he secured Jasmine at the post outside Baba Abdiesus's shop, Ali resigned himself to purchasing a more modest list of goods to preserve both his secret and his life. He stepped to the entrance and paused there as his eyes adjusted to the lower light.

"Ah! The peace and blessings of Allah be upon you, young Ali!" Abdiesus greeted him as he stood there at the threshold. With true joy in his expression the old man came up to clasp Ali's shoulders.

"And also to you, my friend." Ali gave a brief bow to the shop-keeper. "You are well?"

Abdiesus nodded and his smile grew broad. "The Almighty has smiled upon me." He gestured around him with a well-wrinkled hand at the stocked shelves. "Please, see for yourself, only the finest goods in this shop these days…"

Ali smiled as the merchant's second nature eagerly peered out. Dutifully, he made his way through the stacks of goods, trailing his hand over polished metal and perfect glass tubing, running his fingers through baskets of loose gears and testing the tensile strength of the high-grade wire. He drew a breath, his eyes drifting closed as he savored the scents of fine oils used for lubrication.

Though it had been years since he had last entered Baba Abdiesus's shop it was as if he had never been away. The atmosphere embraced him like a friend. From the time he was a young boy, this shop and its owner had fed Ali's fascination with mechanical things. Even now Abdiesus followed behind him reminiscing on the sort of simple tinkering Ali had once done before his apprenticeship.

When Ali had selected his purchases they returned to the counter. As the merchant bundled the goods they chatted of the years gone by. Not much of note had happened in Wadi Al-Nejd…weddings and births, mostly. They did not discuss the funerals. When Ali told the shopkeeper of his time in England studying with the great Charles Babbage the man showed true delight. As the talk shifted to the designs Ali had assisted on, or even constructed on his own, Abdiesus's eyes brightened, as did his smile.

"I still have the coin box you made for me, my boy," the shopkeeper said as he bustled to a shelf behind the counter, wisps of white hair and beard trailing behind him. He held up a small tin box with a crude, articulated figure — Ali's childish interpretation of a djinni — perched on top. When a coin was wedged into the figure's 'hand' it bobbed forward and dropped it in a slot big enough to allow a dirham to slide through. Ali had not realized his friend cherished it still. Given the simple nature of the tinkering, Ali was humbled.

"It gladdens me that this has brought you such joy."

Sobering, the man placed the trinket in Ali's hands. "I am proud of the man you have become, Ali, as would your father have been, had Allah not summoned him home, but do not forget the joy to be found in the working of simple things."

Before Ali could respond, another patron entered the shop. Abdiesus reclaimed the box and shuffled away to assist them. Ali departed, this time with a heart that looked upon his modest purchases with nothing but joy and gratitude.

"Husband," Malakeh asked, her voice petulant, as Kassim sipped his tea after the evening meal. "Did you send your brother to the bazaar with a gold coin?"

Kassim sputtered and smacked his cup down upon the table. "Have I what?"

"Sent your brother to the bazaar with a gold coin..."

His eyes narrowed and he sat forward, his teeth grinding while his wife went on as she dipped her flatbread into the za'atar, not even looking for an answer.

"He disappears all day, coming back so late we scarcely see him pass by, but this morning I saw him in the bazaar, his donkey heavily burdened. He was paying that scrap peddler, Abdiesus, with a gold coin…"

"I would not give that cur even a copper dirham," Kassim said, uncertain which annoyed him more, that his brother had somehow come by gold, or that his wife would think it came from *him*.

"Oh," she answered with studied innocence, drawing figures in the *za'atar* with a small piece of the warm bread. "Well I'd assumed it came from you as I know Ali has none…but the serving girl, Fatemeh, did mention she saw him come out of the desert burdened with two heavy sacks this morning. Perhaps your brother has discovered a cache…"

Kassim spat and fumed, his stomach roiling on rich food and envious thoughts. The diamonds! What else could bring his brother such a windfall? Surely Ali would not be so foolish as to sell the priceless gems, but equally as preposterous was Malakeh's thought that Ali had simply found the coins in the desert. Hatred coiled in Kassim's breast at the possibility the diamonds might truly be lost to him. Those were to be his! No, he would have heard. Such precious rarities would have drawn attention, and gossip.

Whatever the source of Ali's bounty, how dare his brother hide his good fortune, squandering it with no regard for Kassim, who generously saw that he received the best leavings from their table? "He has seemed altogether too happy of late, given his position. Surely there is something going on." And Kassim's expression grew calculating. "Go, wife, and prepare a feast worthy of an emir's visit. Stuffed lamb and dates, persimmon and spices, saffron rice and cashews…the best we have to offer…"

Malakeh gasped, her bejeweled hand going to her breast and her lips pressed tight in distaste that he would ask her to share their *best* luxuries. "But who shall we feast, husband?"

"Why, my brother…how else will we have from him the secret of his treasure?" Kassim rose and went to a small, hammered-bronze chest. Lifting the lid, he removed a vial and pressed it into his wife's hand. "For Ali's coffee after the meal," Kassim told her, a smirk twisting his lips as he presented her a drug which would make his brother inclined to reveal all.

Ali returned home, his donkey burdened by many parcels containing all the things he had sought, though not as in as great a quantity as there might have been. *Better not to draw attention,* Ali reminded himself. It rankled, though. He could have had so much more had he been free to spend both gold coins.

At that thought, Ali felt the heat of shame upon his face. Such greed was unworthy of him. He had more than he ever imagined he could afford, including the tools he'd longed for from Abdiesus's shop and a small, finely wrought copper boiler. Coveting more when his needs were met disgraced him before the Almighty. Silently, he begged forgiveness.

Guiding Jasmine into his work shed, Ali removed the parcels and led the donkey into her makeshift stall in the corner of the room, his hands running lovingly over her ears as he whispered thanks for her service. Ali chuckled as he left the stall, thinking that she must be beginning to like him as she only tried to bite him twice. He then turned and examined each purchase before he stowed them away, that their obvious presence not betray his new good fortune.

Content, he left the shed only to find one of his brother's servants waiting patiently by his front door.

"I beg your pardon, Baba Ali," the young girl spoke, her eyes carefully downcast as he approached. "My master bids you good evening and invites you to dine at his table this night."

Ali frowned at the unexpected show of generosity. There had been only vitriol between them since his return from England. Still, all the more reason he would not insult Kassim by refusing his offer. Bowing his agreement, Ali headed for his brother's larger, more prosperous home, all the while wishing he could continue past and stride away across the desert.

How he wished he'd given in to that impulse.

Hours later he staggered home, his gut sour and his head swimming. His brother argued he should stay with them for tending, but Ali shuddered and broke away, needing the comfort of his own bed. He barely reached it before the nightmares dragged him deep into darkness and refused to let him go.

Ali thrashed in the grip of a feverish sleep peopled by thieves, monsters, artificers, and beautiful women who dissolved into smoke. Over and over, he relived the *ghul*'s attack and spent a lifetime in the grips of the djinni's cursed ones. He cried out for his father and *Ustad*

Babbage as he dreamed of brass camels and fiery dogs swimming through curtains of sand. And gold. He dreamed of gold.

Perhaps that was why Ali did not realize that while trapped in the midst of his drug-induced nightmares, he had woken to see his brother, Kassim, crouched beside his head, a large gold coin pinched between his fingers.

"Holding out on me, little brother?"

Slowly, Ali blinked, struggling to focus on the coin. He let his head roll from side to side in a semblance of a shake. His vision wavered until Kassim himself seemed to dissolve into mist. *Was he like the djinni? No.* The darkened room seemed to waver in and out. Ali blinked again, his thoughts tangled and jumbled.

"Where did you get this lovely coin, Baba Ali?" the specter of his brother whispered, his tone giving lie to the endearment. The words echoed oddly, first low, then painfully high, but Ali had not the strength to cover his ears.

In his half-sleep, he mumbled his tale as complete as he never would have awake, answering questions spoken softly in his ear even as his eyes drifted closed. He did not mention the travel diary and the other goods left to him by their father; even in his sleep, that secret overrode all impulse to speak. He did not hear as his brother slipped from the room, mumbling about preparations for a trek across the desert.

Kassim, mounted on his father's prized stallion, led a string of three camels across the Rub-Al Khali until he came to the oasis his brother had told him about. He had discounted Ali's murmurings of *djinn* and *ghul* and mechanical hawks as drug-induced imaginings, but the oasis he remembered from long ago. It was before his father had forgotten all about him in favor of Ali. He remembered how they had traveled many sweet afternoons together to discover the desert's secrets. They had never found any, but they had frequented every oasis to be found near Wadi Al-Nejd.

Now, Kassim hurried past the palm trees and arta bushes. He skirted the spring without even dipping his hand into the cooling waters. He ignored it all to search for the stones and bush that marked the entrance to vast wealth. When he found the spot he drew himself up and ordered in a loud voice, "Open, Sesame!"

Lizards and rodents scattered through the brush at the noise. Somewhere a branch snapped, but Kassim paid no attention. He watched in awe as the dune fell away to reveal the stone outcrop he only half expected to find. His jaw dropped to his chest when the cavern opened precisely as his brother described, revealing such treasure that Kassim wished he'd brought twenty camels instead of just three. He hurried inside with his beasts, stopping only to utter the words to close the cavern before turning toward the wealth displayed before him. His eyes gleamed with greed as he unwound the sacks he had brought. He did not know how much Ali had carried away, but Kassim was determined to claim even more lest his brother's fortune outstrip his own. Let Ali have the diamonds. Kassim would lay claim to everything else.

He strode deeper into the cavern, cataloging the goods with an avaricious eye.

"*You* do not belong here, foolish Ins," a woman's voice spoke softly at his back.

Kassim spun and searched for the speaker. He scowled at finding no one in sight. "Show yourself, woman. I'll have no games with you."

Silence met his demand.

"Did Ali send you? Tell you to frighten me?" he scoffed. "My brother wastes your time and mine. Show yourself."

"You do not belong," she repeated. "It is worth your life to be found here. You must be gone. For his sake, I will warn you, touch nothing, or you summon misfortune."

"Warn as you like," Kassim said as he continued to search the shadows for her. "I will have my piece of this." He gestured widely around him, nearly spinning in a circle. "You will not bar me from it."

"As you wish, but you have been warned."

Kassim laughed, coming to a realization. "You cannot stop me, can you?" The woman could continue to hide for all he cared, the treasure was what was important. He made a rude gesture to the whole cavern, still not certain where the woman who challenged him hid. Impatient with the interruption, he turned back to his perusal, noting the choicest goods that he might take away. Ignoring the spices and the tea, even the silks, he reached for the best of the treasures only to find he could not budge them. No matter how he tugged or strained, the riches remained where they lay. He screamed in frustration.

"Is this your doing, woman?"

The light dimmed in response and the chamber took on a sulfurous scent. Kassim snapped his jaw closed on any further comment. It seemed his brother's ramblings about magical things were not to be disregarded. Snarling, he turned instead to the lesser jars full of more common gems and, upon discovering that they could be removed, dumped their contents into his sacks. Though they were not the finest in the cavern, Malakeh would be pleased with the quality. She was a shrewd woman with a keen eye for trade. He then did the same for the gold and silver, but ignored the copper, continuing on until all three camels strained under their burdens. There were other things he longed to take…gem-encrusted chalices, gold platters, and — Allah, be praised! — a regal throne that would have kept him in luxury until the Last of Days, but he suspected they too would thwart him. Sighing over all that remained, Kassim vowed to return. He then stepped in the proper place before the rock that marked the way out. So pleased was he with this day's efforts that he crossed his arms and swelled his chest before saying in his most commanding voice, "Open, Saffron."

He stood and waited for the way to open, but nothing happened.

"Open…Saffron!" he repeated, anger sending a rumble through his words. Still nothing, except that the light in the chamber took on a red tinge. Kassim sifted his memories searching for a clue to what he had done wrong. Frantically, he tried other words, the rumble in his voice becoming a quaver. The only result was a deepening of the crimson glow which left the cave appearing as if bathed in blood.

Kassim opened his mouth to try again when hisses and bangs and the grinding of rock upon rock filled the chamber. Fear filled his limbs until his body trembled, knowing that no words from him had commanded the opening of the cavern. As the rock face slid into the earth, he dropped to his knees. The thieves rushed into the cavern, weapons aloft, and seized him.

"Allah's blessings, a visitor," the leader said, his voice soft, almost genial, as it filtered through the folds of his chafiye. His gaze slowly traveled from Kassim to the over-laden camels. He leaned forward in the saddle, the leather creaking.

Kassim shook on his knees, head bowed, not daring to look up. "*Hadji*, forgive me, I had no idea this was not a treasure long-forgotten."

The lead thief dismounted and casually walked over, his boots sounding dully on the stone of the cavern floor. He stood over Kassim. "Oh…but it is, and we wish it to remain so." He laughed, unwinding his scarf to show a face that had seen more than mortal men should.

Kassim's lip trembled and tears scored his cheeks as the thief revealed his face. Too late, he squeezed his eyes shut. "Mercy, I beg you, have mercy!"

"Honor requires retribution…you dared to come into my cavern… to take my hard-won treasure…"

At that some of the men laughed. It wasn't a pretty sound. Kassim's gut clenched. The two thieves holding him tightened their grip as he hung pitifully between them.

"Look at those bags!" Their leader patted them until they clinked in the silence. "This is enough wealth for any ten men to enjoy for a lifetime." At that he *tsk*ed and shook his head, an expression of sorrow on his face that did not translate to his eyes. "Allah does not condone greed."

Kassim started to sputter excuses. Tears fell faster from his eyes, rolling down his cheeks to drip from his beard. His gaze followed as the leader turned slowly, addressing the semicircle of thieves, "Tell me, men, how are thieves punished?"

"Take his hands!" echoed around the chamber.

The leader circled Kassim, who struggled weakly, frantic at being so helpless. His tormentor pulled out a sharp blade that glinted in the light of the cave. "Your hands, brother? Perhaps one finger at a time?"

The band of thieves rallied to the suggestion, calling out jeers or ideas of their own. Several raised arms that ended in stumps or hands shy of the proper digits.

Kassim cringed and turned his eyes away from the sight, only to flinch as the blade tapped against his face, bringing his gaze back. The odor of urine joined that of frantic sweat. "Or your eyes for daring to look upon and covet things that are not yours? We could take your tongue for daring to speak magical words that do not belong on a commoner's lips such as yours? Or maybe I should make you eat all the gemstones and gold you have taken until your stomach bursts and spews forth gold coins like offal…"

All Kassim could manage was a wordless moan, wrenching and tortured.

The leader moved in close, his face inches from Kassim's, pinning him with a hard, flat gaze that held a subtle glow. "Give me the box and you might be spared this torture, perhaps even granted a merciful death."

"Box?" Kassim blinked in confusion. "What box?"

A flash of light on steel caused him to flinch, then yell as a thin crease opened in his cheek beneath the sharpened dagger blade. The cut burned as blood crawled toward his neck until the itch of it woke a twitch in his jaw. The blood mingled freely with his tears.

"It is such a small thing I ask." The leader said coaxingly. Then his gaze narrowed. "Or is it that you have a partner hiding away with the box?"

Kassim could do no more than shake his head.

"Fled with it, then?"

When the thief raised the dagger yet again, Kassim quailed. Frantic, he opened his mouth to speak of Ali. It was *his* fault Kassim was here. He'd known of the cave, after all. Surely, if anyone knew of this box the man sought, it was Ali. Before Kassim could speak the words the woman's voice sounded in his thoughts, low and even, and more foreboding than even the knife-wielder's.

"*You will* not *betray him,*" she threatened softly, like the warning before the earth shakes. "*You will remain silent on this or I will end you in a death for which there is no sufficient word to describe the pain.*"

Kassim felt the truth of her words in the depths of his soul. His knees gave out and he slumped against the grip of those restraining him realizing that only death would free him now.

"We will find it," the leader said, intensity vibrating through words that rose in volume with each one. "Before your death or after."

Though Kassim stammered a response, he blubbered so much as to render the words incomprehensible, even to himself. Not that the leader appeared interested in anything Kassim attempted to say. By his brutal expression, only screams would satisfy his outrage. "Tell me your name, little man, that I may know who I have the pleasure of killing."

Kassim squeezed his eyes shut and clenched his jaw until his teeth hurt, but no words left his lips.

"You choose pain? Let us not disappoint you," the leader said, his expression florid. "Thwart me as you will, I need no name to make of you an example against any others daring to take what is not theirs." At that, the leader's gaze circled the room. The thieves' jeers fell silent, replaced for quite some time by Kassim's screams. And whether due to the djinni's threat or through some last vestige of familial loyalty, only the Almighty would know, Kassim never spoke Ali's name to his tormentors, hiding it away, deep in his heart, until his last breath left him.

Chapter Twelve

Most of the caravan spoke no English. Babbage was less disturbed by this than he might have been if he were more of a social creature. He kept his camel close to Behnam out of convenience and otherwise endured the desert in silent contemplation.

Once Babbage ensured Ali's safety, he swore by the lad's god or anyone else's that he would never again leave England's temperate clime. His head ached with the pounding of the sun and his skin had long ago gone red and tender. Would have blistered even, had not Behnam lent him a salve to soothe the burn and given him a cloth like Ali's to wrap his head.

Around him Babbage noticed the men's conversation had increased and taken on a more energetic note. He shielded his eyes and peered ahead where most of their gazes seemed to dart.

"Behnam, is it real this time?"

The caravan leader laughed and patted Babbage's shoulder good-naturedly. "Ay, *Ajnabi.* That is Wadi Al-Nejd. Your pilgrimage is ended."

Babbage had no idea what the man had called him, and frankly he didn't care, though he expected it was not flattering. He released a shuddering breath, relieved to be

done—for now—with the desert and sand and bloody mirages that had tormented him for six weeks with the false promise that civilization lay in sight. "Get me there swiftly, my friend, and I will buy the tea and sweets."

Again Behnam laughed, but the camels moved no faster than their steady, plodding pace.

Day passed into night and day again. Ali did not stir, so profound was the torpor from the drug, trapping him in a slumber that eventually left no room for even dreams. On the dawn of third day he woke, his throat as dry as dust and lips cracked and bleeding. *What happened?* No matter how he tried, he could not clear his head. He sipped from the water by his bed. The tepid liquid soothed him. He lay back down and drifted in an uneasy doze until, in the dark of night, there came a frantic pounding on his door.

Startled awake, for a moment Ali could not breathe. *Had the thieves found him? Were they at his door, their* khanjars *drawn and death gleaming in their eyes?* Fragments from his earlier dreams fluttered across his thoughts causing sweat to bead his brow. He raised a silent plea to the Almighty.

And then he laughed. The pounding increased and he laughed once more as he tumbled from his bed, staggering on weak legs to answer the door. *As if the cursed ones would bother to knock!*

Ali opened the door and sobered abruptly at the sight of his brother's wife standing at the entrance to his house, her knuckles bloodied from prolonged knocking and her face soaked with tears. She looked up at him with shame and desperation in her gaze.

"My husband...please...tell me where he is..." Her voice broke as she pleaded with him. It surprised him to see the depth of her distress. Always he had thought the marriage more of business than affection, as Malakeh came from a large merchant family known both for the quality of their goods and their advantageous connections. Now, looking into her eyes, he could not deny the love and loyalty that fueled her panic.

Ali knelt to lift her up. He led her to the privacy of his small courtyard and lowered her to the bench outside his workshop. Malakeh clung to him as he sat beside her, sobbing into his shoulder as she admitted what she and Kassim had done. Ali raised his arm to comfort her, glad that she could not see his face. He should be angry, but he had too much fear in his heart to allow room for it. Faint memories surfaced of what he had thought were dreams. His brother crouched by his bed holding a gold coin. Ali telling Kassim of his adventures and of the cavern.

"He left more than two days ago with three of our camels," she admitted. "I have not seen him since. I am frightened, brother. Tonight I dreamt of blood on his bed."

"Allah, preserve us."

His sister-in-law stilled and drew away as the words slipped from Ali's lips.

"What? What do you know?"

"Shhh..." Ali murmured. "Go home, clean yourself up and do not worry, I will bring him back."

She believed him. He saw it in her eyes. He prayed he did not disappoint her, for he feared what he would find.

"It will take me some days," he cautioned her. "And you must tell no one... *no one*. If someone asks after your husband say only that he is very sick and cannot be seen."

She nodded, worry creeping back into her gaze. He patted her arm, then set her on her feet.

"In the morning, go to the bazaar and purchase a tincture from Baba Mustafa so that none may suspect Kassim's disappearance. Allah be with you, kinswoman. Now go!"

Ali watched as she scurried home through the dark. As she disappeared, he reached a hand to his forehead, still smudged with the ashes of the djinni's latest flower. A faint tingle sparked along his finger. Not much. A mere echo of what it had been before, but perhaps enough for Ali to fly swift across the desert after his brother. Though his legs shook and he remained faint from the days of drugged stupor, he dressed in haste and drew out his special sandals. They were kinsmen and as such he would find his brother and bring him home.

Before Ali departed he slid a dagger into his sash, then fed and watered Jasmine who was particularly mulish at having been left for three days. Even so, the donkey brayed an objection and made a half-hearted attempt to bite him as he left. He ignored it. His heart burned with increasing dread as he set off.

It took him until the dawn of the second day to reach the oasis. By the time he arrived he held a deeper appreciation for the djinni's previous assistance. He circled the dunes looking for signs of entry, if any still remained. Breathing deep, he scanned the desert from horizon to horizon. He squinted at what he thought was a dust cloud heading toward Wadi Al-Nejd. His brother? The thieves? Nothing but the wind? Ali sighed and placed his life in Allah's hands.

Careful to leave no sign behind him, he made his way into the heart of the oasis. Out of habit, he plucked a blossom from a nearby plant and slid it into his pocket as he moved to the ill-fated spot between the rocks and the bush. It had been many days. Would the djinni welcome him? His heart beat fast and a frown creased his brow as he stared at the dune before him. What would he find inside? There was no way to know for certain, save for saying the words.

"Open," he said as his eyes squeezed tight of their own accord, "Sesame."

He waited for the reverberation to stop as the earth swallowed the stone, then took one hesitant step forward, followed by another, his eyes still shut. He drew a shaky breath, trying to taste what flavored the air, beside the oasis and the desert beyond. He smelled the perfumes and the teas. He smelled the arta blossoms and a hint of sulfur. If he turned to his right, he caught the heavy aroma of oil such as he used to lubricate his constructs. But that was not all. Those smells he knew from before. There was a scent that nearly made him turn away. Piss…and something else. Something both sweet and foul. Something sharp and earthy, just edging to decay.

Ali continued to walk forward with careful steps until he felt hard stone beneath his feet.

He opened his eyes and snapped them shut once more, but it was too late. The image would be his until Death took him. Just inside, Kassim's body, cut into four pieces, hung from the great brass pipes in the cavern—two on the left, and two on the right.

A sound came to Ali's ears as he dropped to his knees. Great, gulping sobs at first, trailing off to a high keen. It took a moment to realize the cries came from him. As the sun climbed the sky and the flies buzzed in, Ali knelt there, once again locked in grief…and guilt. He could do nothing else, so great was his remorse at having set his brother, the last of his family, upon this course.

"Seek you his fate, Child of Adam?"

Ali scrambled to his feet and turned toward the djinni's voice. She watched him from her glass prison, having formed a face, but no body to carry it. Anguish smothered all gentler feelings within him.

"Did you do this?" he hissed. He pointed at where his brother's body hung in quarters from the latticework of pipes.

The mist surrounding her deepened to violet.

"Foolish *child*, I am djinni, created from smokeless fire by the All-Merciful Himself! I have no need for *khanjars* and knives to claim the end of one such as you. The cursed ones found your brother and served him thus." The hurt in her tone added to Ali's shame.

"What happened?" he asked in a heavy whisper.

The djinni remained silent a long moment, then it was as if the whole cavern sighed.

"He took of the treasure," she murmured, "and he forgot the words."

Ali nodded, unsurprised, then bowed deeply.

"I beg your forgiveness, gracious lady," he murmured.

"It has been many days since you last came." The djinni's voice held no censure, only sadness.

His voice softened even more. "For that too, I beg your forgiveness."

The violet mist rotated slowly in the glass, but did not change color, nor did the djinni appear.

Ali turned away and without another word sought a method to lower his brother's remains, refusing to leave Kassim, even knowing his actions would betray him to the thieves.

Ali crawled over the mounds of treasure until he could reach a length of metal pipe. Carefully testing it against his weight, he climbed. The pipes creaked and groaned, but did not give, as he neared the first quarter of Kassim's body. Wrapping one arm and both legs through the pipes, Ali drew his dagger and sawed at the rope, wincing as the slab fell. Closing his eyes, he said a prayer, then opened them to move on until he'd cut all of his brother down.

Tears slowly dried on Ali's face as he returned to the ground. A search of the cavern revealed a large canvas sack full of glass baubles banded in leather with cork stoppers at one end. Ali dumped it over and shook them all out, finding the smallest bit of satisfaction as most of them smashed. When the sack lay empty, he carefully placed his brother inside and bound the bundle closed tight. Then, numb with grief, he moved to the camelids, which still stood in formation.

"Which is the lead construct?"

"The camelid on the left, with a one scribed into its forehead."

Without another word, Ali tugged the camelid's tail. Once it folded itself down he hefted the sack containing his brother onto the construct's back; he then found the catch keeping the chassis secure and opened it. When he checked the boiler he found that water filled the tank and the embers inside the firebox still glowed. He blew upon them until they kindled and flared, then fed the fire with tar from the barrel he noted on his first visit to the cave. He tugged the tail again and the camelid rose. Then Ali grimaced at the cloudy memory of his own drugged babbling. He bore the guilt of this. Forcing the dark thoughts away, he followed the djinni's previous instructions, marveling as the beast came to life as she had described and began a steady pace forward.

Ali scrambled out of the way. "How do I stop it?!"

"Press down upon its nose," she answered. "When you wish to start it forward, do so again…and ensure you do not stand in its path."

Ali did as she instructed. Without another word, he led the construct toward the mouth of the cave.

"If you take the machine, they will find you."

Ali stopped, but did not turn. "It cannot be helped. I am taking my brother home." *But…might there be another way?* he wondered, remembering the scraps of metal in the back of the cave.

"Do they bother to mark their scraps and mechanical leavings as they do their treasure? Do they care as to the tools and materials?" Ali asked the djinni. His artificer's mind already rushed ahead, planning before she'd even answered 'no'.

Surely he could find enough functioning parts there to construct his own transport in short order. He had some experience working on self-propelled carriages from his time abroad. The thieves would still know he had been here, but perhaps they would find it harder to track him. Maneuvering the camelid back into place, Ali picked through the scrap pile until he had salvaged enough parts. Taking up the dusty tools left out on the workbench, he constructed a rough sledge consisting of several panels of bronze sheet metal affixed to belted runners that stretched from back to front on each side, similar to the pulley system that operated the cavern opening, only of linked iron plates gripped all along their length by large-toothed, steel gears. A boiler—cobbled together from three defunct units—powered a steam engine that rotated the gear shafts, thus walking the belt forward to propel the sledge. Although rough, it reminded him of some of the transports he had seen during his three years in England. He was not certain it would operate in the loose sands of the desert, and he was not certain it would carry both Kassim's remains and himself, but Ali was prepared to try and if he had to walk all the way to Wadi Al-Nejd, then he would do so, as long as he brought his brother with him. Once he had the transport complete he wrestled the sack down into place, then glanced toward the glass pipes framing the entrance.

Heartache wrapped itself around his chest and his shoulders drooped even further. "I will not return."

"No," the djinni whispered as if she expected his words. Then, her voice intent, she continued, "Free me…that I may aid you. I can speed your way and hide your passage from sight."

Despite their many nights of unspoken courtship, Ali experienced a qualm. Countless were the tales of djinn that could not be trusted. Countless were the tales of their anger and vengeance. Few spoke of a djinni volunteering aid. Or holding tender affections for a mortal, no matter how he wished it. True, she offered an exchange for freedom, but how was Ali to know if the good will would last?

He hesitated and then cursed himself for thrice a fool. His mind might be fearful, but his heart had no doubt.

"Tell me," he said, "how to make this so."

"I am trapped by a spell on the glass. It freezes at my touch and the cold burns me. The glass is enchanted such that it can never break."

Ali frowned. "Then how can I help you?"

"If you remove this brass fitting," she answered, floating up to the joint in question, "you will discover the gap by which they ensnared me. Find a sound vessel among those you dumped to the ground and press it to the glass, opening to opening. Once I am inside you must stop the hole quickly, lest Rassul summon me away. Within the bauble, my magic will be unbound."

Ali nodded, his expression stark as he moved to the pile of half-shattered baubles and sifted through until he found one perfect globe the size of his fist. He remained silent as he moved to the glass pipes. First he unstopped the vessel and nestled it carefully among the tools, then he struggled to remove the brass fitting that sealed the djinni's prison. All the while, she swirled and billowed within the pipe in an ever-changing mist, pulsing through every shade of purple from the palest to the deepest dark. The shifting colors dazzled Ali's vision.

Overwrought, he snapped. "Cease this! Let me complete the task." In silence, the djinni settled in a near colorless vapor at the base of the tube.

Sighing, Ali brought the globe into place, then loosened the brass fitting, allowing it to clatter to the stones at his feet as he pressed opening to opening. The djinni lingered below, hesitant, until Ali sighed again and murmured, "I beg you, please forgive me."

The djinni's smoke billowed and surged into the new vessel, a thin tendril snaking around to caress his hand before withdrawing. As the last wisp entered the glass globe the djinni spoke.

"Now," she instructed in subdued tones. "Close it, quickly."

Ali did as she bade, then pressed his forehead to the globe before wrapping it in soft cloth and stowing the bundle in the leather pouch. He paused again, his gaze sweeping the cave. Allah, forgive him, but vengeance filled his heart.

As if sensing his most secret thoughts the djinni spoke, "This treasure is as cursed as the hearts of those who stole it; let its taint neither press your palm nor darken your spirit."

"They deserve to lose what *they* care most for…"

"Don't be foolish, Child of Adam, you deprive them of more than mere wealth this day."

Thinking on her words, Ali realized that while a geas protected the shah's treasure the ill-gotten gains the thieves had stored up would fall to whoever found them. That would serve for now as justice, until Ali could find the means to bring down the cursed ones and avenge the deaths of his family members. He nodded abruptly at her wisdom, though he did, in defiance, retain the tools.

The djinni did not comment.

Ali sat cross-legged on the sledge and pulled the sack that contained Kassim's remains firmly into his lap. He then reached for the lever that worked the engine and set it in gear. The sledge rolled from the cavern. Using a second lever to halt one track while the other still turned, he maneuvered around the lush growth. Ali looked back and grimaced at the thick trail they left in the sand, but even as he watched tendrils of the djinni's vapor swept the signs away.

"Thank you." Ali swallowed hard and resisted the urge to dart his gaze from horizon to horizon seeking thieves across every dune. "Can you ensure no one sees us?"

"No eyes shall see even our dust on the wind," the djinni answered calmly as they rode across the sands. Ali wondered at the strain in her voice, but spied nothing that might be wrong. From time to time a shadow trailed their progress and the falcon's now-familiar cry sounded overhead. It comforted Ali's soul that the other djinni watched over them yet the pouch at his side shuddered at the sound of Shanin's cry.

Even so, Ali muttered fervent prayers to the Almighty that did not end until his brother's home came into sight. Despite the late hour, Malakeh stood in the center of the courtyard beside a single lit brazier. Behind her, the household lay in darkness. At the tears glistening in her eyes, guilt and sorrow weighed Ali's gut much heavier than the burden of his brother's body. He directed the sledge forward.

"Welcome to my brother's home, monument to his wealth." Ali's words were bitter as he brought the sledge to a halt before his brother's widow.

Malakeh stumbled back against the wall of the house, her cry strangled as they suddenly appeared before her. On recognizing Ali she rushed forward, a scowl upon her face.

"You know my husband has forbidden you to bring your infernal machines—" she started to chastise him, her lip curled in distaste, only to stop abruptly when her eyes dropped to the bundles in his arms.

Ali lowered his gaze as he came to his feet. "I am sorry, honored sister," he said out of respect. "I wished to say that I have returned Kassim to you, only his spirit now walks Death's Garden."

Malakeh slid to the ground, the sledge forgotten. Tears fell from her eyes to soak the dusty earth. Ali grimaced when she tore at her hair and beat her breast. But when she began a piercing keen that threatened to wake the household and even the neighbors, he went to her and lifted her to her feet, his hand pressing over her lips.

"No. You cannot mourn. Not yet. First we must hide the true manner of Kassim's passing, lest those who killed him come upon us."

Malakeh's eyes went wide. Ali removed his hand.

"I have done as you bid," she whispered. "Each day since you left I went to the bazaar and purchased tinctures and healing potions for Kassim, telling all that my husband is abed with fever."

"You have done well. Tomorrow you must go and purchase more medicine and let none suspect Kassim has no more need of them."

His brother's wife blanched. "But…he must be buried! You must honor your brother's spirit…his remains!" She pounded Ali's chest with her tight-held fists. "I will not let you dishonor him!"

Ali caught her wrists and stilled her. "Do not let grief overwhelm you. You will do as I say. Were you to fetch your mourning cloths and oils for the anointing all would know Kassim has succumbed to his 'illness' —"

"As it should be," she spat, something of her usual disdain returning.

"No! *Not* as it should be. The moment word spreads of Kassim's death it might come to the ears of those responsible for this crime. Such knowledge might well bring them to *your* threshold."

"Good," she said. "I would have them brought to justice."

Ali's heart longed to agree, but his wiser self shook his head at her short-sightedness. "And how would this be so? They would know of your misfortune, but you would yet be ignorant of the blood on their hands. Would you place this household…*yourself* at risk of their further vengeance?"

If he'd thought she had gone pale before it was nothing compared to her response to his warning. Malakeh's eyes widened and her arms trembled in his grip.

He shook her. "Do you understand?"

Malakeh nodded, fear in her gaze.

"Then return to your bed, my brother's wife, I will see to him."

With no more words, and no more tears, Malakeh retreated inside.

Weary beyond imagining, Ali sighed, his eyes aching with unshed tears. Despite his brother's ill-fated treachery toward him, Kassim held a place in his heart.

"Djinni?" Ali called out, sounding lost even to his own ears.

"No one shall disturb you," she said, her voice kind.

As she spoke a tight net of sparkling dust rose to span the courtyard. Another settled over the sack containing Kassim's remains, cloaking it and the sledge from outside view.

"Not even time shall disturb your brother's remains as long as my magic shrouds the body."

Ali smothered his own sob. "I thank you."

With that he carried his brother's body into the house, as tenderly as he would a child.

Though he ached for rest, Ali could not close his eyes without reliving the moment he discovered his brother's fate. He now stood responsible for Kassim's household, from the least servant to his wife. Ali rolled over in the bed, it was soft and luxurious, a rightful testament to his brother's wealth, but Ali's discomfort was of the spirit, rather than the body. He threw an arm over his eyes, and yet his thoughts continued to plague him. There was no affection between him and his brother's wife. He would honor his responsibility as required by tradition, but Malakeh would have to content herself with being a widow, for Ali would never make her his bride.

Shuddering at the thought, he got up. Cradling the djinni's globe, he climbed to the roof of his brother's house to find comfort beneath the stars. He lay, hand idly stroking the glass. "What am I to do?" he mused half to himself. "I must honor my brother's memory and protect the household. I must safeguard the treasure. I must, as an apprentice tinker also provide for my own household and future family." Ali gritted his teeth. "I must find justice for my kin."

"Were you not gifted by both your father and the Almighty?" the djinni spoke softly in reply, "Skilled hands, and a kind heart. Of such are heroes of legend made."

Ali nodded. "Such are characters in children's tales."

"Like djinn?" she challenged, not unkindly.

Ali felt a smile at his lips and resolved to face this challenge. He thought back to his time in England. His mind had always worked best on recalcitrant problems when his hands worked on more tangible materials. Perhaps if he retired to his workshop his thoughts would settle enough to uncover a solution. But dare he leave his brother's household with no one to watch over it?

As if summoned by his musings a bell-like cry sounded overhead. Ali peered upward.

"*Go, young Ins,*" the falcon-bound djinni spoke as if directly into Ali's ear, though the clockwork bird continued to fly high above. "I will watch over your household that you might prepare yourself for the challenges to come."

He watched the clockwork falcon dip and circle above, dawn's light glinting off brass pinfeathers. And then Ali knew what he would do with his hands while thoughts chased themselves about his head. His shop waited, filled as it never had been before with the finest of supplies. Already Ali could envision the design he would make: a body to house the djinni. A vessel of beauty and grace, articulated enough to grant her the freedom of the world, while yet sheltering her from the foul sorcerer who would control her.

Ali sat up, sending quiet thanks skyward to the clockwork falcon. He then raised his djinni's globe to his eyes and gazed within. The mists swirled with jagged sparks shooting through it. "Djinni, what is wrong?"

The mist grew heavy and sullen as again the falcon cried. Ali took this as confirmation of what he already suspected.

"Shahin is the one you spoke of, is he not? Your brother…"

"Yes," she answered softly, shocking him that she answered at all as her mist had drawn in on itself until it resembled a dense thundercloud. "Though I knew him by another name when we shared guardianship of the cavern."

She drew herself tighter yet until she was no more than a small, black marble in the center of the globe and Ali realized she would say no more.

He stroked the globe as if to comfort her and then thought back to his intentions and realized his plans might comfort her spirit. "Allah, grant me the skill, but come…" he told her, as if she'd any choice. "While my mind ponders what action to take, I will build for you a body. Neither task will be quick, but I am determined."

The mist in the globe brightened like a star flaring in the sky. Though she remained contained, Ali felt the caress of her pleasure and delight.

"I oft assisted my master with his constructs," she told him.

Laughing, Ali cradled the globe to his chest and descended into the household. After instructing a servant to fetch him at his shop should they have need of him Ali hurried to his home.

Chapter Thirteen

HOOFBEATS PUNISHED THE DESERT WITH A FIERCE POUNDING as the thieves rode up to their lair. Rassul led the throng, his face twisted and harsh, eyes bright with the rage burning in his breast. From clear across the Rub-Al Khali his magic warned him the djinni had been freed. He had not wanted to believe it possible, but now, as their steeds trampled the oasis, he could not deny the cavern lay open. But was the treasure within unguarded?

He galloped right through the entrance and spun his mare around until it reared, its hooves striking sparks on the stone as it came down. Clear, empty glass taunted Rassul. He dismounted. Chanting harsh, guttural words none of his men understood, he attempted to summon the djinni. Though the ring on his finger glowed ember-bright, and Rassul sensed a draw upon his magic, she did not appear.

The cavern echoed with his fury as the sensation faded. He cursed until every one of his men cowered. Without control of the djinni or one who shared the blood of the old guardian, the mechanism that secured the cavern would not open once closed. It was part of the spell that safeguarded the treasure. Until control was restored, one of them would have to stay in the cavern at all times.

Spinning again, he raked his gaze over the cave, noting first the crunch of glass beneath his prancing steed, and then, looking up, he bellowed loud enough to rival Ibliss, the Evil One at the Day of Judgment.

Wheeling to confront his lieutenant, he pointed at the severed rope still dangling above.

"You *will* find the one responsible."

Then, moving to the workbench, the leader narrowed his gaze, noting the old guardian's tools were gone. Uttering a curse, he rummaged underneath the bench where all manner of clockwork contraptions gathered dust.

Rassul grabbed a little mechanical pigeon from the tangle. The clockwork messenger resembled those from his time at the Persian Court, only those had been in the form of fanciful songbirds with vibrant plumage. This one held a glimmer of magic at its core. Once the key in its back was wound tight it would fly back to this cavern no matter the distance it had been carried. At its belly was a thin tube that held a scrap of paper upon which to scribe a note.

"When you have found him, send a message by this bird that we might deal with our intruder. I would speak with him before we make of him a more permanent example."

The thief held the pigeon in his hands as if it might break.

"Find me the one responsible, Juyan," Rassul ordered in low, rumbling tones, his gaze flat and deadly as a viper's, "or suffer the death due him!"

The thief paled and headed immediately for Wadi Al-Nejd.

Once inside his shop, Ali placed the djinni's globe in a safe place on his workbench, then drew the shutters over the windows. After lighting the lantern, he laid out all the supplies he had purchased with the djinni's coin, assessing the resources available for this new creation. He then took a charcoal stick to a piece of parchment and sketched the skeletal infrastructure, refining the design based on the Langstroms' clockwork doll with elements inspired by the falcon's near seamless motions. He then diagramed the support elements, a pump to run the hydraulics coursing through the framework and bellows in the place of lungs, to cool the boiler.

Beside this foundation he drew a fanciful outer form that closely matched the djinni's appearance when she wore a body. He noted the materials he would use for each element, from sturdy brass and copper for the inner workings to tiny flecks of gold leaf for her nails. Smiling as he scribed the final line, Ali set down his stick and turned to take up his tools. His hand hesitated over those he'd bought himself before drawing away and dipping into the pouch he had taken from the thieves' cavern. He laid those tools out one by one upon his workbench and put the others away.

"My master's tools." The djinni's voice held a mix of delight and longing.

Her emotions seemed to shiver down Ali's spine. Yet he merely said, "My *grandfather's* tools. They were wasted where they were. I shall put them to the best use."

She did not argue or scold.

Ali started by assembling a framework of rods and pistons, pulleys and gears, with his small copper boiler and its tempered glass reservoir at the heart of it all. All the while, his thoughts roamed, wearing away at the other issues weighing on his mind. *How will I protect the household? How will I depose the band of thieves? How do I hold fast to the dreams of my heart, against the onslaught of these new responsibilities?* Ali expelled a hard sigh and shunted that last, selfish thought to the back of his mind.

The tinkering went faster than his problem-solving, with the djinni's will acting as a second set of hands and her magic replacing his small forge. Where he had need, she heated the sheets of metal until they glowed that Ali might shape them. When he asked, she fused joins in the metal skin as if the two surfaces were always one, with nary a seam visible, until a lithesome form stood near complete before them. The only time Ali's efforts slowed was when the djinni insisted he pause for a meal of tea and saffron rice sprinkled with cashews and raisins, which she had summoned. But now…now they were done. The construction, anyway.

As Ali's eyes roamed over the clockwork form at least one solution to his ponderings came to mind. If his brother's body were but whole perhaps they could fool all into believing Kassim had newly passed, which would divert the thieves attention should they somehow learn of his death.

Content to have at least the start of a solution, Ali stepped back, his face dark with stubble, his skin covered in grease, and allowed himself to stare in wonder at what he and the djinni had wrought. Before them stood the most amazing construct he had ever built. Its pale copper skin burnished satin smooth and flawless, fused with a light dusting of crushed rubies across its cheeks and lips. Its silky hair of bronze wire so fine and supple Ali's breath swayed it. The limbs were graceful, the features delicate and beautiful. Only those blank, glass eyes betrayed its engineered nature. Ali released a weighty breath. He wanted perfection for his djinni and mere glass marbles would not do.

And then he remembered his inheritance.

Moving to the corner of his workshop, he pried out one of the cobbles that made up the floor. Beneath it, nestled in the hard-packed earth was the puzzle box. Drawing it out, Ali carried it to his workbench and worked the pattern to unlock the puzzle. Breathing deep, he uttered the words, wincing as the hidden pins once more pricked his skin, then watched the box unfold to reveal the pouch containing the two gems nestled inside. He drew it from the box and shook the contents into his palm, matching black diamonds the size of plump, round dates. At any time he could have sold these and had ten times his brother's wealth, but as signs of his father's love, they had meant more to him than coin and comfort. Looking from the gems to the djinni's near-complete body Ali could think of no better purpose for them. Unhinging the jaw, he reached inside and extracted the glass marbles, then carefully slipped the diamonds into their place.

"Please," he said to the djinni, "just a touch of heat to mold the holding rings." Through his leather glove he felt the metal soften and swiftly shaped the rings to hold the gems firmly. The jaw moved back into place and the construct stood, near perfect, but still not quite.

"It is done!" Ali clasped the small glass globe tightly and gazed into its depths, "Djinni?"

The mist darkened to almost black, "I am afraid."

Ali smoothed a hand over the glass. "I was told once, that djinni were made from smokeless fire, by the All-Merciful Himself. I should think one such as that would fear nothing."

"What Allah has fated, let none question." Her melodious voice trembled only slightly as she murmured the old adage. "Release the stopper, Ali."

He drew off his gloves to manage the delicate task. The plug popped free in his grip, as if the djinni assisted from within, and Ali quickly moved the globe near to the boiler valve. The dark mists swept from the glass ball and into the clockwork woman. For the barest of moments the construct seemed less machine and more…alive. Then suddenly a tendril of mist seeped back out from the valve like steam. Ali felt the djinni's panic as she cursed in her own tongue. The vapor stretched and thickened into a defined line, more drawing out as Ali watched, confused.

"Rassul summons me!" the djinni called out, the words high and tight, as if she struggled to speak. Her fear pierced Ali's heart like shards of glass. He reached for the mist and it clung to his hand, only to be sucked away.

"Quick, you must seal the chamber!"

"But you are not all within," he said.

"I am more than a puff of smoke. The essence will fade, but I will not."

At her reassurance, Ali reached for the valve only to hiss and snatch his hand away, his skin burned near to blistering. Grabbing a rag he tried again, though his hand throbbed.

Ali twisted the valve closed and held his breath until the dark diamond eyes kindled with an inner flame. Relieved, he laughed and hugged her body close, amazed at how soft the metal felt, and warm. He could barely distinguish the construct from flesh.

The djinni gripped his arms as awe unaccountably transformed her features. "Ali?"

He stepped back and closed his eyes, feeling shame at his lack of propriety.

Without looking, Ali reached out his arm to the workbench where a neat pile of clothes waited. He handed her the embroidered linen tunic dress that had belonged to his mother, then a rusari to cover her hair.

Ali turned away as she put them on over her perfect form. He felt the beginning of physical stirrings. He flinched as her hand came to rest on his arm but laid his own overtop before she could draw away. Opening his eyes, he turned and smiled at her in wonder. She appeared of flesh. It was only as she touched him that her metal nature came evident. In some ways, she was more real to him than ever in this moment. In others, she was yet a dream. His heart ached to ask the question gone unanswered for so long. "Gracious lady, I would ask… please…your name?"

The face he had crafted for beauty reflected sorrow. "None…"

He beseeched her with his gaze. "Your name?"

She lowered her eyes and fisted her new hands tight. "Hami," she whispered, bitterness thick on her lips. "*Protector*. Only I failed and my master is dead for it. I will no longer lay claim to this name."

Ali doubted that his grandfather would have held blame against her, but he did not point this out. Instead, he indulged himself aloud as he had only done silently before, calling her by the name he used for her in his deepest, most private thoughts.

"Then gracious lady, with your permission, I would call you *Morgiana*," Ali said.

Her head tilted slightly to the side as she lifted her gaze. "Morgiana?"

"It means 'great queen'…a name of power and strength…and beauty," Ali told her as he spread salve on his hand.

She nodded. "It is a good name," the djinni…*Morgiana* said decisively.

She turned a little too swiftly and caught herself against the counter, not yet used to her new body. She gazed at her hands, the nails small and perfect. She ran her fingers through her hair, long and lustrous. "It has been so many years, decades…since I have truly assumed a physical form." The joy glimmering in her gaze outshone any she had exhibited before.

Ali looked upon the beautiful woman in front of him and felt affection swell within his heart. It didn't matter that the body was built and not born. It didn't matter that the soul within it was Djinn rather than Ins. All he knew was that no other had understood him so well.

Morgiana raised a hand to his cheek, daring to touch him. "I haven't touched another since…" Her eyes misted. Water and oil, but still tears, "Thanks be to God."

Ali reached into his pocket for a kerchief and encountered something soft. "Ah…I have something for you," Ali said with a smile as he pulled out a pink kudu and gently pressed the flower into her palm. The tears fell faster, but now Morgiana smiled, revealing delicate, mother-of-pearl teeth.

He looked upon her with wonder, her beauty bringing him both joy and consternation. As his reaction of moments ago proved to him, they must proceed with great caution or bring censure down upon them both. Unless one looked very closely indeed, it was nigh impossible to tell her body was constructed. If he were to bring her into his household there would be talk, or worse. When he explained this, Morgiana nodded slowly and considered him a moment before speaking.

"Would any comment if I were to serve in your household?"

Ali shook his head but still pressed his lips in concern. "You have no husband or home of your own. Even as a servant, there would be talk were you to make your home beneath my roof."

Again Morgiana nodded, her expression remaining serene. "And if I were to stay here?" she asked, gesturing toward his modest home. "When you have moved on to your brother's house?"

Ali smiled broadly, relief settling in his belly. "You are both wise and clever, Morgiana. This would be acceptable, granting that the two of us are never here alone together."

"Then this we will do," she said with an answering smile, one of the rare few he had seen.

Content, they returned to his brother's house to tend to Kassim's body.

Before Ali and Morgiana had even crossed the threshold Malakeh confronted them, agitation clear in her abrupt motions as she stalked toward them. "Ali, where have you been? Why have the rites not been ob…" She fell silent her face paling as her eyes went wide. For a moment Ali thought she might fall as her body swayed before going rigid.

"What is this? My husband is dead and you bring a strange woman into my home? Have you no decency?" She then turned to Morgiana, "Leave this house," she hissed, looking ready to strike the djinni. "Your presence offends me."

"Malakeh, no."

"Am I to be deposed from the household so quickly, then?" she asked.

Before Ali could refute her words, Morgiana stepped forward.

"I am djinn, good woman, what know I of households? I do not seek your place, only to serve my master and keep guard over him and all he holds dear."

Ali sighed, wishing, perhaps, that she had not been so open about her nature. He stepped between them and laid his hand on Malakeh's arm, concerned by the alarm in her gaze. "Please, I will explain all, but first allow me to see to my brother."

She jerked away, her lip drawing back. "Now you have a care for him? He has been waiting how long for the respect due him, and now you put me off to see to it? Now that you have pleased yourself?"

"Woman," Ali said, glaring at her. "I do not like what you imply. Do not try my patience in this. We will speak after."

As she stalked away, Morgiana laid her hand on his shoulder.

"I am sorry to have brought dissention to your household."

Ali could not hold back his laugh, a harsh sound tinged with sadness. "Allah forgive me, Morgiana, but you cannot bring what was already here." He sighed again. "I need to remember that Malakeh speaks from pain more than anything else. Come, let us see to my brother."

Trepidation knotted Ali's stomach as he and Morgiana entered the chamber where his brother's body lay. A faint, over-sweet scent of decay teased his nose. It had been several days since Kassim met his end, though only one since they had retrieved his remains. Death had already begun to consume the flesh before the djinni worked her magic. They could deny decay no more.

"Please, gracious lady," Ali asked in a subdued voice. "Remove your protection."

Morgiana nodded and drew away her magic.

His face set in tight, grim lines, Ali then used his dagger to cut away the sack, gasping at the odor that rose from within. Bile fought its way past his throat to bang against the back of his clenched teeth. He closed his eyes and brutally restrained his grief, glad that he had forbid Malakeh from entering the chamber.

"We cannot bury him in such a state," Ali said, his gaze going to Morgiana. "Is there nothing you can do?"

The djinni shook her head, the glow in her eyes subdued. "Magic has no power over flesh, only that which influences flesh."

Ali stepped back. "I must fetch Baba Ahmed to stitch the body whole." Amongst all the tailors of the Wadis along the edge of the Rub-Al Khali, Baba Ahmed was the most gifted. It was rumored that his skill was so great that he had stitched the wings back on the Sultan's nightingale, restoring flight to her, after she had been maimed by a hunting hound.

"But…" Morgiana said, then fell silent.

He turned to her and marveled at the subtle frown on the clockwork body she sheltered in.

"Please, go on," he told her gently.

"If you go to him, others will know. They will speak of how you first had your brother's body restored before consecrating him for burial." Her eyes met his and he felt the worry dimming her gaze. "If Rassul hears of this, he will surely know it was you that trespassed on the cavern…you who stole away the body, and… me."

Ali felt the wisdom of her words. "It must be done—" he started only to have Morgiana interrupt.

"Then allow me to fetch the tailor, master. None will know me, nor that I am of your household."

At her use of the word 'master,' Ali's frown deepened. He wished to love her, not rule her. He nodded.

"You are wise, Morgiana. And I would ask that you call me Ali. We are…friends, are we not?"

The djinni smiled, her fingers going to her mouth the feel the movement as if surprised. "Yes…Ali."

The joy he felt buoyed his spirit. Ali then told her how to find Baba Ahmed's shop, and what she should say to him. He finished by handing her first three coins from Kassim's coffers, and then a linen blindfold.

"If he wishes the coin, he must allow you to bind his eyes, else our secret will yet be revealed. He must not know which house you bring him to, or who is within." Ali instructed her.

"I shall veil my face with my *rusari* that he does not come to know my features." Morgiana added.

She bowed and did as he bid her, returning soon after, leading the tailor.

That night, Ali watched in silence as Baba Ahmed spent the hours of darkness blindfolded, sewing together the body parts of a man he could not see. Ali marveled at the tailor's skill. Clearly the rumors had been true. By the cock's first crow, Ali could scarce even see the seams where Kassim's body had been hacked asunder. When Ahmed was done, Ali handed Morgiana three more gold coins to be given to the tailor in thanks for his skills, and for his silence, then instructed her to return the man to his stall.

As there were no other male relatives, Ali alone performed the *ghusl*, the ritual bathing of his brother's body. Even within the shroud wrapped around Kassim's stitched-together corpse, Ali imagined he could see his brother's face. Fighting to remain impassive, he willed the image in his mind to reflect peace. He washed the body three times, and then wrapped it in the *kafan*, three pieces of plain cotton cloth. It was a simple, modest wrapping. When he was done he tied the open ends. In deference to his brother, Ali opened a bottle of perfumed oil he knew Kassim was fond of and allowed a few drops to scent the cloths.

Heart weighed with sorrow, Ali cleansed his hands and put away the items used for the ritual. With a final prayer over his brother's body he lowered his head respectfully and left the chamber. As he drew the door closed behind him someone softly cleared her throat. Ali looked up. Outside the chamber stood a middle-aged woman, still slender and pretty, but with a crook to her left leg.

"Paknoush, Allah's blessing upon you," he greeted the servant with a smile. The first thing he had done on assuming responsibility for the household had been to send servants in search of this woman and Old Hamza, the gardener, whom his brother had cast out. Both gladly returned , but only upon hearing Ali now ruled there. Of all that had happened in recent weeks, this brought him the most joy.

Paknoush limped forward, her head lowered respectfully.

"Yes?" Ali prompted her when she remained silent.

"Baba," she spoke in tones near too soft to hear. "Please forgive me for disturbing you, but *she* has ordered so very many things and the housekeeping coffers are near exhausted already."

Ali frowned. 'She,' no doubt, was Malakeh. His lips thinned and his expression grew tired. Paknoush touched his face, her own expression worried. Ali offered her a rueful smile, faint, but apologetic.

"It will be fine," he tried to reassure her.

She relaxed and bobbed her head. He saw understanding in her gaze. All of the household knew of the silent—and not-so-silent— battle between Ali and Malakeh. Finances were not what they should be and Ali insisted the luxuries be curtailed until solvency was restored.

His hidden gold would help, but he must use it sparingly lest it draw unwanted notice.

Malakeh regularly flouted his edict. While she enjoyed her pleasures, he knew she was not usually so wasteful. Grief had broken her judgment.

"Send the goods back and instruct the merchants that no purchases are to be accepted from this household that do not have my approval." Ali pressed his lips tight lest he speak more than he ought before the servant. "We must content ourselves with more simple fare for now."

Paknoush nodded then backed away, returning to the kitchen.

Ali spun and headed for the courtyard where his brother's widow liked to take her morning tea.

"Malakeh, you can no longer order as you wish. We have not the coin to pay for it."

"You are turning into an old man, Ali, we must find a way to relax you." Malakeh stared at him boldly, fluttering her lashes. She shifted her body in subtle suggestion.

Before he could school his reaction, Ali's discomfort caused him to step back.

He saw a flash of worry in Malakeh's eyes before they went cold and her expression reverted to the haughty sullenness to which he was accustomed. "Would you deprive me a few simple indulgences in my grief? You are the head of this household. It is your responsibility to keep me in the manner to which…"

"…we can afford!" Ali cut her off, his head aching as he dealt once more with her sense of entitlement. It could not go on. Reaching down he took her arm and drew her from her lounge, leading her through the house and into the chamber where he had been re-viewing accounts earlier. Malakeh resisted, her voice shrill as she objected his manhandling. Ali sighed and pulled her forward until she stood before the desk strewn with parchment. Two books sat open side-by-side, one the business accounts, the other the household.

"Look at them, Malakeh. You are a clever woman. Look at the decrease in business since my father's passing. Look at the expenses."

He saw some glimmer of surprise at his compliment. Even so, she glowered at him and yanked her arm away. Though she turned up her nose, as if ignoring the books, her eyes did glance at the numbers. "You will never be the man your brother was."

Without thinking, Ali answered, "Thank you." Immediately, he dropped his gaze, shamed at his response. He had not spoken ill of the dead…his very brother, no less…but had certainly implied it.

His brother's widow slapped him soundly and stalked from the room.

Ali groaned as he looked down at the tallies, noticing the household account had not even been updated for some time. He closed the books and left the chamber. Tomorrow he would mourn his brother. After that he would rebuild the household.

Perhaps in his old age there would be time again for invention.

Chapter Fourteen

Juyan trod the streets of Wadi Al-Nejd, listening at every quarter. Surely there would be word upon the lips of the people and fear in their hearts at the death the intruder had met in the oasis lair. Strangely, Juyan heard no word at all. It took him three days of subtle questions to discover a tailor who bragged of stitching together a corpse without even benefit of his sight, using such fine stitches that even his own fingertips could scarce feel the seam.

Disguising himself as a man of modest wealth, the thief entered the tailor's shop and spun him a tale of unrequited love and a challenge put forth by the woman he would marry.

"*Hadji,*" he said. "I am told that your stitching is so fine that any garment you sew is as of one solid piece of cloth…is this so?"

"You have not heard falsely of the skill of Baba Ahmed," the tailor answered, his chest swelling as his chin lifted. "Why just this week I mated four pieces of a body together as if they'd never been cleaved asunder, and this with my eyes bound shut. Imagine how much finer my work is with open eyes, stitching cloth."

Juyan let his brow furrow with uncertainty. "And how am I to know the truth of this? I must be certain, for my Priya will

not consider my suit unless I present her with a wedding garment with no seams."

The shop keeper sputtered. "Do you doubt my word, honored patron?"

With a calculated look, Juyan shrugged. "Forgive me, *Hadji*, but my heart would break to be turned away from my love. You understand I must be certain. I will pay handsomely for your service, but I am not a wealthy man and must ensure what coin I spend is not wasted. If I could but speak to those for whom you did this work…might you tell me their name that I might ask them of your great skill?"

Baba Ahmed deflated at the request. "I do not have a name…"

The thief frowned. "Then tell me, at which home did you work this wonder?"

"I cannot. My eyes were bound in this very shop and the cloth not removed until I was returned to it."

It took great effort, but Juyan restrained his impulse to strike the man down. However slight, this was his only clue to find the trespasser. Letting his expression slide into sorrowful lines, he turned, as if to leave.

"Wait!"

Pausing, the thief looked over his shoulder.

"My memory is as skilled as my fingers," the tailor said. "Bind my eyes and lead me from the shop. I am sure I know the way for I counted each step just as I count the stitches I take up in a garment."

And so Juyan bound Baba Ahmed's eyes and led him from the shop. Following the old man's guidance through the city to the merchants' district, they stopped before a fine home that spoke of great wealth. White cloth draped the gate to show the household was in mourning.

"You are certain?" he asked of the old man as he drew the blindfold away.

Baba Ahmed nodded.

Juyan handed him a coin. "Go back to your shop, old man."

"But…what about the wedding garment?" the tailor said, his words almost a whine.

A glare from the thief sent him hurrying back to his shop.

When the old man was gone from sight, Juyan marked the wall with charcoal and walked away.

Morgiana watched the two men standing before the gate of Kassim's household. She stood in the shadows of a neighbor's home, having just returned from the bazaar with foodstuffs. One of the men she recognized as the tailor. The other's face she could not see, though the way he stood echoed something familiar. For a moment the two talked, gesturing at the household of which Ali was now master, then the stranger sent the tailor on his way. When the old man left, the one remaining took chalk from his pouch and scribed a symbol beside the gate, then turned to leave.

Morgiana's grip on her basket tightened until the reeds creaked. She knew him, one of Rassul's men. Backing even further into the shadows, she tugged the edge of her *rusari* higher over her features and watched the thief walk away. Once he was gone, she stepped forward and drew upon her magic. Weaving an illusion no mortal could see through, she cloaked every gate on the street in mourning and scribed the thief's symbol on each wall, even the one that bore those signs in truth, then continued on her way to Ali's house, unsure if she should tell him now or wait until after the mourning ritual.

At dawn, four days after it had departed, the mechanical homing pigeon returned to the thieves' lair. Guards had been posted at the mouth of the open cavern. One remained at his post while the other bore the pigeon inside.

He crossed the chamber to the cache and stood before the ornate throne.

Rassul looked up from where he lounged, staring moodily into the jeweled canopy. He glanced from the guard to the ground with hooded eyes and one raised brow. The man flinched, then fidgeted before gingerly lowering himself to his knees. Rassul allowed himself the semblance of a smile as the guard shifted on the uncomfortable surface presented by the piled riches.

When the man was situated and had waited a sufficient length of time Rassul spoke.

"Read it."

The guard bobbed his head and fumbled with the bird. He extracted the scrap of paper and read a single word: "Come."

Rassul surged to his feet and called his men to assemble. As they readied their mounts and strapped on their weapons, he strode out onto the sand breathing deep of the perfumed breeze. One by one the men joined him. The greybearded thief held the reins to Rassul's mare in one hand and those of his own in the other. Rassul mounted, sitting heavily in the saddle. The mare danced under him, anxious to be off.

As the last man exited the cave, his booted steps carrying him between the pile of stones and the arta bush, the sound of grinding stone rose. Rassul spun, fury transforming his features. "Inside, you fools!" he cried, "One must remain!" But it was too late. The cave remained locked to them forever unless they secured the djinni.

Rassul kicked the mare hard. She lunged forward half-trampling the man who triggered the cavern to close. The man yelped and strove to protect his head from her sharp hooves. Rassul's dark expression didn't change as blood stained the man's *besht*. "Get up, cur. We ride for Wadi Al-Nejd."

Finally, the mourners had taken their leave and only a couple of men remained. Ali sighed with relief. Exhaustion dragged at his limbs. The *Janazah* had taken most of his energy, Kassim's loss striking him a deeper blow than he realized. Now his spirit and his brother's would never find peace between them.

"Baba Ali."

Ali turned to see Tutak Afsahani, a local tradesman, waiting respectfully behind him. The man wore a solemn expression on his lined face. Ali smiled, polite but weary. He didn't know Tutak well, but he had been a colleague of Kassim's and was well-known and respected in the community of Wadi Al-Nejd.

Tutak tugged at his white beard. "Allah's blessings upon you and I ask that we forget the trivialities of life and remember that the All-Merciful is all that prevails beyond Death."

Ali nodded at the familiar condolence still unsure as to why Afsahani had remained.

"Alas, Ali, I would speak to you of your dear brother Kassim's debt." Tutak shook his head, as if unhappy to bring up the subject. "I know that you would not wish his debts to prevent his ascent to Paradise."

Dread struck Ali like a stone. "Of course, of course. Please, Baba Tutak, tell me of this."

"I too would speak to you of Kassim's debt."

Ali turned finding another merchant waiting to speak to him. His sense of foreboding deepened. "Please, sit and refresh yourselves. We will speak over coffee and Allah grant me the ability to do what I may to ease my brother's path."

Rassul paced in a secluded alley not far from the merchants' quarter of Wadi Al-Nejd. Each time he pivoted, his eyes blazed as he looked down on the bloody remains of Juyan. Rassul gave the body a kick, deriving some small satisfaction as his booted foot connecting with the still-warm flesh. The man would have been wiser to flee rather than pretend to have found the intruder's home—Rassul kicked the body again—though fleeing would have been just as futile. Not only had the man's summons resulted in their loss of the cavern and the treasure, but when Rassul had followed him to the street he claimed held the home of the intruder, every gate had been cloaked in mourning white and marked with the thieves' sign. Beating the man to death had done little to assuage Rassul's fury.

Turning his back on Juyan's remains, Rassul scanned the handful of men who had come with him, looking for one to do his bidding. He had tried depending on youth and cunning to no good effect. This time age and experience might serve better. If nothing else it showed some sense and skill at survival that transcended strength or luck.

"You," Rassul said, pointing to a lean man with scarred hands and a beard showing more grey than the others. "Old brother, you *will* succeed where this man failed."

The old thief—a rarity to be sure—looked uneasy but wisely gave a hurried bow before escaping into the night.

In his wake, Rassul left the alley with three other thieves as escort. The rest of his men camped outside of the town. Taking the quartered body was a direct insult, but worse yet, they could no longer wait in comfort to see what news bore fruit. That the intruder had reduced them to such circumstances fanned Rassul's rage until he blazed with it. He had worked hard and long to secure that treasure, his only guarantee of one day being restored to Persia and his place at court. Now it had been snatched away, leaving him trapped in this cursed place. He would not allow this to transpire. He would find the rat responsible and reclaim the djinni—the very key to the treasure cave—as well as the box. Until that time, Rassul entertained himself planning the torments he would inflict on the one responsible.

Within a week, the old thief returned.

"Master," he said as he genuflected, his head touching the ground where he knelt.

Rassul didn't even wait for him to rise. "What did you find?"

"A woman took the tailor to a home—"

"I know all this." Rassul's hand sat more heavily on his bone-handled *khanjar* as his impatience grew. Juyan had said as much.

The old man's eyes fixed on the weapon. "I found the home and marked it with broken stone."

Rassul smiled. "Then perhaps tonight we will pay our trespasser a visit."

Suddenly, his head snapped up and his gaze went to the ring on his right hand. The stone glowed in the low light. The djinni used her magic nearby. It was not the first time he had sensed her, but before her spells had ended too swiftly for him to act. What she worked now lingered as if more complex.

"Oh, you'll not escape me this time, little one." Rassul smirked and whispered words that made the thief tremble and edge away, not even bothering to rise from his knees.

Once again, as she went about household duties, Morgiana spied one of Rassul's thieves watching the street too closely. When he marked the house where her beloved was, there was no question she would have to warn Ali. But first, she must hide this thief's marker. Closing her eyes, the djinni felt her magic well up within her. Focusing, she concentrated on the broken stone. Once more, she mirrored the sign before every house on the street, and then again on the streets to either side to better confuse the matter for the thieves.

As she did so a familiar feeling gripped her. Morgiana cried out as Rassul's magic latched on. Like the prison she'd endured for so many years, it burned with a cold that caused her soul to ache. Her new body twisted at the pain. Dropping her bundle, she lowered herself down beside it before drawing her essence into a hard, tight ball within the glass walls of her copper boiler. There she waited until Rassul's magic lost its grip on her. He could not take her from this body. And once she had withdrawn her magic he could no longer reach her, yet the memory of his dominance kept her trapped within herself, huddled on the walkway just inside the gate, until Ali came to find her.

Abdul Asad found the stone walls of Wadi Al-Nejd a pleasing sight. After weeks of trailing across the desert in the wake of the caravan he had lost patience with the journey. He was amongst the newest of the thieves to have sworn loyalty to Rassul. He dreamt of treasures and immortality and power beyond imagining. But instead he was traipsing through the desert following the Englishman. Alone he would have traveled more swiftly. Instead he had the annoyance of both moving slowly and hiding his presence.

Though, truth be told, their slowness aided him now. The caravan had at least another day's journey to reach the city and night would soon be upon them. As they made camp, Abdul Asad seized his chance to break away and report to Rassul while the teacher, Charles Babbage, slept.

The thief secured his horse among some bushes well away from the caravan's camp and unfurled his bespelled carpet. He laid it upon the sands and sat in the center with little more than fringe to each side of him. Once he was settled, with his legs folded and his hands on his knees, he placed his left hand over the silver band bearing Rassul's mark and murmured the man's name. Slowly the carpet lifted and Abdul Asad restrained himself from grabbing for the edge as he flew low over the desert.

…*toward* the city.

He gasped and did clutch at the carpet then, fearing something had gone wrong. The magical transport dipped and nearly rolled, but he released his grip in time.

"Fool!" he cursed himself, then forced his hands back to his knees and waited impatiently as the carpet neared the city walls, then veered toward a *saif* nearby. His confusion further deepened as it deposited him beside a large camp sheltered in the corridor between the dunes. He flinched as Rassul himself stepped out of the shadow of the largest tent as if he had been waiting. If the carpet had not dumped Abdul Asad on the ground he would have left again at the murderous look in Rassul's gaze.

"Where is he?"

Abdul Asad blanched. "The teacher? He camps just outside the…" His answer cut off as Rassul grabbed him by the throat.

"The apprentice…where?"

"I do not yet know," Abdul Asad answered, his words strained. "But I have no doubt the teacher will lead us to him. Tomorrow he will reach the city and we have only to trail him to find our quarry."

"You had best pray he does," Rassul said as he tightened his grip. "For our quarry has barred us from the cavern, robbing us of our treasure as surely as if he carted it away on a hundred camels."

Abdul Asad would have cried out, had he the breath for it. He tumbled as Rassul cast him back onto the carpet.

"Return to your *teacher* and do not lose him, or you will long for death as if it were a comely woman's arms, and you a leper."

Late that evening Ali returned to the office to find Malakeh examining the accounting books. She looked up at his entrance. Her dark eyes flashed with dislike briefly before they returned to the books and a more thoughtful expression replaced the emotion.

"Malakeh, what are you—"

"I would know for myself the state of this household," she snapped. Malakeh flipped a page, one finger following the numbers.

Ali watched as she calculated in her head and made a correction in dark charcoal. "I did not know you had an interest—"

"You never knew me at all, nor did you wish to." Her words were harsh, but true, filling Ali with shame. "You assumed much, but I was raised in this trade even as my brothers were, to be a helpmeet to my husband…who likewise did not know me and would not hear my counsel."

Ali winced, guilt once again slicing into him.

Malakeh continued as if she did not notice Ali's pained look, "And now we are little better than paupers and must pay debts taken by Kassim…" She made another mark in the book, her brow furrowing.

Ali's hand tightened on the door until his knuckles were white. "Kassim chose the path destined for him by Allah."

"Did Allah choose to make me a widow?" Malakeh's voice cracked and the eyes that gazed up at Ali were filled with tears. "No, a man did that. You made it possible."

"I am truly sorry for your loss," Ali said stiffly. "And I thank you for your assistance."

He wondered briefly if Malakeh would make a true accounting. But she would gain nothing in cheating them both.

"I do not do this to help you, Baba Ali, but to reclaim my household," She waved him away. "I will bring you the accounts when I have finished with them."

"Allah preserve you." Ali said, backing from the room.

"My husband's honor and legacy is all I care for Baba Ali," Malakeh said, her voice now sad, "This household, this business is all that remains of him."

Leaving the cries of the market behind him, Charles Babbage made his way down a short lane until he saw a cluster of tables on the walkway, which Behnam had told him marked the local teashop. Once he had the landmark in his sights he turned expectantly to the opposite side of the lane to find his destination, a shop that among other things, supplied artificers with raw materials for their invention.

Massoud had told him of this shop long ago. Babbage prayed that there had been no change in proprietor. Ali's father had talked of his good friend Abdiesus Al-Mohamed, had even shared tales of the man's encouragement of Ali, providing bits of scrap for the lad to experiment with and teaching him little tricks of the trade that had made Babbage's task as mentor easier than it might have been. Now he approached Baba Abdiesus's shop with a dry mouth and a sour gut, afraid to enter and learn he was too late.

Stepping from the bright dusty street to the dim shop disoriented him. He blinked and peered about him, seeing more raw supplies than he would have expected in this far-off land. As he let his gaze travel in wonder, noting several brands of tools and other supplies clearly imported from his own land, there came a shuffle behind him. He turned to spy a man coming toward him old enough to be a contemporary of his father.

"Allah's blessing upon you, good sir," the man said in careful English as he stopped before Babbage. "I am Abdiesus, your humble servant. How may I help you this day?"

For the first time in weeks, Babbage smiled, almost laughing with his relief. "You speak English!"

The old man bobbed in acknowledgement. "A little." Then he quirked and eyebrow, "Do *you* speak Arabic?"

Babbage snorted. "That lapse in my education has been pointed out to me."

"Baba Abdiesus," he added, using what he knew to be an accepted honorific. "I am Charles Babbage, I'm here seeking—" Before he could continue the man cried out as if in celebration.

"*Salaam*! I had not thought to be blessed with meeting you, *Ustad* Babbage," Abdiesus said as he came close. "This is truly a blessed day!"

Babbage stiffened, his eyes widening as the man engulfed him in a massive bear hug, and kissed him on each cheek.

"Allah, be praised! I have heard so many tales from Ali of your good care and teaching of him. You have my deepest gratitude in the absence of the boy's father …"

Etiquette aside, Babbage grabbed the man's shoulders and cut him off. "Please…you must tell me how to find Ali. He is in grave danger."

Abdiesus' smile vanished like a mirage in the desert. "Come…come! I will take you to him."

Rassul walked boldly down the street in merchant's quarter with Abdul Asad at his side, their chafiyes slung low on their necks. Swirls of magic streamed from Rassul's hands to dance around them and confuse the casual observer's eye as they trailed the Englishman and his guide. Finally Rassul had a name, gleaned from the chatter of the men before them: Ali. A common name, but soon he would know of this man who would steal from him with impunity; who would take away his djinni.

As the men before him approached a familiar street with one house yet draped in mourning, the magic wreathing Rassul's hands spiked and crackled and his teeth gnashed as outrage flooded his soul.

"I have been here before," he said, the words rumbling like the earth about to shake.

Wisely, Abdul Asad remained silent.

"For weeks we have sought this desert rat, sending men to search the city and beyond for news. I was forced to kill two of them for failing to track this man, yet each had brought me to this exact spot where I might find my quarry." He heard Abdul Asad gulp at his words. "*You* have not failed me, though. See that it remains that way."

"Yes, my master."

Rassul stopped, and Abdul Asad with him. Across the street, the shopkeeper knocked at the gate. Shock, then rage flowed through Rassul as the door opened to reveal what appeared to be a young woman in modest dress. Beautiful, yes, but otherwise unremarkable, had he not recognized the face he had often seen dissolve into smoke. She stood there, bold, conversing freely. Barely did he restrain the urge to send lashes of magic across the intervening distance to strike the djinni down. She carried herself as if no one could touch her. He would prove to her how wrong she was in her thinking.

Without turning away from the sight before him, Rassul pulled Abdul Asad to him. "Fetch me ten camels and thirty-five of the largest jars you can find, large enough to fit a man inside. They must be of the best quality. Fill one with the finest of oils. Bring the others to the camp and tell the men to prepare their blades…"

"This is Charles Babbage—Ali's teacher," Abdiesus said, his hands gesturing effusively, "He would speak with Ali."

"I must see him immediately," the stranger said in English, his odd cadence not quite obscuring the anxiety in his voice. For a moment he looked at her closer with puzzlement in his gaze.

Morgiana nodded, grateful her magic blessed her with understanding any tongue. She responded in Babbage's own language. "Allah's blessing upon you, *Ustad* Babbage, welcome to Wadi Al-Nejd and my master's home," Morgiana said as she looked at the peculiar man, noting his hair, like a mingling of white sand and black ash, and his pale, lined face. He stood straight and stiff beside the old shopkeeper, Abdiesus, whom Morgiana had met in the market once or twice. Both trusted friends of Ali. And yet something made her uneasy.

Morgiana glanced beyond them at the street, a slight frown bending her lips. She saw no one, sensed no one, but a chill stiffened her motions despite the shimmer of oil at her body's joints. The sensation called to mind Rassul's efforts to claim her, yet she felt no tugging upon her spirit, no clamping down of his will. Her frown deepened.

Ustad Babbage took a half-step forward. "Thank goodness! You speak English. Please…Ali?" he repeated with more urgency.

Morgiana nodded and stepped aside to let them in, closing the gate firmly behind them. She led them out to the garden, which Old

Hamza had been patiently restoring as best he could with the resources available. When she glanced back she saw the confusion in their expressions though they followed politely. True, it would be more usual for her to have welcomed them inside, but in the garden they were open to the skies, which meant Shahin could reach them should danger intrude, though with each step away from the door her anxiety eased.

And still she continued to the garden. She wished to surprise Ali and draw him away from the worries of the household. The garden served better for this. Other than his workshop, it was where he seemed the happiest.

The guests followed in silence but she was certain their eyes lingered where the removed statues had left scars in the tattered landscape. She quickened her steps and brought them to the heart of the garden where Hamza had been focusing his best effort. The footsteps behind her faltered as the clearing came into view, nearly restored to its former splendor, with tender young ferns softening the pathways and a pair of young ring-necked parakeets bathing in a tasteful basin under the remaining palm tree. Other basins spread around the foliage cooled the air and lent the music of their trickle to the garden, pleasing the ear as they flowed one to the other.

"Lovely," the one called Babbage murmured behind her. "Absolutely lovely..."

She smiled as he stopped to finger a blossom on an arta bush next to the granite bolder at the center of the clearing. Unusual for a courtyard garden, but Ali had planted the bush himself just for her.

A sudden grunt came from the far side of the garden, followed by a quiet groan. Morgiana frowned and turned to the sound to see Old Hamza lowering himself to kneel on a mat of woven reeds. Beside him was a seedling waiting to be planted. The old gardener looked worn, but resolute. He worked too hard, determined to return the garden to its former glory.

Morgiana showed Babbage and Abdiesus to an awning-covered area with cushions and pillows that had also been newly restored and bade them wait. The shopkeeper settled in comfortable repose, but the Englishman paced, a frown returning to his brow. She hurried, stopping only briefly at Hamza's side, knowing Ali worried over how hard the older man worked to restore the garden.

"Peace be with you, *Hadji*," she murmured.

He looked up and smiled as his hands gently pressed the soil over the plant's roots. "And also with you, child."

"I go to fetch Ali for his guests." She gestured toward the waiting men. "It would please me very much if you would join us for tea."

He narrowed his eyes well aware of her continued efforts to get him to rest. "Will Paknoush's sweets be served?"

Morgiana smiled. "They will be brought by Paknoush herself, I assure you."

Hamza's gaze brightened at the mention of the kitchen servant, whom Morgiana knew he found pleasing of nature and form. The gardener looked upward, as if seeking divine guidance, his head slowly nodding.

Morgiana offered her arm to brace him, somewhat surprised when he availed himself of it. He pressed her hand in thanks, but said nothing as he went to join the others.

Well pleased, Morgiana hurried inside to request the tea and convince Paknoush to join them in the garden, even if only for a few minutes. The woman took some persuading, uneasy with taking tea with the guests rather than the servants. With everything in order, Morgiana went to fetch Ali. A soft smile graced her lips knowing the joy this news would bring him.

Chapter Fifteen

A TAPPING AT THE DOOR DREW ALI FROM THE BUSINESS matters he sorted through. Glancing up, he smiled to see Morgiana waiting in the doorway. Her eyes glimmered brighter than the luster of the diamonds that made them until he wondered what mischief she planned.

"Yes, gracious lady?"

"Come, Ali, we are to have tea in the garden."

He lifted one brow and looked from her to the orders he needed to review. "Are we?"

She ducked her head shyly. "It would please me greatly and the fresh air would do you good."

Ali smiled and rose from the desk. "I cannot argue with your reasoning, Morgiana." He gestured for her to precede him. As they passed through the door she dropped behind him. "And where are we taking our tea?" he asked, amusement coloring his words.

"At the heart of the garden."

He nodded, then stopped. When she drew even with him he offered her his arm, as he had seen done in England many times. Though she was made of clockwork, she was an unmarried woman, and not of his family. In public, he would not dare bring censure upon her by doing so, but in the

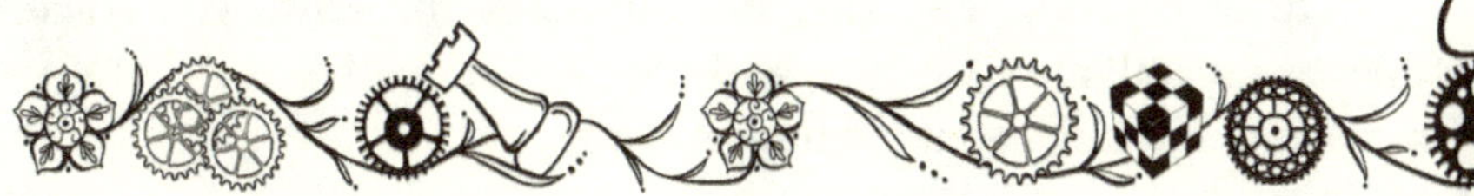

privacy of his home he could enjoy her company as he pleased. She looked at him oddly until he reached over and placed her hand in the crook of his arm. Her cheeks warmed causing the crushed rubies there to deepen their hue as with any maiden's blush.

Entranced by the sight, and reminded of a surprisingly pleasurable moment of his time in England, on impulse Ali asked, "Will you dance with me?"

Gasping, Morgiana snatched her hand away, her head shaking forcefully. "A djinni's dance is a terrible thing, though beautiful beyond imagining. It is not meant for mortal eyes."

He assured her he understood, and tried to explain more genteel dances such as the Moulinet, the Polonaise, and the Landler but she continued to cast nervous glances his way as they proceeded to the garden. She did not again place her hand upon his arm.

Rather than relax as the incident passed, Morgiana seemed to tense further the closer they drew to the clearing, but more as if with excitement than with concern. As they came even with the granite rock at the center of the garden she spoke.

"Look who has climbed out of his books to join us."

For a moment, her words confused Ali, until he realized she spoke of him, not to him. In response, two men rose from where they sat beneath the awning. He also noted that Hamza and Paknoush offered soft smiles from a quiet corner of the garden, a little away from the others. Baba Abdiesus lifted his bulk from where he was ensconced on a pile of cushions fanning himself. The other guest was a man in a *chafiye,* but dressed in a lightweight summer suit such as Ali had often seen in England.

He gasped as the man turned.

"*Ustad* Babbage!" Ali hurried forward; shock, laughter, and tears fighting for dominance.

Babbage's own eyes glistened, though a smile did grace his lips. Each hurried toward the other, clasping briefly before Ali stepped back, still gripping *Ustad* Babbage by the shoulders. "I cannot believe you are here…Why? Why are you here?"

Ustad Babbage's expression sobered.

"I had to warn you," Babbage said, urgency threading his voice. "The thieves are still after the box, and they mean to kill you."

"But you could have sent a letter."

"And never know if it reached you? Or have it arrive too late? I had to see for myself that you are well…"

"Are you?" he asked, his gaze trailing over Ali. "Well?"

"At least two of them have died in the trying, and my brother at their hand, but yes, I am as well as any without family might be."

This time *Ustad* Babbage grabbed him, his expression fiercer than Ali had ever seen, almost angry. "Never believe that in any way applies to you, my boy. Never, do you hear me? You slight every one of us standing here."

Ali felt his heart swell. "How long before you must leave?"

"The Langstroms will stop for me on their return, so if you will, I must impose on your hospitality a month or two."

His teacher look embarrassed to say so, but Ali smiled, feeling his chest well with joy.

"Come, tell me of your journey." "Tell me what has happened."

Laughter peppered the air as they spoke one over the other.

Glancing toward the others, Ali remembered they were there and thought perhaps that conversation would have to wait for a time. "Please, *Ustad*, we are well. And well protected." He added with meaning. "But tell us all of your adventuring." Ali gestured toward the cushions.

His teacher nodded, understanding in his eyes.

And with that, they sat to tea. Both Abdiesus and Morgiana proved to be able translators so that Paknoush and Hamza could understand the conversation. *Ustad* Babbage revealed himself well versed in the telling of tales, until everyone nearly laughed themselves to tears as he shared his harmless missteps along the way from England to Arabia.

Through it all, Ali wondered if perhaps *Ustad* Babbage's skill was in the *spinning* of tales and not their telling, as he noted a somberness to his teacher's gaze that gave lie to his laughter.

Not to be out-done, Ali told of his donkey, Jasmine, and her fondness for nibbling. Then Abdiesus shared the story of a monkey who tormented the owner of the teashop across from his store. They were all laughing at his account of the creature pelting the man with overripe dates when someone insistently cleared her throat.

"I must speak with you, my husband's brother."

Ali looked up to find Malakeh standing at the edge of the awning, her lips turned down and her body rigid. He fought to retain his light spirit but his muscles tensed and his stomach clenched unhappily. This morning he found a thread of silver in his hair. He well expected there would be a score of them by the time the conversation was done. For a moment he considered putting her off that he might enjoy this unforeseen visit, but he had found within himself a kernel of respect for Malakeh. Since she had taken over responsibility for the books, the household's finances and organization became clearer. And there was no doubt her skill with the business would quickly address many of the debts Kassim had amassed.

"Please," she asked softly.

Rising, Ali looked toward his guests, smiling to see *Ustad* Babbage begin a passionate discussion with both Baba Abdiesus and Morgiana on the potential use of mechanized cooling systems similar to those in aerostat engines, within architecture other than the traditional wind towers. Beyond them, Hamza and Paknoush had moved together to speak quietly over their teacups before slipping away, no doubt back to their duties. Rather than disturb any of them, Ali led Malakeh to a small bench nearby.

His brother's widow settled on one end of the bench and looked up at him expectantly. Ali did not sit beside her.

"What troubles you, Malakeh?" For indeed worry pinched the corners of her eyes and her demeanor bore signs of strain.

Her eyes dropped to her hands, which gripped each other in her lap.

"I am with child," she said softly. "We must marry soon."

Ali felt a spark of joy at her good news, glad that the Almighty had blessed them with something of Kassim to carry on. But the happiness quickly faded as the rest of her words struck home.

"No, Malakeh, that will not be," he told her, his voice firm, but not cruel. "You and your child will always be provided for, but I will not take you to wife."

"You would shame me so?" Her voice rose until he feared the others might come running. Panic was evident in her gaze and he sought a way to soothe her.

"You are honorably widowed," he told her, remaining calm in the hope she might as well. "There is no shame in this."

"You must! It is your duty. I-I don't want to be outcast."

"It is my duty to provide for you, until you marry again or the end of your days, but I cannot wed you."

Ali, sensing the fierce emotion within her, spoke softly, "Malakeh, surely you want more than to be a wife. You could —"

She wasn't listening. Caught in her own fears and futures, Malakeh's breathing grew shallow and her gaze narrowed, darting in the direction where Morgiana entertained his guests. "It is unnatural," she spat at him. "She is a made thing!"

Ali scowled and drew himself up, barely reining in his fury. With effort he kept his voice low. "I may have made Morgiana's body, but you would do well to remember that the Almighty Himself made her soul and found it beautiful."

Malakeh shrank back and fear crept into her expression. Her lips trembled. *And small wonder*, Ali thought with a fresh measure of shame. He was never stern. He never raised his voice. He knew some of his brother's treatment of Malakeh had been less than kind. To serve her with violence, even in word only, was harsh.

"Oh, Malakeh," Ali's words were a whisper of sound. "She is not the reason we will not wed. I respect you, but I will not marry one whom I do not love. With your help, I will hold my brother's legacy in trust for your child, and you will always have a home here, should you wish it, but to commit our lives to each other would be to wrap us both in chains."

He turned from her soft crying and started to return to his guests, but paused at the edge of the walkway. "Allah has gifted you with much, you have beauty and strength and cleverness. Trust in that. Trust in your own heart, but I cannot give you mine." He turned to glance at her over his shoulder, a smile spreading across his face. "And do not doubt this, sister… your blessing fills me with joy."

In the hours after the evening meal, when all save he and *Ustad* Babbage had gone home or taken to their rest, Ali sat at a low table with his teacher, a *shah-mat* — chess — board between them. They sipped at cups of warm milk with cinnamon as Ali shared the more perilous aspects of his journey home. He spoke low and briefly, wishing to be done with the bitter memories.

"Are there none to deal with these ruffians?" his teacher asked, his expression grave.

Ali shook his head. "They are powerful enough to rule the desert, outside of the cities. Who would risk retribution? They keep their activities to the desert and so the magistrates have no care for them." Almost he smiled as *Ustad* Babbage *humph*ed.

Finding it unwise to dwell on such dark matters before sleep, Ali turned the conversation to all the mechanical wonders he had seen since leaving England. When he told of the camelids from the thieves' cavern, Babbage lifted a skeptical brow, until Ali retrieved his grandfather's travel diary and showed the diagrams from which the machines were built.

However, when Ali began to describe his djinni's body—with nervousness jumping like a mouse in his belly and pride swelling his chest—Babbage gave a laugh and brought his hand down on the table. Shaking his head he sat back on his cushion.

"For a while there you had me, lad. I did not realize we were back to telling tales."

Ali looked down a moment to hide his hurt. It took much effort to smooth his expression. "Honored teacher, I tell you no tales. As Allah is my witness, I speak only the truth."

Again, his teacher scoffed.

"Bah! More of your talk of magical beings. I dare say this is just like the fairies you insisted on feeding back home." Ali noted that *Ustad* Babbage's gruff manner had resurfaced. "The stray cats were grateful, but nary a brownie showed its face. Not once have I seen with my own eyes reason to believe in otherworldly beings."

"But, *Ustad*," Ali interrupted, his tone respectful. "You had tea with one today."

"The hell you say!"

If the situation were not so tense, Ali would have found amusement in his teacher's rare curse.

"Morgiana is the djinni."

Babbage paled. "That is not possible."

"With Allah all things are possible."

At that Babbage scowled. "I believe in science, in technology, in knowledge; not poppycock nor wishful thinking."

Ali raised an eyebrow, "Did not your own good friend Lady Clara Langstrom not say that 'Impossible is a limit we place upon ourselves based on 'reason' and an imperfect understanding?' "

Babbage opened his mouth, clearly about to object. Ali raised a hand stilling his response. "Please."

Ali reached for the king from the game board.

He placed it before him. "Alone, a man stands on two feet and must withstand all things by his own power." He flicked the piece and it fell.

Ustad Babbage watched, silent. Ever had his teacher been fond of philosophical debate. Ali stood the king back upright, then reached for three more pieces. He set them down, one by one. The queen, "Love;" the bishop, "Faith;" and the rook, "Knowledge;" all three formed a close triangle around the king.

"You have a point, lad?"

Ali nodded, his expression patient. "If a man has these three things then nothing may stand against him. The obstacles of life crash against him as waves crash upon the sand. And when the tide retreats, the sand remains."

Babbage *humph*ed again, but seemed to consider his words, though Ali had no doubt, it was on no more than an academic level.

"If one of these three is removed, or held more closely than the others, stability is lost." He demonstrated. "Take one away," Ali went on, "and a man is vulnerable from that direction, and again might fall. If he finds his balance," —he restored the original grouping, then took up the same pieces of the opposing color and began to place them along each side of the first— "then passion, hope, and wisdom, may be attained." As he finished, Ali traced the pattern the triangles would form if the pieces were linked, the shape of a six-pointed star.

Ustad Babbage leaned forward, his frown deeply creasing his face. "Wrong religion, isn't it?" he said, nodding toward the arrangement.

Ali bestowed his best frown upon his teacher but did not address the comment meant to deflect him. "You have knowledge and love," he said quietly his finger brushing first the rook, and then the queen, before coming to rest on the bishop, "and I pray that one day you will find faith."

His teacher's expression grew pained and he offered a sardonic smile. "I have had faith, my boy, and been broken for it. Have you not considered that sometimes faith may be wrong? Love self-serving? Understanding flawed?"

"There is truth in what you say," Ali answered, "but no man's truth is complete. Only Allah knows all." Ali smiled. "And is that not the reason for faith?"

Babbage blew out his breath, as if in frustration. "We can reach no resolution on this, I think, and certainly not tonight. Now is the time for rest. We can battle anew tomorrow."

Ali nodded and did not press the matter. In Allah's time all things destined would come to be.

"Rest well, my friend. If you have need of anything you have only to ask," he said with a bow before turning toward the sleep chambers. He stopped as his teacher spoke softly.

"Ali…you want me to believe the young woman is 'other'…if that is so, how can you trust you do not already have danger among you?"

Before Ali could respond there came a knock at the door. He excused himself and hurried to answer, that the household would not be disturbed. He peered past the door to see a man, travel-worn and weary, with ten camels behind him.

"Peace be with you," the man said with a humble bow.

"And also with you," Ali returned the greeting.

"I am Mu'Tamid, and I have journeyed far. Might you have a place for a weary traveler to lay his head?"

Hospitality dictated that Ali shelter the man. He stepped back and opened the door wide. "Please, be welcome in my home."

"Allah's blessing upon you, honorable sir. You have my gratitude." The trader said, with just a look of concern as he glanced back at his camels. As Mu'Tamid waved his hand toward the animals, the lamp light glimmered off an onyx ring on his right hand. "Please, my beasts will do well enough where they are, but have you a room where I might keep my wares for the night? The jars of oil are precious and worth much to me."

"Of course," Ali answered. "Let me summon my servants."

It was late and though she was a creature of fire and not flesh, Morgiana found herself weary. Taking tea in the garden had been enjoyable, but she was not use to dealing with so many people at once, and for a prolonged time. Anxiety had plagued her throughout the afternoon. The gathering made Ali happy, though, and she could not begrudge him that.

She was not best pleased, however, when a stranger arrived at the door and imposed upon her master's hospitality. By the time he knocked, Morgiana had already hidden from the press of mortal souls and their incessant talk. She listened from beyond the door to the kitchen as the servants were roused and the man's goods stored away. All she wished was for the household to go back to their rest that she might return to her own sanctuary, where Ali kept his workshop. But not yet. There was one more task to complete.

Finally, as she heard Ali lead the trader to a sleeping chamber, Morgiana crept through the house, checking to make sure all was secure before leaving for the night. Ali did not ask it of her. Likely, he did not even know. She took the task upon herself for, though her circumstances had changed, still she was a protector.

Her efforts took longer than usual this night. The body Ali had made for her resisted every movement at first. She brought her hand up to check the lock on a window and her lips twitched in annoyance, noticing her arm moved slowly as the gears ground rough against one another. Was this body a blessing or curse? To be neither Ins nor Djinn, neither flesh nor fire, but something else? Something that lacked the easy grace of either form? She creaked like an old woman where before her movements had been nothing but fluid.

She shook her limbs and rubbed them, but movement remained difficult. In her haste to see to the hospitality of Ali's visitors this afternoon, she had neglected the day's necessary care for her constructed body. She grimaced. Desert sands were unforgiving toward machinery. Fine sand and dust gathered in the gears and cogs. Unlike Shahin, she had not the decades of existence in a mechanical body. She did not know how to use her magics to better maintain her new form. However, once she oiled her body she would again move freely. And that was the key, not how it was done, only that it *was* done. She resided within a fabricated body, but she was free. Ali had released her from the dominion of the cursed ones.

Annoyed at her own forgetfulness, Morgiana headed toward the storage area only to find the oil jar empty. She then checked Ali's workroom and the kitchens, but could find none. The stiffness spreading through her body, Morgiana limped to the storeroom that held the trader's jars of oil. Surely he could not tell should she borrow a little cup of lubricating oil. It was a small liberty to weigh against her master's hospitality. In the morning, she would tell Ali that he might purchase more and pay for what she took.

When she came to the first jar, a voice whispered from inside, "Is it time to attack? The jar is small but my knife is ready."

Morgiana started but did not scream or call for help. Inside the amphora was a man who had entered their home with malice in his heart and death in his hand. She recognized the voice of one of the cursed ones, a weasely man called Abdul Asad. Her gaze thoughtfully considered the other thirty-four amphorae. She took a breath, the bellows in her chest drawing in the night air, cooling her boiler as she gathered her thoughts. She answered quietly, deepening her voice, "No, but soon."

Still stiff and unbalanced by the sand grinding in her gears, Morgiana slowly made her way to each and every jar. At all but one, a voice asked if it were time and each time she responded, "No, but soon."

The voices were all familiar to her ear.

Her internal pump raced out of rhythm as she realized that Ali had unknowingly welcomed the thieves into his home and even now harbored Rassul himself, disguised as the trader, for his voice alone she had not heard come from the jars. Kassim's mutilated body surfaced in her thoughts, only the face bore Ali's features. Morgiana's stiffening body shuddered and a moan slid past her lips. Should the thieves succeed she would once again be alone...perhaps a prisoner of the cursed ones. But worse, Ali, a good and virtuous man, would be no more.

Fury kindled behind her eyes until they glowed, while the purple mists at the heart of the construct swirled with the violence of a desert storm, darkening to the veil of night. These thieves would not have her Ali. The construct body might have stiffened, but for the first time in millennia, Morgiana's magic was unbound and she was free to use it. These cursed ones had taken her last master, a man she cared for. She would not allow them to take Ali, the man she...Morgiana could not finish the thought for she had not the words.

She spoke ancient phrases, commands so dark and terrible that the air around her shivered. Sparkling dust rose to cover the walls and each of the amphora containing men until all glowed with purple flame, ensuring nothing — not sound nor thief — would escape the chamber. Morgiana could not work her magic upon the thieves' flesh, but she knew its delicate nature, so susceptible to outside influence. With a satisfied smile and the focus of her will, Morgiana first sealed the ceramic jars, then, using flame so hot it was transparent, she heated the air within. Each thief howled in mortal terror and unending pain as she steamed them, flesh and blood and bone. Outside none sensed the horror that took place within.

The effort drained her, leaving her weak. She stumbled, and her arm knocked against one of the jars. It toppled to the ground and shattered,

sending clay shards and fine ash into the air to settle over everything. In the remaining wreckage, the dull gleam of a *khanjar* caught her eye, the metal warped and blackened.

For a moment she could not move. Something closed around her, gripping as firm as one of Ali's vises. She fought against the paralysis but did not have the strength to break it, then suddenly the sensation faded away as if never there, and she wondered if perhaps she had pressed herself too far.

Shuddering, Morgiana turned away from the broken container. Careful of the remaining jars, she made her halting way to the sole vessel that bore oil and bathed her body until it glistened and each gear gripped the next in soundless, fluid motion. Then, without glancing back, she went to find Ali.

Rassul paced his chamber, impatient to begin the night's bloodshed. Energy sparked from his fingertips. He loosed a bolt of magic against a costly chair. It collapsed, the rare wood rotting and decaying into dust within seconds. Fate had both blessed and cursed him, for Ali—who vengeance dictated must die for his offenses—bore strong resemblance to the old guardian, whose life Rassul had ended long ago, the original human protector of the cave. The boy was surely of the same blood, and if so, then perhaps it was more than just chance that led to the loss of the puzzle box, the intruders in the cave, and the presence of the djinni in this household.

The mystery fed Rassul's ire. Before he could indulge himself in further destruction, the onyx ring on his hand warmed uncomfortably.

His head snapped up and his gaze narrowed. Somewhere nearby he sensed that the djinni used her magic. Muttering a spell beneath his breath, he summoned her, to no avail. His teeth clenched and he reached out more forcefully, his essence following the thread of her magic. Another spell showed him her image, allowed him to see what he had overlooked when he had first spied her at the door. Her form was not flesh or the seeming of flesh, but metal. Somewhere within, desert glass insulated her from his will. Rassul's eyes narrowed and his cleverness saw past her defenses. She might think herself beyond his reach, but the same could not be said for her clockwork body. Exerting more power he expanded his other sight until he saw her surroundings. He nearly screamed in outrage as he spied his jars and the steam seeping from beneath the blackened lids. There was little doubt as to the fate of his thieves secreted within.

Knowing he had been found out, Rassul swiftly wove a spell over the djinni's body to bind it to his command. At first something repulsed his effort. Recklessly, he pressed more energy into his magic until his muscles screamed and bile rose into his throat. Determination tightened his brow as he clamped down and increased his focus. He would not let his own body cause him to fail. By the time the resistance faltered, then fell away, sweat slicked Rassul's skin and his *thobe* clung to his body. Moments after the spell took and Rassul ended his efforts, sick covered the tile floor. Spitting the remnants of acid from his mouth, he crept out the window to flee through the garden and over the wall. He could not claim his success this night, but he now had the means and his spell would wait, dormant, until he called upon it.

In the morning, Ali woke to a house in turmoil. Outside in the courtyard, the camels growled their displeasure and beyond his chamber, Ali could hear the servants murmuring as they scurried. He rose from his bed and completed quick ablutions before going to discover the matter. As he opened his door, he found Morgiana kneeling in wait before his chambers.

"Gracious lady, what is the matter?"

She lifted her eyes, then rose to stand before him.

"Master, I must inform you of a grave matter."

Ali scowled and nearly reprimanded her for addressing him thus. She rarely did so, especially after he had made clear his feelings that there would be no debts between them. No master and no servant, equals before the Almighty. Ins and Djinn.

Ali stretched and rubbed his face to hide his expression. He was already out of patience with the day, but it was not fair to her when all she had known were masters or those who sought to master her.

"What is it, Morgiana?"

"Please, come."

Ali followed her through the household, his nose pinching at an acrid odor he could not place, that had not been there the night before. It grew stronger as they neared the kitchen. Before Ali could ask about it, Morgiana led him into the room where the trader's jars had been stored. He gasped and staggered back at the sight of the blackened lids still curling wisps of steam. The stench here gagged him until he fled to the kitchen and waved for Morgiana to close the door.

"I ask you a third time, what is this?"

She did not flinch at his stern tone.

"We were out of oil. I thought to borrow a measure as my joints stiffened," she told him, her gaze solemn upon his. "When I came to the first jar a voice whispered out to me, asking if it was time to escape from the jars and rain death upon all in this household. I told that voice, and the thirty-three after, that it was not. I knew them all, Ali, cursed ones, and I used my magic to sear them where they hid."

Ali felt a chill at her words.

"You killed them…all of them?"

Morgiana dropped her gaze. "I fear not. The trader, who surely must have been Rassul himself, has fled."

Ali paled at her response. The djinni did not seem to notice, for which he was grateful. He watched her from the corner of his eye. Before he had freed her from the glass pipes in the cave, there had been doubt in his mind at the wisdom of his act. Those doubts, fanned by *Ustad* Babbage's comments of the night before, rekindled in the light of day. Ali found his heart conflicted. That she could kill so many without any remorse concerned him, but, he could not dispute that he and his household were safer for her actions. Would he have chosen any differently in her place? He stared at the smoking jars and felt ill.

He could not help but think better had she killed them all. Then he would never worry again who might hide in the shadows. He grimaced, not certain what was worse, that he too could feel no remorse for the death of such evil men, or to admit that he had been so foolish as to welcome the very man who sought to kill him into his house.

With effort, he set his doubts aside, nodding his thanks to the djinni before going to inform the servants and instruct that precautions were taken to ensure such deceptions would not occur a second time. And, as the stench again struck his nose, something would need to be done about the jars and their grisly contents. With that reminder, the flame of doubt licked again at the back of his thoughts.

Ali pressed his lips thin and turned his contemplations to more practical matters.

In the end they dumped the ashes—all that remained of the bodies—in the garden, and smashed the jars in the garbage pit. It was Malakeh who suggested they sell the camels at market, resulting in a more than tidy sum. This represented an unexpected bounty for the household from those who would have slaughtered them in their beds. As for Rassul, the servants were instructed to allow no one entry who was not a trusted friend or member of the household.

Then, worn out with worry, Ali went to find *Ustad* Babbage and make sure that at least with him, all was well. He found Babbage in his private chamber already dressed for the day and taking tea. Ali was relieved to note that the aromatic floral scent masked the faint, acrid odor pervading the rest of the building.

"Good morning, Ali! Come to draw the battle lines once more?" his teacher greeted him.

Ali offered a weak smile, knowing he must tell his mentor all that transpired.

"Good morning, *Ustad* Babbage, I pray you slept well?"

Ustad Babbage waved the question off. He sat forward and peered intently into Ali's face.

"You are distraught. What has upset you?"

Ali grimaced and told him of the thieves and their intent. *Ustad* Babbage looked shocked.

"Abdul Asad, you say?"

"Such is what Morgiana has told me."

His teacher abruptly stood, his fingers clutching at his hair as he paced the room, cursing fervently beneath his breath.

Ali rose as well, concerned by the uncharacteristic language. He continued to explain, though hesitantly, of the djinni's measures to deal with said thieves before harm could come to the household. It surprised him when, rather than press his point from the night before, *Ustad* Babbage proceeded to thank the God he did not profess to believe in.

"I am sorry, lad, so very sorry. I see now I have played the fool in this. Can you forgive me?"

Ali's brow wrinkled in confusion. "I do not understand, what is there to forgive?"

Again *Ustad* Babbage cursed. "Ali…I led them to you. I encountered Abdul Asad and another man ransacking my home the day you departed. In my foolish insistence to come and prove to myself you were well, I guided them to your very door!"

Ali shook his head. "Set that fear from your heart, my friend. They have proved well able to find me on their own, on more than one occasion." Then, before *Ustad* Babbage could persist to argue, Ali waved him toward the door. "Let us not dwell on blame save to set it at these thieves' feet—may Allah grant them mercy. We should have more concern at this moment for what Paknoush has prepared to break our fast."

Chapter Sixteen

NEVER BEFORE IN HIS LIFE HAD ALI FELT THE URGE TO STRIKE a woman. Never. He knew it was a common thing for some, but such was not the way his father had raised him or his brother. The Prophet taught—all glory to His name—that whenever tolerance is added to something it beautifies it, and whenever it is withdrawn from something, it leaves it defective.

And yet, Ali struggled at that moment to find any lenience in his heart for Malakeh. He searched the gardens for her, having already gone through the household. Clearly she knew this, for he could find her nowhere.

"Malakeh!" he bellowed. "I have no more patience."

At his yell, a whimper rose from somewhere behind him. Slowly he turned, his gaze narrowed as he searched the foliage, which had attained enough of its former glory to afford many places to hide. When he spied a shimmer of golden silk behind a squat date palm he slowly moved forward, careful not to disturb the undergrowth.

"Woman, you will show me the respect due as head of this household." He kept his tone low, but startled even himself at the chill of his words. "Stop hiding like a child or have no doubt I shall treat you like one."

She rose from behind the tree, her eyes wide and her lips pressed tight until a thin pale line ran around them. "You are a good one to speak of respect, *brother*."

"Did you not believe me when I told you we would not wed?" he demanded, his words striking like steel. "By all that is sacred, did you believe that if you planned for it I would have no choice?"

Her gaze dropped but not before he saw the shame in them.

"No, Baba Ali," she answered, her body taut and her hands flexing. "On my honor, I had begun to plan the wedding before we spoke. I canceled what I could, but some things were too late."

Ali groaned and held himself still only through great effort. They had spoken two weeks ago. At first, items that arrived were merely put away, none realizing they were anything more than household goods. Then more and more luxuries were delivered, fabric and jewels and ornate rugs.

That had been yesterday morning.

Today there had been a surprise of a different sort.

"And the guests? Did you not think to cancel the guests?"

"Those I could," she answered, her voice barely heard. "Please… please forgive me."

He leaned forward and held her gaze with his. "Your family awaits us inside."

Malakeh swallowed convulsively, her eyes rolling in panic. "I am sorry. I could not stop it and was so afraid I said nothing."

Everything about her spoke of fear, from her expression to the way she flinched as he drew a deep breath. Ali was reminded once again that brother had no compunction against beating women. He let his breath out slowly and closed his eyes. At times, he found it very difficult to resist wishing for the return of his simple life in exile.

"Mind me, Malakeh, we must have trust between us. If we continue to do battle, it will tear this house apart." He waited for her to nod in agreement before continuing.

"Come, sister. Let us both speak with your family."

Malakeh wrung her hands, but without complaint, followed him.

Abruptly, he stopped and turned to her. "Tell me, do they know of my brother's child?"

Some of the fire came back into her gaze as she straightened and gave him a look of offended disdain.

"They are well aware I am with my *husband's* child."

Unashamed, Ali nodded. "Good, then there will still be reason for celebration."

They entered the house in silence on stiff strides to find her father and her two youngest brothers waiting. Malakeh's family sat rigidly on plump cushions with tea, untouched, cooling before them. Their expressions were not encouraging.

"The Almighty's blessing upon you, honored Sayyid. You and your sons are welcome here," Ali said with an effusiveness he did not feel.

Malakeh's father did not return his greeting. "What is this I hear that there will be no wedding?"

"I cannot marry where I do not love," Ali answered simply.

"Love? Bah! What of honor?"

"There is no honor in being a poor husband to a woman, with little thought to her beauty or her wisdom. It would be as putting a wild bird in a cage to keep it safe, while denying it the freedom of flight." He gestured to Malakeh. "We are of one accord on this."

Her eyes lowered, she nodded her agreement.

"And how will you provide for my daughter, whom you will not marry, and her with child? I will not leave them to be destitute." Malakeh's father's gaze was hard and his hand rested heavily on the decorated *khanjar* at his waist.

Ali noted Malakeh's panic at her father's words and nodded at her in reassurance before turning back to Sayyid. "They will not be destitute. I am a skilled craftsman, and your daughter…you have taught her well."

Ali looked at Malakeh and noted both pleasure and concern in her expression at his words. He shared both feelings, but he could not let that show. Ali drew himself up, his stance respectful, but determined, mind frantically searching for the words that would make everything right.

Malakeh knew much and could teach him, but there were certain tasks for which he had no skill and a woman with a child could not do, no matter how able she might be. As he considered her and how well she had been trained, the Almighty's Own inspiration came to him.

"Please, honored Sayyid," he said, bowing in deference to her father. "I have a proposal I humbly request you consider. My father's trade is well established and of good repute, but alas, being the second son and destined for other things, I did not benefit as much from his knowledge and wisdom in this, as your sons have from you." Here he nodded at Malakeh's brothers, who stood nearby. "I would be a hindrance to your daughter in this. Might you consider leaving one of your sons to help her as she manages our humble business? Such would allow him to better his skills and an opportunity to work as a part of a thriving trade."

Liban, the youngest of all the brothers, straightened and leaned forward, his expression eager. Perhaps too much so. Ali interjected before he and the household indeed found themselves destitute, with the power in another's hands.

"I retain my responsibility as head of both household and my portion of the trade, held in trust for my brother's child, but would value his knowledge and counsel to ensure the business prospers."

His comment tempered a small measure of Liban's eagerness, but the young man nodded.

"I wish to consider this proposal, Father."

Sayyid eyed them all closely for a long, silent moment.

Anxiety twisted Ali's gut as he waited and the others seemed to hold their breath.

"I will sanction this agreement on the condition that my son receives half share in the business."

Ali narrowed his gaze and lifted his chin. "One quarter of my share, with one half in trust for the child and the remainder going to support the household."

"One third to my son," Sayyid countered. "And the rest as you have said."

Malakeh opened her mouth to protest the cutting of the household funds, but both Ali and Sayyid silenced her with a glance. *She will have to content herself with* simple *luxuries in truth, or go without,* Ali thought as he and Sayyid shook on the agreement.

"I thank you for your benevolence," Ali addressed the older man, then turned toward Malakeh. "I will leave you to visit with your family, sister. Peace be with you all."

"And also with you," they answered as he left the room.

Ali was well pleased and for the first time since his brother's death he knew true hope.

Word of the wedding debacle traveled through the market like a caged songbird set free. On hearing of it, Rassul smiled with satisfaction and he too began to plan.

One night, several days later, Ali came upon Morgiana in the garden, her eyes scanning the sky.

"Should the cursed ones start to come at us from above, then we are truly at Allah's mercy," he teased without realizing his words were in poor taste.

The djinni tensed and jerked her gaze toward him, silently watching him through unfathomable eyes that for once he had no difficulty recognizing as hard diamond.

"It has been some time since you have sought out my company, master. Have you some need of me?" Though her tone was nothing but respectful, hurt shone in her gaze. He winced at her return to the use of 'master'.

"No, gracious lady, merely your company," he answered chagrined to realize, that despite all, he felt peace in this moment for the first time since peering past the storage room door. "And please, I am not your master."

Morgiana looked away from him, sorrow marring the beauty of her smooth copper mien.

"What I did, killing those men, it disturbed you."

Though he could not dispute her words, Ali's heart ached to see the trail down her cheek. He struggled, searching for an answer that would return them to the easy companionship they shared in the cave.

Her gaze hardened. "I would ask you, have I done anything which you would not have likewise done to protect this household?"

Ali remained silent, thoughts and feelings warring within him.

The djinni turned and walked away and Ali found he could not bring himself to call her back.

The next evening the household was disturbed yet again by a knocking at the door. Ali could not think who it might be, except another of Malakeh's interminable wedding guests. Waving off Mateen, come to answer, he opened the door.

"Allah's benevolence be upon you and yours," the man patiently waiting outside offered in greeting.

Ali answered in kind, though he grew weary of the constant intrusion of guests who then had to be told that there would be no wedding. An uncomfortable experience for both guest and Ali, who was then usually forced to host them until arrangements could be made for the return home. *How long would this go on?*

"I am called Izad al-Din," the man went on. "A business partner of Kassim bin-Massoud. I am here for the…"

"I am afraid you have been misinformed, there is to be no wedding," Ali said, who, after almost a week of these arrivals, found even his courtesy strained. He glanced ruefully back to where *Ustad* Babbage sat in the garden. Malakeh's family—with the exception of her brother Liban—had returned to Jeddah and Ali had been looking forward to this time of quiet to visit.

The merchant frowned and smoothed his beard, which was perfumed with rosewater and bedecked with tiny gold adornments.

Ali could not help but notice the quality of Izad's silks—surely from the great Khan Empire—and the plentitude of jewels on his fingers. The man clearly enjoyed success in his business.

"Ayee! And I have come so far," Izad moaned.

Ali raised a plea for forgiveness to the Almighty. It was disgraceful that he would be so inhospitable. After all, it was not this man's fault Malakeh had overstepped herself. "Please, forgive me. I regret that your journey was for nothing. I would offer you my hospitality that you might rest."

Smiling benevolently, the merchant bowed his acceptance and stepped over the threshold.

"I thank you and in truth, I had hoped to speak to *you* on a matter of business. I trade in mechanical devices. I have heard of your skill as an artificer."

Ali smiled and drew himself up, well pleased to have his technical skills receive praise. Likewise, he was eager to hear the nature of this business Izad would discuss. After Ali's conversations with Kassim's debtors, and the impact it had on the household coffers and his own cache of gold, it relieved him greatly to have a merchant trader such as this seek him out. Even Malakeh's clever accounting and financial reorganizing could only help for a short time. Until Liban revived their family's trade and the caravans were traveling again filled with merchandise, they would need something to fill the coffers.

"If you would wait here, with *Ustad* Charles Babbage," Ali said, gesturing toward the cushions surrounding a low table set for the evening meal. "He is English." Ali added, as if that explained much. Izad nodded.

Ustad Babbage raised a hand in greeting. "*Salaam*, traveler. Peace be upon you."

Ali felt his lips quirk into a smile, Babbage showed inordinate pride in the few words he had picked up in Arabic. "I thank you for your generosity, Ali," Izad said as he eased himself down to a cushion, covering a yawn and looking embarrassed to have done so. "Pardon my rudeness. I am afraid my journey has been long."

"No need for pardon. Let me offer you respite," Ali assured him as he summoned his brother's wife.

"Malakeh, inform the cook we have another for the evening meal. And tell Mateen to prepare a chamber for our guest." Ali then turned to the merchant as he gestured to the table, "*Tafathalo*." *Do me the honor*.

Izad smiled. "You are too kind. But please, do not salt the meat."

Ever the courteous host Ali acquiesced, though the request took him aback. "As you wish."

As Malakeh hurried to the kitchen to relay the request, Izad sat forward.

"Perhaps we might come to an arrangement, you and I?" Izad said. "I have done business with the Beni Zayed and the Artificers' Guild, but from time to time my customers request something unique. A design none of the others can provide, a mechanical device both functional and artful. In these lands of magic and desert sands, often I despair of meeting their mechanical needs." He sighed dramatically. "Might such work be suited to your skill?"

Ali looked from Izad to *Ustad* Babbage realizing his teacher could not hope to understand the discussion. "Please, good Izad, I would translate our conversation. *Ustad* Babbage does not understand our tongue."

Izad showed mild annoyance at the request. "I speak the tongue of the foreigners," he said, distaste clear in his tone, but he repeated his query in English.

Babbage's bushy eyebrows rose at the request.

Ali nodded in assent. "I have built many machines and constructs, both from others' designs and original workings of my own."

Ali pressed his lips together to hide his smile as *Ustad* Babbage *humphed*. "I have never had a better student."

"Ah, then you are a Master Artificer," the merchant said, his smile broadening, but his gaze remaining flat.

Reluctantly, Ali shook his head. "Well, I have not sought commission with the Guild," — he had not had the coin to do so — "but..."

"Then you have apprenticed under another? Learning from the great builder tribesmen, such as the Beni Zayed, perhaps?" the merchant interwove his fingers, his expression earnest but his gaze mocking.

Ali masked his own annoyance. Izad's words reminded him of the many taunts Kassim had made about his constructs. "No, I have not learned from the Beni Zayed."

"He learned from me," Babbage snapped. "And you'll not find a better student between here and Cambridge."

"From *Ustad* Babbage I have learned the ways of working technical marvels such as few from our world have ever seen. Surely, you have seen the great machines of the West."

The merchant clapped his hands in feigned surprise. "Forgive me, my esteemed host, I would not insult your hospitality…or your guest—" His manner, however, pled otherwise.

Babbage face reddened and his jaw went tight.

"No, no." Ali said soothingly. "Please, allow that I may show you my humble skills, and you will know the quality of my instruction." He stood and motioned his guests to join him. They toured the house as Ali pointed out the modifications he had made to improve the efforts of his servants, such as the self-filling lanterns and the baffles in the kitchen that kept the heat from the cook fires on the food and not in the room. He even showed them the sledge that had carried Ali and his burden across the desert on that ill-fated day not long ago. Sadly, all were simple workings as he had not the coin to purchase supplies for grander work. Then, when Ali despaired at what else he might show as evidence of his skill, Izad spoke.

"Have you nothing grand to rival the workings from those foreign lands you hold in such high esteem?" His lip curled just enough to be noticed.

Babbage muttered almost inaudibly under his breath, "As if you would know of the greatness of Victoria's England."

Ali sighed. This was not going as he had envisioned. He did not want to see Babbage and Izad enter into a verbal conflict. He thought longingly of the doll the Langstroms had commissioned. If only he could show *that* to Izad, surely the merchant could not help but be suitably impressed. Then Ali realized there was one more thing he might show the man, and *Ustad* Babbage too—who still doubted—that would convince them of his great skill.

With a slight frown, he paused and wondered at the wisdom of what he considered. Was this truly for the good of the household and securing new trade or was it for his own pride. Ali shook off the thought and waved over Mateen who had been passing by on his way to the kitchens. Ali felt a quaver of shame in his stomach as he whispered in the servant's ear.

Morgiana frowned as Malakeh ordered the cook to set aside their salt and remake any dish that had already been seasoned thus. To share bread and salt was sacred. It was a sign of hospitality, but more than that, since the oldest of times, it was a peace bonding. That one man would refuse to share salt with another did not bode well.

"Who is this man who will not have salt his hosts?" Morgiana asked.

"Stupid girl, it is not your place to question this," Malakeh said harshly, forgetting herself so much as to raise her hand.

Morgiana's bright diamond eyes flashed in fury.

"And you are a foolish woman to speak so," she said, her voice soft and her tone gentle. Yet there was no mistaking the "otherness" that even Malakeh could sense. The briefest of flames kindled at Morgiana's fingertips.

"I-I-I must refresh their tea," Malakeh stuttered and all but ran from the room.

As the woman fled, Mateen entered the kitchen. He looked around then came toward Morgiana, his steps hurried and his expression superior as he ordered her to attend their master. Her eyes darkened. She had chosen the role of servant in this household as anything else would have been suspicious, but at moments like this she found herself sorely tempted to prove to them to what degree she transcended this position. Morgiana sighed in regret and told herself to have patience. Her emotional balance had not been so bad when she and Ali had been at peace, but lately matters had been strained between them. She missed their quiet time together and their talks such as had taken place in the garden, under the stars, she even missed their talks from when she had been imprisoned inside the glass pipes in the cavern. She felt more alone now, surrounded by an entire household of people, than she had when it was just the two of them together in the darkness.

The largest dinner platter was piled high with lamb and succulent fruits on a bed of couscous. Malakeh could not heft it herself. Morgiana slid a carving knife beneath the edge of the meat and bent to lift the tray. Spying the bowl of salt which had not been used, she frowned. Perhaps their guest would dishonor his host by foregoing salt, but she saw no reason for Ali not to partake. Knowing his pleasure in the seasoning, she placed it beside the knife before lifting the platter high and proceeding to the chamber where Ali and his guest awaited.

Ali schooled his gaze as Morgiana entered the room where he, Izad, and *Ustad* Babbage lounged on embroidered cushions, bolsters at their backs. In her arms she carried a platter piled high with roasted lamb and other delicacies, so heavy, the strongest manservants would have struggled beneath it.

Her steps slowed as both his guests fixed their gazes on her, ignoring the feast.

"Morgiana is a djinni, a woman born of smokeless fire," Ali said to his guests, refusing to meet her shocked gaze as he did so. "This body you see is the most complex clockwork I have ever engineered, even above the Langstroms' commission." This last he directed to *Ustad* Babbage. As he spoke, the platter of lamb thudded down onto the table between them. He could not help but look up into Morgiana's eyes knowing he had caused the upset visible there. In that moment, Ali realized what he had done—he had betrayed her trust.

She glanced toward Izad and Ali saw her gaze widen until she appeared panicked. Her limbs trembled faintly and she opened her mouth, as if to speak, but no words came forth.

Confused, Ali turned his gaze to the merchant, noticing a smirk upon Izad's lips as he fingered his large onyx ring.

"It is pretty enough, but shall we see what it can do?" the merchant said, malice seeping into his words. He gestured and Morgiana jerked upright.

Ali half-rose with her, his heart tightening in his chest, realizing something was very wrong. Before he could react further, Morgiana grabbed *Ustad* Babbage by the neck and dragged him to her. Her hands moved with grace, viper-quick. Babbage barely had time to yelp before his breath was caught within his lungs.

All the while, her mouth moved silently, and her eyes darted this way and that in frantic helplessness. Her hands tightened and Babbage's face grew redder as they began to squeeze even tighter. Babbage's hands pulled at her wrists, but the djinni's brass and copper body was unyielding.

Ali spun back to the merchant sensing that the real threat came from him. "What is this?"

"This is vengeance," Izad hissed as he stood, the sullen glow of sorcerous magic swirling from his fingertips. "This is retribution for your offenses. This is myself, *Rassul Maroun*, master of the Rub Al-Khali crushing an upstart tinker boy beneath my heel.

"If you value your *esteemed* teacher's life, you will fetch the cursed box….and *nothing* more."

Ali paled. *Ustad* Babbage stood rigid in Morgiana's grip, a hostage, with her gold-tipped fingers pressed hard against his windpipe. Rage mixed with panic blazed in the Englishman's eyes and he'd clenched his teeth so tight Ali heard them grind. The djinni's grip tightened even more and small traces of blood welled from *Ustad* Babbage's throat.

"Morgiana—"

The djinni gave only the faintest shake of her head. She looked horrified and the truth Ali read on her face told him she acted against her will.

"She cannot help you, *Baba* Ali," Rassul said, showing a sharp smile. "And your friend does not have much time."

Having no other recourse, Ali hurried to his chambers to collect the puzzle box. For a moment, he considered bringing another of less import, but he could not risk his teacher's welfare. Rassul was behind all the attempts on his life. All the effort, all the death, and all the heartache. No, he could not risk Babbage. Snatching up the *Himitsu-Bako*, Ali regretted the day Shahin had ever brought it to him.

As if in response, the falcon-bound djinni's screech sounded from outside. But there was nothing the falcon could do here. There was no way open for the falcon to strike at Rassul that did not lead to Babbage's death at the hands of Morgiana. Ali returned quickly to the others, conscious of the subtle prick against his palms from the puzzle box. He smothered a smile as a plan came to mind.

Devoid of expression, Ali approached Rassul, putting himself between the thief and both Morgiana and Babbage. He held out the box, careful to keep his bloodied palms turned away. The moment the thief gripped the box Ali stepped back and bit off the words, "Open, Sesame!"

At the same time the falcon shrieked again, the sound echoed by Rassul as spikes much larger than those that had merely pricked Ali's palms shot through the thief's hands, dark metal emerging from the backs. Blood spattered the cushions and the walls as Rassul cast the box aside. The spikes tore his flesh, leaving gaping wounds as he ripped his hands away from it.

From behind Ali there rose a gasp, and the sound of a body crumpling to the floor. Ali glanced over to see the djinni stalking him and *Ustad* Babbage on the floor unconscious.

Slipping out of the way, Ali looked frantically for something to use as a weapon, but nothing lay within reach. And then he saw it, the lamplight glittered off the pure white surface of a bowl of salt.

Salt and bread shared between men created a bond. So said the Almighty. But that was not all. The sharing of salt was more than just a tradition for meals, it was more than a symbol. Salt preserved the dead. Salt repelled demons. Salt protected against evil. This man, without doubt, intended evil.

As Ali's hand closed around the grains, Rassul screamed his fury and lunged for Ali himself. Bloody hands clawed at Ali, ripping at his *thobe* and then his skin, but not catching. When his hands would not hold, Rassul snared Ali with magic, the words breaking from him between groans of pain.

Ali struggled as his body magically lifted from the floor and was slammed against the wall.

Rassul leered into his face. "You have caused me much trouble, *boy*. You have cost me my men, and blocked me from my treasure; you have stolen away my slave and caused me pain. No more."

Behind Rassul, Ali could see Morgiana. Completely still. Trapped by Rassul's magic; trapped in the body Ali had made for her. Again the falcon screamed in the distance and suddenly the building shook as if struck by a boulder. At the sound of the falcon-bound djinni, Rassul's control seemed to slip.

"Shahin," Ali whispered, but the mechanical falcon did not appear. Ali fought to free himself, but the thief merely shoved him higher on the wall, the magic again pressing him so he could barely breathe. He tried to raise his hand and fling the salt at the sorcerer, but the magic held him immobile.

"Now I will destroy this household and all within it, but I shall start with you." Despair gripped Ali's heart as he saw Morgiana, once more bound as a prisoner to Rassul. He regretted that he had given any consideration to *Ustad* Babbage's fear that she was a danger. Even now, when Rassul forced her body against her will, Ali could see tenderness in her gaze as she looked at him. From the oil-slick tears glistening in her eyes and the frantic twitches in her body, he saw how mightily she fought the magical compulsion. If Allah willed it and they survived, he would not let her doubt his trust of her again. He had been such an arrogant fool. He had spoken to *Ustad* Babbage about achieving balance in *his* life, and yet Ali had ignored the very wisdom he had sought to impart. He did not merely have a care for Morgiana. He *loved* Morgiana.

With that acknowledgement, peace wreathed Ali and freed him from dread.

He watched Rassul, waiting for any chance to attack. He noticed the thief's smile deepen in wicked lines as he looked in speculation from Morgiana to Ali. In the end, he merely said, "You shall watch as I make her dance." At his words, Ali's grip tightened until the grains of salt bit into his flesh as he remembered the djinni's caution at his earlier invitation. He tried to close his eyes only to be thwarted by Rassul's command of his body.

Resigned to whatever the Almighty had planned, Ali prayed, beseeching only that Allah spare the household and set his djinni free.

Morgiana tried to cry out at Rassul's words but no sound escaped the metal body. She was as trapped within her clockwork form as she had been within the glass-and-copper pipes of the treasure cave. Regardless of her own desire, her body would do as Rassul commanded and dance. For mortals to watch a djinni's dance, it was beautiful and powerful and terrible all at once. It would rend their soul and shrivel their flesh. No common man could survive the experience. Rassul's sorcerous nature would likely preserve him but Ali…she could not speak to his fate.

She tried to refuse the command, but Rassul compelled the body itself, not her spirit. Something in her clockwork chest seized even as her limbs wove and dipped in sinuous grace, like an asp upon the sands. The diaphanous silk of her clothing shivered and danced in the air, the delicate cloth mimicking the lavender mists of her native form.

As she swayed and whirled, Morgiana closed her eyes and bent her will toward breaking Rassul's spell. With all her heart she wished her body to become flesh that his magic could not compel it. It was not possible, but she did not cease to lift her prayers to the Almighty and His Prophet, her heart crying in supplication, her soul abasing itself with every dreadful step. She pled not for herself, but that Allah might have mercy on Ali.

The thief laughed as the smell of warm oil permeated the air.

Ignoring him, Morgiana did not cease her prayers, nor her efforts to resist, even as her glistening body sent up fine tendrils of smoke. Rassul's laughter grew louder; the tone hardened.

No longer able to help herself, Morgiana opened her eyes to see Ali pressed up the wall, his body lax but for his right hand, which was clenched in a fist. She met his gaze and begged him to know this was not her will. Ali gazed back and she saw him struggle to move his lips, trembling with the effort until she heard the barest of whispers forced past Rassul's spell. "I love you, gracious lady."

Then Ali's dazed eyes closed.

Her steps faltered and she felt ablaze with joy. Morgiana cried out to the Almighty as Ali gave her the word her heart could not name: *love*. She *loved* Ali and he her. With this new understanding her heart broke free. For an instant her brow blazed as if the Almighty pressed a kiss upon her. At that touch, she realized Rassul's magic no longer commanded her dance. With her eyes on Ali's limp form, and praying the moment had not been left too late, she swayed and dipped, her steps her own. She stepped past the platter of forgotten food, and there espied the bone handle of the carving knife.

As if sensing something awry, Rassul released his hold on Ali, whose body slid boneless to the ground. Rassul and Morgiana lunged for the blade in unison, the thief joining her in a new and no less deadly dance. She blocked him from the knife but failed to secure it herself. He struck at her with magic, his fingers twisting from the dark shards of power that sought to pierce her breast. Her skin burned as if bathed in acid, then suddenly, the sensation faded away. The sorcerer snarled and dove again for the blade on the serving platter. He snatched it up before she could intervene. Instead of striking at her as she expected, Rassul lunged for Ali. Enraged, she shrieked, the cry echoed by Shahin. The thief flinched, distracted. At that same moment Ali raised a shaking hand from the floor and cast a stream of salt into Rassul's face.

The thief screeched and clawed at his flesh, which smoldered everywhere the salt had landed as if he'd been struck by hot coals.

An unseen wind whipped through the room, knocking furniture aside, pulling tapestries from the walls, twisting rugs, smashing the fine glass tea cups, and filling the room with an evil stench. Glaring, with bloody furrows torn in his skin, Rassul surged forward and drew even more magic.

As Morgiana watched Ali threw the rest of the salt at the sorcerer-thief. Rassul screamed but continued forward, his magic swirling around him like a sickly dust storm.

Righteous anger flared in the djinni's breast. Rassul meant to destroy Ali, to destroy their love. Flexing her magic and commanding her limbs, which now moved with a very different grace, Morgiana lashed out. Flame grew at the end of her arm, bright and clean and righteous. She was a djinni, built by the All-Merciful himself from smokeless fire. With a flick of her fingertips she flung the fireball at the most cursed one. It struck him and wrapped his form, bright orange and white flame licking his flesh until Rassul became, briefly, a living pyre.

Ignoring his cries, Morgiana fell to the ground beside Ali and gathered him into her arms, barely noticing how the hard floor bruised her now flesh-and-blood knees. Ali groaned and gave a weak shake of his head, Morgiana cried her first salt tears, laughing with joy, though she barely had the strength.

"Any other man would have perished to witness a djinni's dance. You are an uncommon man, my love." She laughed harder as more tears flowed. "Surely, I must have you to husband."

At her words Ali's eyes widened. He reached up a hand to wipe away a tear, his callused fingers rough against her own now-soft skin. "Allah be praised! It is His miracle," he murmured, the words faint but his gaze clear and direct. "I accept, gracious lady."

Epilogue

"AH, LAD, IMPOSSIBLE THINGS, YES? IMPOSSIBLE THINGS." Babbage's voice was chipper, though still hoarse even several weeks after Rassul's attack. He slapped Ali on the back as they headed past the workshop in Ali's small home. Already the sun was setting.

Ali nodded, his attention and focus on the wedding processional to take place. He would walk from his home to his brother's house where Morgiana and her attendants awaited.

"What is this?" Lady Clara couldn't hide the surprise from her voice as she joined them from a nearby chamber. Dressed in a long skirt and long-sleeved dress, veil covering her head, she looked as comfortable as if she had returned from a walk in the English countryside.

"How the devil did you convince the old reprobate?" Fitz said coming up beside his wife.

"Shouldn't you be with the women?" Babbage groused at Lady Clara good-naturedly.

"You know, you're not helping Ali here," Fitz said, kissing Ali on each cheek as was the traditional custom.

Ali blinked, seemingly in a daze.

Babbage *humph*ed. "He's fine."

"Where's Sadie?" Clara asked.

"Some old man showed her sweets in the garden and is teasing her with trying to discover where he has hid the rest of them. I think he's the gardener."

Ali chuckled. "Hamza has done that for all the children in the household, servant and master alike. Even I never found all of his hiding places."

Outside there came a rising noise and Malakeh's youngest brother, Liban, opened the door. "Are you ready?"

The men of Wadi Al-Nejd had come to escort Ali. Torches flickered in the fading sunlight. The men held aloft candles. In addition to Liban, Ali recognized Abdiesus, the tailor, Ahmed, and a number of others. He could hear the *bendir* drums, bagpipes, and horns. Ali stepped out and the volume rose.

Shaking off his daze Ali laughed and shouted, "Tonight I go to wed my beloved, Morgiana. She is the most beautiful and rare of jewels and with a heart as true as any man could ever desire. Her eyes are like the dark of night, her courage like the hunting falcon, and her beauty like the full moon."

Thus began the chanting and singing of poems. They walked through the night, their white *thobes* almost glowing in the flicker of torchlight. And as they passed each home, the people of Wadi Al-Nejd assembled on the balconies and flat roofs of the houses; they waved from the windows. The men continued to chant and sing of Morgiana. From time to time women in the buildings would trill their joyful ululations until their voices were hoarse.

Ali felt his heart beat faster as they approached the house where Morgiana awaited. His pace quickened and the clapping and dancing increased in frenzy as voices took up the call, "He is coming, he is coming!" And when he first stepped into the garden and spied her waiting at its heart, beside his grandfather's stone and the arta bush, Ali felt his breath catch at the sight. Morgiana wore a silken dress with gold embroidery thick across the front. A girdle of gold coins embraced her waist, while about her head draped a black head cloth of crepe with gaily-colored fringe. When she stepped toward him, she clinked with the many bracelets, gold chains, and finger-rings that adorned her body. Her hands were dyed henna red for luck. In fact, all the women's hands showed red designs. Even Lady Clara had succumbed to tradition.

The evening moved as a blur. The imam was a short man with piercing eyes. He looked sharply at Ali and Morgiana and in a stern voice reminded them about how the Prophet honored his wives, how to honor women, and how women should treat their husbands and honor them.

"I do so swear." Ali said.

The *imam* opened the *Katb el-Kitab*, the book, for Ali to sign his name. *Ustad* Babbage and Fitz Langstrom signed as witnesses. Morgiana was expected to sign later, in private.

Ali allowed himself a small smile as he considered that little in their time together had gone as expected. After Fitz had handed the quill back to him, Ali dipped it back in the ink and then held it out to Morgiana. "I would be with you, in all things."

There was a sharp intake of breath from those present and the holy man pursed his lips but there was no objection. Although unusual, it was not forbidden.

Ali saw Morgiana's eyes light up and her smile shone like the sun itself.

Hours later, Ali and Morgiana lay together in the new bower near the stone set there by Ali's grandfather. They were finally alone. Thick new pillows and cushions cradled their bodies, and fresh green fronds waved over them in the last breezes of the night. There were but a few hours until dawn. Already the songbirds had begun to stir and the stars faded from the sky. Ali held close his djinni-wife and whispered, "No more going swift and sure across the sand, gracious lady. I would spend my life beside you always." Her soft laughter and dark eyes caressed him as he opened his hand.

"It is appropriate upon marriage, that the husband give a gift to his wife. Something that is hers and hers alone. I would give an offering of my trust and of my love," he murmured.

Cupped in his palm lay her djinni's ring, the dark onyx stone nestled among tiny, perfect arta blossoms.

...and so, Best Beloved,

they lived the rest of their days together,
beyond even the number allotted
to mortal men..

What?

Wise child... foolish child, now you dare
to ask am I Ins or Djinn? Ah, you are too
late. It is for you to decide if I have shared
what may or may not be my story, for the
night is for the telling of tales of which the
morning may bear Truth.

Now hush yourself, Child of Adam,
and pass me the sweets.

Glossary

Abdul Asad (servant of the lion) – one of the three thieves first sent after the falcon and the puzzle box. He is the only one to survive the initial effort.

Aerostat – a craft that gains its lift through the use of a buoyant gas. Aerostats include unpowered and powered.

Afsharid dynasty – one of the Persian ruling dynasties of the time.

Ali bin-Massoud – (high) Kassim's younger brother, favored by their father. Sent to England for schooling so he could have a better life, since he would not inherit. Apprenticed as an artificer under Charles Babbage a noted engineer of the Victorian Era.

Al-Jazari – chief engineer at the Artuklu Palace, the residence of the Mardin branch of the Turkish Artuqid dynasty in the 13th century, author of *The Book of Knowledge of Ingenious Mechanical Devices*.

"Are you Ins or are you Djinns?" – A traditional greeting upon meeting a stranger, found in several folktales, asking whether the stranger is human, or not.

Arta bush – Calligonum comosum – Also called the fire bush. It has stiff broom like branches, flowers and edible fruit. For most of the year it appears dead, then in February and March it blossoms and fruits.

Artificer – 1. A skilled worker; a craftsperson. 2. One that contrives, devises, or constructs something.

Baba – an honorific that can mean father or old man. Though this can also be a name we have elected to use this solely as an honorific in this story, rather than use it in both of its capacities, as it was in the original tale where the primary character is Ali Baba but other characters are called Baba before their name given name.

Behnam – (reputable) – caravan guide.

Beni Zayed – a clan known for its skill in engineering and mechanical works.

Besht – a robe worn over a *thobe*. It can also be formal wear or indicate wealth, royalty, or religious position.

Biaban Govad (desert wind) – Massoud's treasured stallion.

Book of Knowledge of Ingenious Mechanical Devices, The – written in 1206 by Al-Jazari, chief engineer at the Artuklu Palace, the residence of the Mardin branch of the Turkish Artuqid dynasty. The book detailed 100 mechanical designs, all of which Al-Jazari built himself. Some were modifications on the earlier works of others; some were his original concepts. Many of the methods and techniques resonate with the steampunk tradition.

Camelid – traditionally any of a family (Camelidae) of 2-toed ruminant artiodactyl mammals having a 3-chambered stomach and including the camels, llamas, and vicuña. For the purpose of this story these are mechanical constructs modeled after biological camels.

Caravanserai – a roadside inn situated on the trade routes where travelers could rest and recover from their day. They provided food, drink and accommodations for people and animals. Places to buy supplies or sell goods.

Chafiye – a traditional Middle Eastern headdress fashioned from a square, usually cotton, scarf. It is typically worn by Arab men, as well as some women. It is commonly found in arid regions to provide protection from direct sunlight, as well to protect the mouth and eyes from blown dust and sand. Ali's use of the term indicates his family is of Persian origin, using *chafiye* rather than the regional *ghuttra*.

Charles Babbage – (26 December 1791 – 18 October 1871) an English polymath. He was a mathematician, philosopher, inventor and mechanical engineer, who is best remembered for originating the concept of a programmable computer. He taught at Cambridge University and had a series of financial setbacks that led to his design for the difference engine not being built until after his death.

Desert glass – Found in Libya, desert glass is a geological mystery as to its origin. However it has been considered valuable and used as jewelry for thousands of years. One of the most famous pieces of desert glass is found in Tutankhamen's pectoral.

Djellaba – a long, loose-fitting outer robe worn by both sexes with long, full sleeves and a baggy hood that comes to a point. Generally made of wool, the color of the robe indicates marital status.

Djinn (hidden from sight) – spiritual creatures mentioned in the Qur'an and other Islamic texts who inhabit an unseen world in dimensions beyond the visible universe of humans. Together, the djinn, humans and angels make up the three sapient creations of God. The Qur'an mentions that the djinn are made of a smokeless and "scorching fire", but also physical in nature, being able to interact physically with people and objects and likewise be acted upon. Like human beings, the djinn can also be good, evil, or neutrally benevolent and hence have free will like humans and unlike angels. djinn have the power to travel large distances at extreme speeds and are thought to live in remote areas, mountains, seas, trees, and the air, in their own communities.

Farzeen – (learned) Ali's grandfather and protector of the hidden treasure. For the purpose of this story, he was an artificer in the court of Shahrokh, the last shah of the Afsharid Dynasty. He was sent away to protect the treasure until the shah's descendants claimed it.

Ghul – There are lower orders of djinn, one of which is called Gul or Ghul (from which the English word ghoul is derived). These are regarded as a kind of female or evil djinni (the male is called Qutrub). Guls are said to be solitary demonic creatures resembling both man and animal; they inhabit cemeteries where they feed on the dead, or lay in wait for a traveler to pass where from they entice and trick him by changing their shape to resemble another traveler, and lead him from his course till lost.

Ghusl – The ritual bathing of a body for burial by relatives of the deceased. Men must be washed by men, women by women, and children by relatives of either sex. It is permissible for one spouse to wash another if needed. The washing is performed three, five, or seven times if needed, but always an odd number. See the following website for more detail.
http://www.islamicity.com/mosque/Janazah.htm

Hadji/Hadja – (m/f) honorific similar to sir or madam, used for an older man or woman. Traditionally only used for those who have made a pilgrimage to Mecca.

Henri Giffard – (8 February 1825 – 14 April 1882) a French engineer. In 1852, he invented the steam injector and the powered airship. His American cousins Tommy and Hugh are fabricated for the purpose of this story.

Himitsu-Bako (personal secret box) – a traditional Japanese puzzle box, which was developed over 100 years ago in the Hakone region of Japan. Hakone was a relay station on the main road to Edo (present-day Tokyo), and the puzzle boxes were popular souvenirs for travelers.

Today there are only nine National Master Craftsmen producing *Himitsu-Bako* in the Hakone region. The youngest is over 60 years old. It is impossible to say whether this magnificent artwork will survive to another generation.

Hami (protector) – The djinni Morgiana's original name.

Harâm (sinful) – In Islamic Jurisprudence, haram is used to refer to any act that is forbidden by Allah, and is one of five that define the morality of human action.

Howdah gun – a large-caliber handgun, often with two or four barrels, used in India and Africa from the beginning of the nineteenth century, and into the early twentieth century.

Imam – a Muslim leader of the line of Ali held by Shiites to be the divinely appointed, sinless, infallible successors of Muhammad.

Ibliss – the Islamic Devil. A djinn who refused to bow to the Almighty. The primary characteristic of the Devil, besides , is that he has no power other than the power to cast evil suggestions into the chests of men, women, and djinn, although the does mention appointing djinn to assist those who are far from in a general context. "We made the evil ones friends (only) to those without faith."

Ins – a term for humans, non-supernatural beings. Also called Child/Son/Daughter of Adam.

Izad al-Din (god, angel) (of the religion) – Name Rassul uses the second time he comes to Ali's house disguised as a merchant.

Janazah – Islamic Funeral ritual. See website for more in depth detail. http://www.islamicity.com/mosque/Janazah.htm

Jannah (garden) – an eternal paradise for Muslims akin to the Christian Heaven.

Juyan (seeker) – the fourth thief sent after the box.

Kafan – three pieces of plain cotton cloth used to wrap a body for burial.

Kassim bin-Massoud (divided) – Ali's older brother, heir to their father's fortune.

Katb el-Kitab – the Muslim wedding ceremony and signing of the contract.

Khanjars – The traditional dagger of Oman. It is similar to the Yemeni jambiya. The khanjar is curved and sharpened on both edges. It is carried in a sheath decorated in silver, on a belt similarly decorated in silver filigree.

Khizr (green) – one of the three thieves first sent after the falcon and the puzzle box.

Kufr – An act of ingratitude.

Language – Because of Ali's mixed ancestry with clear connections to Persia, Ali uses both traditional regional Arab words and Persian words.

Liban (successful) – Malakeh's youngest brother who comes to help manage the merchant trade.

Lingchi (slow slicing/slow process/lingering death/death of a thousand cuts) – a form of capital punishment practiced in China from roughly 900AD to 1905. The one being punished was tied to a wooden frame in a public place and a knife was used to slowly remove parts of the body. Punishment was a humiliation, painful death, and desecration of the body.

Ma'a Salaama – Arabic for goodbye.

Malakeh (queen) – Kassim's wife. Knowledgeable and well-trained in business, but relegated to a frivolous life without purpose by her husband's disregard for her abilities.

Mamilla – neighborhood of Jerusalem established in the late 19th century outside the Old City, west of the Jaffa Gate. It was a mixed Jewish-Arab business district. In the late 19th century, the area around the Old City walls was barren and undeveloped. It was only notable for the junction of paths that would become Jaffa Road and the highway to

Jaffa, with the road to Hebron outside the Jaffa Gate. Among its first structures was the Hospice Saint Vincent de Paul, part of the emerging French Compound. The early building developed as an extension of the adjacent souk along the city walls at the Jaffa Gate as a quarter for merchants and artisans.

Massoud (prosperous) – Kassim and Ali's father, a wealthy jewel merchant killed by the thieves in the desert.

Mateen (strong, firm) – in Kassim's household the servant in charge of the other servants.

Medreses – Arabic for an educational institution of secular or religious nature.

Morgiana (great queen) – the name Ali has given the djinni.

Mu'Tamid (trustworthy) – the name Rassul uses when he comes to Ali's house disguised as a merchant.

Onager (mule) – the young boy that worked as a part of the caravan that brought Babbage to Wadi Al-Nejd.

Qajar Empire – a Persian dynasty of the period.

Rashid (brave) – one of the three thieves first sent after the falcon and the puzzle box.

Rassul Maroun (messenger) (granite) – The leader of the forty thieves, he was sent by the Qatar Shahanshah to retrieve Nader Shah's fabled treasure.

Rub-Al Khali (empty quarter) – the largest sand desert in the world covering a quarter of a million square miles.

Ruqa – incantation, words said or written in the form of dud or Dhikr for the purpose of protection or cure.

Rusari – a scarf worn by women as a headdress.

Safarnameh – a travel diary popular with Persian travelers in the late 18th century through the early 20th, documenting the lands, peoples, and cultures visited. Considered the most popular literary and historical genre of Iran in the 19th century.

Sahhaar – a witch practicing evil magic that is not sanctioned by Allah or his followers.

Saif – corridor between dunes.

Salaam – Arabic for hello.

Salting the meat – a sign of peace, truce between two individuals who sit down to a meal.

Sayyid (a lord) – Malakeh's father, a merchant from Jeddah.

Shahin (falcon) – the name given to the male djinni residing in the clockwork falcon. He is a protector of Ali and deliverer of the puzzle box that is the key to Ali's destiny. The falcon is made in part from the lamp that used to anchor the djinni.

Shah-mat – Literal translation, Persian for "the king is defeated". A game similar to chess.

Shahrokh – The last shah of the Afsharid dynasty.

Shamal – northwesterly winds that generally occur in the summer but can happen in winter as well. They are very strong during the day but lessen at night. They cause great dust storms.

Shisha – a hookah or the molasses-based tobacco concoction used in it.

Simsim – the Arabic word for sesame. In the traditional tale from Ali Baba and the Forty Thieves, the words are "Iftah ya simsim" which translates to "Open Sesame."

Tafathalo (do me the honor) – An invitation to come to the table. Food holds great importance in connection with the rules of Hospitality.

Tahtib – a martial art originating in Egypt, that incorporates traditional forms of stick fighting and defense or dodging techniques with aesthetic flair that has, over time, been transformed into a dance that imitates a fight. The complete Arabic name of Tahtib is "Fann el Nazaha Wal Tahtib" which means "the Art (Fann) of Uprightness and Honesty (Nazaha) through the use of stick".

Thaddeus S. C. Lowe – (August 20, 1832 - January 16, 1913), also known as Professor T. S. C. Lowe. An American Civil War aeronaut, scientist and inventor, mostly self-educated in the fields of chemistry, meteorology, and aeronautics, and the father of "Lincoln's Air Force." By the late 1850s he was well known for his advanced theories in the meteorological sciences as well as his balloon building. Among his aspirations were plans for a transatlantic flight. His flight failed, but in homage to him, and to reflect the acceleration of technology in this steampunk world, the authors chose to name the successful aerostat in the novel after him.

Thobe – an ankle-length garment, usually with long sleeves, similar to a robe.

Tutak (money chest) – a merchant to whom Kassim owed a debt.

Ustad – a Persian honorific literally meaning master or teacher.

Wadi – Arabic for valley.

Wadi Al-Nejd – the fictional city where Ali is from. Translates to Highland Valley.

Za'atar - mixture of sumac, sesame seed and herbs frequently used in the Middle East and Mediterranean areas. It is often mixed with olive oil and spread on bread.

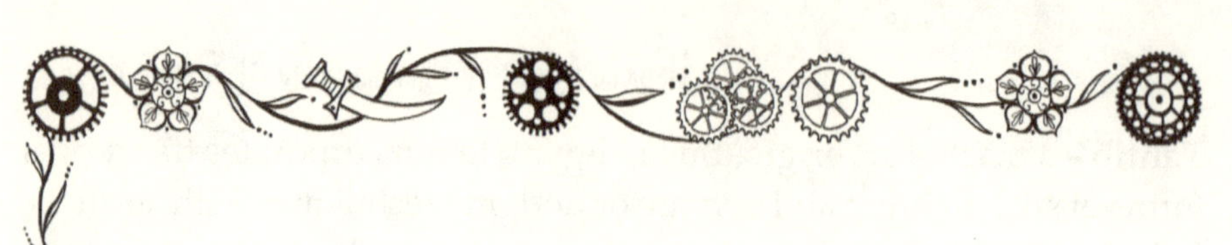

Danielle Ackley-McPhail

AWARD-WINNING AUTHOR DANIELLE ACKLEY-MCPHAIL HAS worked both sides of the publishing industry for longer than she cares to admit. In 2014 she joined forces with husband Mike McPhail and friend Greg Schauer to form her own publishing house, eSpec Books.

Her published works include six novels, *Yesterday's Dreams, Tomorrow's Memories, Today's Promise, The Halfling's Court, The Redcaps' Queen,* and *Baba Ali and the Clockwork Djinn,* written with Day Al-Mohamed. She is also the author of the solo collections *Eternal Wanderings, A Legacy of Stars, Consigned to the Sea, Flash in the Can, Transcendence, Between Darkness and Light,* and the non-fiction writers' guides, *The Literary Handyman* and *The Literary Handyman: Build-A-Book Workshop.'*

She is the senior editor of the *Bad-Ass Faeries* anthology series, *Gaslight & Grimm, Side of Good/Side of Evil, After Punk, Footprints in the Stars, In an Iron Cage,* as well as many others. Her short stories are included in numerous other anthologies and collections.

In addition to her literary acclaim, she crafts and sells original costume horns under the moniker The Hornie Lady, and homemade flavor-infused candied ginger under the brand of Ginger KICK! at literary conventions, on commission, and wholesale.

Danielle lives in New Jersey with husband and fellow writer, Mike McPhail and three extremely spoiled cats.

To learn more about her work, visit www.sidhenadaire.com or www.especbooks.com.

Day Al-Mohamed

D AY AL-MOHAMED IS AN AWARD-WINNING FILMMAKER, author, and disability policy executive. She is a host on Idobi Radio's Geek Girl Riot (https://idobi.com/show /geek-girl-riot/) with an audience of more than 80,000 listeners, and her most recent novella, *The Labyrinth's Archivist*, was published July 2019. Her recent publications are available in Daily Science Fiction, Apex Magazine, and GrayHaven Comics' anti-bullying issue "You Are Not Alone."

She is an active member of Women in Film and Video and a graduate of the VONA/Voices Writing Workshop. Her most recent film, the Invalid Corps (https://invalidcorpsfilm.com) is screening both nationally and internationally. However, she is most proud of being invited to teach a workshop on storytelling at the White House in February 2016.

Day is a disability policy executive with more than fifteen years of experience in both the public and private sector. She is currently a Senior Policy Advisor with the Federal government. She has also worked as a lobbyist and political analyst. For more information on work in disability policy, please check out: www.DayinWashington.com.

Day presents often on the representation of disability in media, most recently at the American Bar Association, SXSW, and New York ComiCon. A proud member of the Coast Guard Auxiliary, she lives in Washington DC with her wife, N.R. Brown and guide dog, Gamma. She can be found online at www.DayAlMohamed.com and @DayAlMohamed.

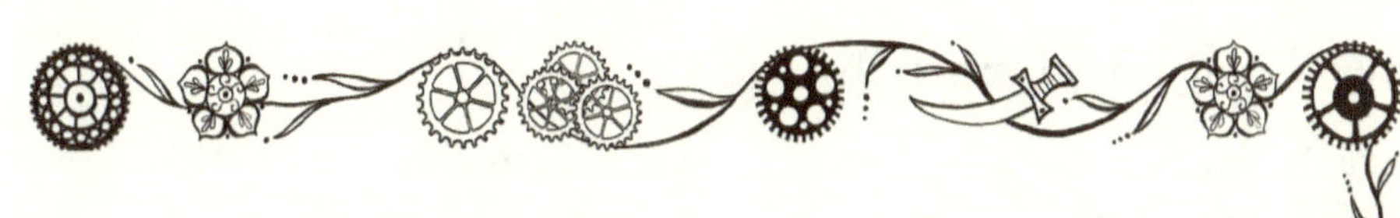

Enchanting Supporters

Alan Danziger
alicat
Amelia Smith
Anders Håkon Gaut
Anonymous
Barb and Carl Kesner
Bec Smith
Becky B
Brad Roberts
Brian Dysart
Brooks Moses
C Foreman
Carol J. Guess
Catherine Gross-Colten
Cathy Green
Chad Bowden
Chris Matosky
Christopher J. Burke
Christy Biggs
Cindy Matera

Craig "Stevo" Stephenson
Craig Hackl
Curtis & Maryrita
    Steinhour
Dagmar Baumann
Dale A Russell
Dancing Emerald
    Green Falcon
Daniel Lin
Danielle Wolf
Dave Hermann
David Gian-Cursio
David Lee Summers
    and Kumie Wise
David Perkins
David Zurek
Deborah Hartigan
Debra Lieven
Ed Ellis
Ergo Ojasoo

Eric S. Schaefer
Erik T Johnson
Erin Hudgins
Eryious
Gary Phillips
H Lynnea Johnson
Harald (Germany)
Hrvoje Bukša
Ian Harvey
im just lori
Isaac 'Will It Work' Dansicker
Jakub Narębski
James Rowland
Janice M. Eisen
Jasen Stengel
Jd Michaels
Jeanne Hartley
Jen Myers
Jenn Whitworth
Jenna E. Miller
Jennifer L. Pierce
Jeremy Audet
Joanne Burrows
John "Shadowcat" Ickes
John Fiala
John Idlor
John Kerecz
Jörg Tremmel
Joshua C. Chadd
Judith Waidlich
Kate Deibel
Kelly Pierce
KellyShannon Pierce
Ken "Merlyn" Mencher
Kerry aka Trouble
Kris Mayer
L.E. Custodio
Lark Cunningham
Lewis Phillips
Linda Pierce
Lisa Kruse
Lori and Maurice Forrester
Lorraine J. Anderson
Louise Lowenspets
Mackie
maileguy
Margaret Bumby
Margaret St. John
Mark Carter
Mark Chick
Mark Featherston
Mark Hirschman
Mark Lukens
Megan K. Ward
Megan Real
Melissa Shumake
Mike Bundt
Mike Smith
Mitchell A Johnson
Morgan Hazelwood
Moria Trent
N/A
Nathan Turner
Oliver James Minall
Pam Halter
Paul May
Paul van Oven
Peter D Engebos
Peter Thew
pjk
R.J.H.
Ralf "Sandfox" Sandfuchs

Raven Oak
Regis M. Donovan
RJ Hopkinson
Rob Menaul
Robert Claney
Robert Dallas
Russell Ventimeglia
S Jeff Nelson
Sam Stilwell
Scott Early
Scott Elson
Scott Schaper
Sheepy!
Sheryl R. Hayes
Stephen Ballentine
Stephen Lesnik

Sue Carlson
Svend Andersen
Tanya K.
Tasha Turner
The Archive
Tiffany Hall
Tina M Noe Good
Tory Shade
Tracy 'Rayhne' Fretwell
Trina L Bork
Vespry Family
Victoria Kay Steele
Wes Rist
Wil Bastion
Zoro58

www.ingramcontent.com/pod-product-compliance
Lightning Source LLC
Chambersburg PA
CBHW062019190726
48284CB00012B/729